UPCOUNTRY

A NOVEL

CHIN-SUN LEE

The Unnamed Press
Los Angeles, CA

For my parents, who brought me into this world—and for Nance, who helped me live in it.

UPCOUNTRY

1
THE ETERNALS

From outside, the house looked run-down and not quite to Claire's taste. It was a remodeled Greek Revival with blistered white clapboard walls and gray shutters missing several slats. A large bow-and-arrow weathervane tilted slightly askew on the peaked roof. Grass ran wild in the yard, patchy and thin in some parts, and overgrown in others. An old green flatbed pickup was parked in the driveway.

The buzzer was broken and she had to knock several times. When the door jerked open, she cried out, "Oh!" The woman before her looked so different from what she'd imagined. She had sharp hazel eyes and thin skin with faint vertical creases above her top lip. Smoke from the cigarette she held at her hip drifted up into Claire's face.

"April Ives? Claire Pedersen." She held out her hand and turned to cough. "Thanks for letting me come by."

"Sure," the woman said, giving the hand a single shake. "Watch out, that board's loose."

Claire stepped gingerly through the hallway and then more boldly into the living room. It was late summer and humid, with only warm air circulating from an ornate candelabra ceiling fan. There were boxes everywhere, a few still open in the center of the room. "Wow, it looks more spacious than in the pictures."

"I sold some furniture last week. You always buy things like houses just from pictures?"

"No!" Claire laughed. "But my uncle told me about this place, and it was such a good—" She caught herself and said, "Opportunity. We knew we had to act quickly."

"My great-grandpa built this house," April said, her eyes wandering over the room. "Been in my family three generations. It'll be weird, having someone else live here." She gave Claire a sudden sharp look. "I thought Karl wanted the place for himself. He knew my dad, so I thought, okay, at least it's not going to a stranger. He only mentioned you after we signed the contract."

"I don't know why. We weren't trying to be secretive. It just made sense, since he's family and here. When we sell our place, we'll do the transfer." Claire was annoyed with herself for feeling defensive. "We're not strangers to the area. Actually, you and I once knew each other."

April frowned. "I don't think so."

"Yes," Claire insisted, "when we were kids. I spent two summers at Karl's farm in Westerville. We used to play in the creek here in Caliban . . . you, me, some other little kid named Eddie. You had a friend . . . Jenny? Janine?"

"Shit," April said finally. "Yeah, Janine and I were tight up till middle school. That's so weird. I don't remember you at all."

"Well, it was only a couple of summers. Then we moved to Florida. But my husband and I've lived in Hell's Kitchen for the last fifteen years."

"I thought he was coming today."

"Sebastian's just up the road. He got sidetracked at the nursery, but he'll be here soon."

April's mouth made a twitchy, anxious pucker. "My kids'll be home in a little while."

Claire had heard her kids were from different fathers. "How old are they?"

"The girls are fifteen and twelve. And my boy's eight. You got kids?"

"No." Claire turned abruptly to peer out the front windows, searching for signs of Sebastian.

"Maybe you should start looking around? You need anything, I'll be over there." April pointed and walked toward the open kitchen at the other end of the room.

Claire felt put off by her curt manner, bordering on rudeness. Of course, the situation was awkward. But if the house had to be sold, she should be glad to have a buyer. When Karl told Claire about the house, she'd jumped on it. She could live closer to him and her aunt, and get Sebastian away from the city, with all its reminders of his failures and misfortunes. The proliferation of galleries only blocks from their apartment was an especially cruel taunt.

"We could have a real garden," she said in her pitch to convince him, "and build you a huge studio." She always equated the country with the last joyful moments of her childhood—before divorce and shuttling between Tampa and Bridgeport, before her father's new family and her mother's depression and early, swift demise from ovarian cancer.

She remembered April as a pretty, towheaded child with a wild streak she found heroic. She was curious to see her again, had even thought they might reconnect. But the woman standing beyond the kitchen counter was bitter, un- friendly, markedly changed. Her face was worn, though her body in a tank top and cutoffs was still slim-hipped and youthful. *How did she keep her figure like that after three kids?* Claire wondered. Meanwhile, she couldn't shake off the ten or so pounds she'd gained in as many years. Her body no longer fit her small head and short hair, which began to gray in her late twenties, with a pronounced streak near the temple. That streak with her side-parted, marcelled bob had a deliberately retro effect that, in her youth, was dramatic. At forty-three, she worried it actually aged her.

She pulled out her phone to call Sebastian. It had only one signal bar, so she sent a text: *Where are you? Think she wants us in and out.* Sometimes she wondered why he even owned a phone. She felt the old resentment chafing and pushed it down while she inspected the rest of the house. In the entrance hall, under the narrow stairwell leading to the second floor, she entered a tiny half bathroom with a tankless toilet and pedestal sink. Both worked, though were none too clean. The floral wallpaper on one wall was stained and buckling. On the dark linoleum floor were nail clippings and swirled clumps of blond hair. She heard April cleaned houses in the area and wondered how she could live like this in her own home.

Shuddering, she turned to leave but caught a strong whiff of something metallic, like rusted iron. She turned back and examined the faucets and toilet for leakage. There was nothing obvious. "Weird," she said out loud, hoping they wouldn't need a plumber. She was just starting to realize what an undertaking it was to buy an old house. She left the bathroom and walked farther down the hall. At the rear of the house was a large bedroom that could be converted into Sebastian's studio. Clothes and shoes were strewn on the floor, and random boxes piled into corners.

Claire had been warned but was still unprepared for how decrepit everything was. The wood floors creaked and the walls and ceilings were dusty, with the plaster cracked in several places. Still, even with the liens on the house, they'd be getting it for less than $30,000. They'd bought a sturdy used station wagon for only $2,000. Karl figured it would take another $80K or so to get the house fixed right. The mortgage crisis the year before torpedoed the housing market, but if they could get $650K for their apartment, even after paying him back, they'd still be ahead almost $300,000.

Karl suggested a reasonably priced contractor who could, he said, "deal with most personalities"—tacit acknowledgment of her husband's mercurial moods. Sebastian would oversee the renovation, living in the house full-time while she stayed in the city during the week, going to the midtown office where she worked as a civil attorney. She hoped it would be a temporary arrangement until she could find something closer to Caliban. Jobs were scarce, but she'd had two promising interviews with a firm in Albany. She'd likely take a salary cut, but the lower cost of living should compensate, and the firm mostly handled property law, which would be less stressful than the personal injury cases she dealt with now.

She returned to the living room, deciding to wait for Sebastian before going upstairs. April was sitting in the kitchen, wrapping up dishes in newspaper. She looked up and said, "So, you having buyer's remorse?" Her voice was so flat, Claire couldn't tell if she was joking.

"Not at all. The house has good bones." Claire crossed the room and opened the door leading to the side deck. "Oh, wow, look at that."

"What?" April scraped back her chair and walked toward her.

Claire looked out at a rectangular swimming pool, long drained of water and enclosed by a chain-link fence. The plaster walls were a bleached chalky blue. A blanket of dried leaves covered the shallow end, while the rotted wooden base of a diving board jutted over the deep end. Dandelions pushed through fissures along the pool's seams and corners, with taller weeds around the edge. Beyond the fence, several yards back from the pool, stood a large maple tree with wide outstretched branches.

Years ago, she gave up photography when she realized she'd never be able to earn a living from it—but there were moments like this when she missed it. "It's kind of beautiful in its way," she murmured. "So ruined."

April stared at her like she was crazy. "It was beautiful thirty years ago, when we could swim in it. When we could afford the maintenance."

Claire reddened. "I'm sorry. I didn't mean to be insensitive." She knew April had a brother in California who'd paid most of the taxes and utilities the last several years but was now going through a costly divorce.

April shrugged. "I just don't get your idea of beauty. Karl didn't mention the pool?"

"He said it wasn't—he didn't take any pictures." To change the subject, Claire asked, "Where will you be going?"

"Not far. I found a rental just a mile up in Pine Hollow, so the kids don't have to change schools."

"Well, it's nice you'll still be close." But in fact, the thought of April's proximity disturbed her. She didn't feel the house could be fully hers with the former owner hovering nearby.

They stood awkwardly, with nothing more to say. She could palpably feel April's impatience. Then, to her relief, she got a text from Sebastian saying he was on his way.

The woman was young and hugely pregnant—so young her pregnancy seemed almost obscene—and yet so benign in her aspect, so graceful in her movements, he couldn't imagine her any other way. On weekday mornings, Sebastian often went to the Horizon Café for a latte and muesli with yogurt; she was usually the one who waited on him. Her name was Anna, pronounced *Ah-na*, and she was a member of the Eternals, a religious group founded in the seventies that practiced an archaic form of Christianity rooted in Judaism. They believed that between the two categories of mankind—the unjust and the holy—only the latter, those willing to serve God, survived mortal death for a second unending life. They weren't eager to engage new converts and were even known to oust unfaithful members. A quiet community of carpenters and farmers, they owned the café and had become a fixture in Caliban over the last twenty years, though some locals were still suspicious and considered them a cult.

They didn't cut their hair and dressed in modest, unadorned clothing. The younger men, with their full beards and plaid shirts, could almost pass as visiting hipsters from Hudson—but the women, with their natural faces, long braids, and ankle-length dresses, seemed distinctly of another era. Anna stood out even more as the only Asian among them.

Sebastian could not understand his fascination with her. He didn't find her ethnicity exotic per se; she wasn't beautiful or even striking, the way Claire had been. Her skin was poreless, but her face round and plain, and she usually had a slight sheen of sweat around her hairline. Moreover, he'd always been somewhat repulsed by pregnant women. He found their lumbering ambulation bovine-like, inducing in him a feeling of claustrophobia. Nor was he particularly fond of children.

When Claire found out in her early thirties that she was prone to her mother's type of cancer, she made the difficult decision to have her ovaries removed. Part of him was relieved. But it was wrenching to witness her anguish and subsequent breakdown. It got so bad at one point, he thought she might actually harm herself. He made her shower, eat, take walks, and help him garden. One day, watching him pot dahlias on their tiny terrace, she asked with a wry smile, "Am I one of your difficult plants?"

"Yes," he said, "exactly."

It was the beginning of her getting better. Afterward, she became militant about self-care. Any sign of gloom—and lately, specifically, his—spiked her anxiety and compulsive need to find a solution. *Leave me alone!* he wanted to scream. *You had your depression, let me have mine.*

Sebastian had constructed installations for the Guggenheim. Eight months ago, a stack of plywood fell off a ramp and onto his left side, breaking his collarbone and dislocating his shoulder. After a prolonged dispute, the museum finally decided to settle. It hardly felt like a victory. Despite surgery and months of physical therapy, his left shoulder now drooped lower than the other and moved with obvious stiffness. He was morose and in discomfort, popping Wellbutrin and Percocet, the latest combination of meds his doctor had prescribed. They killed his libido; he and Claire hadn't had sex in five months. And his worker's compensation would last only another year, through the end of 2010. He wasn't sure this move would be the change they needed, but having some time alone was a relief.

Anna came and stood by his table, her small hands cupped lightly under her belly, which in the last two weeks had begun to protrude more prominently. She pointed to his half-eaten bowl of muesli. "Would you like me to wrap that up?"

Sebastian usually disliked takeaway leftovers, their sad, diminished appearance once reopened. But he didn't want to seem wasteful. "Thank you. And another latte when you can. How are you feeling today, Anna?" It was the closest he could allude to her condition. The week before, he overheard a woman at the next table ask if she was expecting a boy or girl. Anna, clearly flustered, mumbled, "Oh, I don't know," before she hurried away. He embarrassed her too once by asking if she was Chinese or Korean. She said, "My birth parents are Korean, but I've never met them." Then a look of panic crossed her face. "Please don't tell anyone I told you. I shouldn't be talking about my past." It confused and pleased him that they shared a secret.

"I'm very good, Sebastian," she said now. "This morning has been quiet. And you?"

She had a gentle, melodic voice, without a trace of an accent. It was one of the qualities that most deeply affected him; that, and the calm expression in her long dark eyes, suggesting wisdom beyond her years. Anna's youth provoked in him a feeling of acute self-loathing. He'd never been one of those idiots who chased after young girls. He never even cheated on Claire in their seventeen years together. Once or twice he was tempted, but in the end, it didn't seem worth the hassle. Claire was a possessive woman. Sebastian, while slight in height and build, was handsome, with a thick sweep of blond hair and piercing blue eyes. Before his accident, he never gave his appearance much thought. Now he felt self-conscious and, on bad days, even deformed.

"I'm all right. And Luke—I hope he's well?" He'd met her husband once, outside the Eternals' large communal farmhouse a few doors down from the café. Luke worked on their dairy farm nearby. Anna was sitting with him on the front porch swing, and when Sebastian walked by and waved, she stood up to make introductions. Then Luke stood too. He had to be at least six feet five inches, with a pink face, pale eyes, and white-blond hair, though unlike the other Eternal men, he had no beard. Next to Anna's graceful repose, he seemed like an ungainly, overgrown man-child. For Sebastian, their mismatch went beyond their disparate height and coloring. They didn't touch each other affectionately or even casually. He could not imagine them fucking.

"Luke is very well, thank you. I'll pass on your greeting to him," she said with a smile, before walking away. The usual careful, formal exchange. He could never tell if her diffidence was her true nature or if she felt unsettled by his company. He was aware some people found him intimidating and tried hard not to have that effect on her. Despite their almost daily interaction the past month, he knew only that she and Luke came from some town in Massachusetts to "help grow" the Caliban branch. Some Eternals, he read, were born into the community and never knew another way of life. She was likely adopted at an early age. He imagined her as a small child growing up in this peculiar cult, insulated from the real world like some kind of earth-born alien. This otherworldly quality was disrupted by her pronounced belly with its jarring, unwanted eroticism.

For months, he'd lost all sexual feeling, only for it to come back in the form of this ridiculous fetish. Either he was on the verge of a mental crisis or he needed to start a new project. But he was unable to paint and had barely set up his studio, which would be temporary anyway, like everything in the house, until the renovation was complete. For now, he slept in the living room, on the new mattress they purchased, while Claire searched for the perfect antique bed of her country fantasy. When she came up on weekends, going to flea markets and yard sales seemed to be her main occupation. She was also trying her damnedest to ingratiate herself with the locals, which irked and embarrassed him.

He had built a vegetable bed and planted lettuce, beets, kohlrabi, and garlic. By next winter he hoped to have a greenhouse. He also had the contractor pull out the chain-link fence around the pool, a task he normally could have done himself in a few hours. They'd have to deal with the pool later, but the fence was an eyesore he couldn't live with. Claire's pet peeve was the weathervane, which their roofer straightened the week they moved in. They compromised on the candelabra ceiling fan. She wanted to get rid of it, but he declared, "No. It's an amazing monstrosity. Every house needs an odd showpiece."

He'd always yearned for the time and space to make his art. Now he had it, and all he could do was waste that time drooling over some knocked-up child-bride Jesus disciple. Young and Asian, of all midlife clichés. Did he want to paint her? He painted dense, psychedelic landscapes on small canvases. A decade earlier, he was on the cusp of real recognition, with solo shows in local galleries and group exhibitions in Chicago, Los Angeles, Miami—even Art Basel. Then the momentum shifted to other, younger artists, leaving him stuck in a mid-career trough.

Briefly, he indulged in the vision of a rejuvenated buzz around his lush new canvases of Anna's body, the sphere of her clothed belly and breasts abstracted in sections, her long, thick braid floating along a perimeter. Then he snorted in disgust. Even his daydreams were banal. No, he didn't want to paint her. What he wanted to do was more simple and base.

He bolted his latte, paid the check, and left the café. Really, he was losing his mind. Next, he'd be lusting after llamas and burros. At least out here he'd find one.

Walking back home on the narrow highway, he passed the usual storefronts and small businesses, all open at random hours: the secondhand store run by Brooklyn transplants, the post office, and the historical brick B&B. Spotting some old MCCAIN/PALIN signs still stuck on people's lawns, he thought of Claire with all her sucking up, now having to squelch her liberal views. "The audacity of indifference" was his motto when it came to politics; it was all the same bullshit, regardless of party.

Up the road he saw his neighbor Duncan through the open gate of his yard, sitting in his underwear on his back porch, a large brace over his right knee. He was the town drunk, the rumored black sheep of the McAuleys, a wealthy family who subsidized but shunned him. Grizzled and skinny except for his potbelly, he had long dirty-blond hair beginning to thin at the top. In his youth, he had been a promising hockey player, reportedly good-looking. Then he got busted selling pot to minors, lost his sponsors, started drinking, and never stopped.

"Hey, man!" Duncan yelled, lifting a bottle of scotch. "Want a shot?"

"No thanks," Sebastian said curtly. He made the mistake once of taking him up on his offer and barely extricated himself after an hour. He heard Duncan tripped over his bathmat later that day and passed out, waking up with a fractured kneecap. The next time he saw Sebastian, he tapped his bad shoulder and said, "See, buddy, you jinxed me. Now we're both busted up." Sebastian tried to avoid him since.

Walking up the hill to his house, he saw a large green pickup just by the curb, its flatbed facing him. The truck looked familiar. It took him a moment before he realized why, and then April's eyes flashed on his through the rearview mirror before she peeled away.

———————

Anna collected the bills Sebastian left, along with his check, and took them over to Zebiah, who was working the cash register at the front of the café. The older woman glanced at the check and money, then said dryly, "Does he think the tip all goes to you?"

Anna, sensing judgment in the woman's tone, kept hers neutral. "Maybe he's just generous."

Zebiah snorted softly. "Too appreciative, I'd say. We depend on the patronage of outsiders, Anna, but there's no need to be overly friendly."

"I'm not," Anna said, feeling her face grow warm. "I treat him the same as all the customers."

"Well, he seems to be extra attentive to *you* . . . It might behoove you to be less amiable."

Anna couldn't see how or why she should modulate her behavior, but she only nodded and said, "Yes, I'll make note." In the five months since her arrival in Caliban, she realized that Zebiah considered questions to be challenges, which provoked her disapproval. Zebiah was her assigned counsel and, as the wife of their community's first elder, Hiram, also the first matron, so it was important to have her sanction. She'd never before felt so unsure of her place. Before relocating, she had assumed all Eternals, regardless of where they lived, would act the same, but this was not the case.

"Imagine spending so much money eating out every week," the woman went on, "though since his wife is hardly here, I suppose he has no choice. What an arrangement, having her work while he does nothing."

Anna was about to say he was actually an artist but caught herself; it would reveal she knew too much about him. To appease Zebiah, she said instead, "Their ways are strange indeed," before walking away to clear Sebastian's table. Reaching for his utensils, she paused. He'd left another sketch on a napkin. This one was of his fork, drawn with a black pen. The lines were bold and confident; she liked the diagonal way they cut across the paper. The week before, he'd drawn a spoon, and she marveled at how he captured its shine and contours.

She'd always liked looking at drawings but seldom had the opportunity, except for the occasional illustrations she came across in books about gardening, cooking, or farming. Aside from Scripture, those were the only texts she knew. The Eternals didn't necessarily boycott art, but only holy images were revered. These secular sketches were simple things, but it felt wrong to just throw them away, so as she did with the first, she folded this one carefully and put it in her pocket. She wondered if he left them for her, then felt ashamed at the idea, as it would confirm Zebiah's suspicions.

He did seem especially kind to her, always making pleasant conversation, whereas with others she noticed he was reserved. But he was also respectful and considerate. Unlike other outsiders, he never stared rudely or made sneering comments about her faith or appearance. In Milton, where she'd lived most of her life, she rarely encountered outsiders, as the Eternal community there was even more rural and isolated. They sold apothecary items, goat milk, and produce at nearby farmers markets, but only the matrons were permitted to interact with the locals. Here in Caliban, she was shocked to see how integrated the Eternals were with their surrounding community. Their farmhouse, goat pasture, and café were right along the main highway, with the latter business catering mostly to locals and tourists.

One weekend, a group of young Asians came into the café for brunch, and though Anna didn't wait on them, she could sense them watching her whenever she walked by. She was curious too, having never seen so many of her kind, and her age, all together. When she snuck glances at them, she'd sometimes catch their eyes, before quickly averting her own. Then she overheard one of the girls whispering, pointing at her, "What do you think *happened*?" As if something about her was wrong.

In Milton, the only Asians she knew besides her adoptive father were the Yuans, a Chinese couple. Over time, they all blended in with the community and became so familiar with one another she was hardly conscious of her race. But in Caliban, she felt how she stood out from the locals, and sometimes, if she was honest, even from her fellow Eternals. When she expressed this to Luke, he tried to reassure her: "I don't think they view you as different so much as new. I don't feel entirely settled myself. It's probably more about them getting to know us than anything else."

She wasn't convinced but didn't argue. And then, seeing this group of young people who looked like her but also saw her as different, wrong, even pathetic . . . it left her with a raw, painful sense of confusion.

That confusion increased with the changes in her body, which began to feel more alien to her, as did the life she carried. Motherhood was a woman's divine purpose, but above joy and anticipation, what she felt most keenly was fear. It made no sense. She loved children; she was good with them. Why should she be so nervous about having her own? As her belly grew more pronounced, she

noticed a welcome shift among the Eternals, the women especially: a protective-
ness and warmth that had been absent before. But in recent weeks, Zebiah had
become more watchful and critical of Anna's behavior. Now she knew why. It
felt unfair for the matron to judge her based on how frequently Sebastian came
to the café and how friendly he was toward her.

There was nothing inappropriate about their cordial exchanges. Why was it
wrong to be pleasant to someone, even if he was a man and an outsider? He was
the first person she'd met in Caliban who neither pitied nor judged her. He was
kind and conciliatory, and she couldn't deny she was soothed by his attention.
She had always been plain and looked especially so now, being so huge with
child. She knew she shouldn't care, that vanity was a sin, but he made her feel
that she was nice to look at. Dare she imagine pretty. Of course, he never said so.
But his eyes seemed to shine when he saw her.

Later that night, with Luke in their room, she pulled out Sebastian's sketch
and said, "Look, that man left another drawing. It's quite good, isn't it? I wonder how he learned to do that."

Luke took the napkin from her and examined the sketch. "I imagine he studied somewhere. Are you collecting these? Do you mean to keep them?"

"I—I'm not sure. It seems a shame to throw them away."

He gave her a strange look. "But we aren't meant to have keepsakes. Our
possessions should serve a practical or spiritual purpose. This does neither."

His expression was perplexed and, she realized, disapproving. Just like
Zebiah's. In that instant, she saw that she was stupid, and knew nothing, and
needed to be careful. "You're right," she said, "they're just trifles. Give it to me
and I'll dispose of it now."

"It might be best to flush it down the toilet. That would be safest."

So it was really that bad; so bad he wanted to destroy any evidence. "Yes,
Luke. That's what I'll do." She didn't tell him the first sketch was tucked away
between the pages of her Bible. The thought of it now filled her with horror—
that he might discover it and that she could have done something so blasphemous. Tomorrow, when he wasn't looking, she would flush that one too.

All day long rain fell over the valley, turning everything flaccid and heavy with moisture. Cicadas in the meadow were finally silent, leaves had begun to change color and drop, and Claire could feel a sharp nip in the air. She ran all her errands that morning, getting in and out of the car in her mackintosh, trudging through mud and wet grass to the vegetable stand, the poultry farm, and the organic store. Next on her list was a big outdoor flea market in Pine Hollow she'd heard about. The weather was discouraging, but she hoped it might keep other people away and give her a better selection.

Besides, there was nothing to do back at the house. Sebastian was in his studio, deep into something he wasn't ready to share, and rainy days inside always put her on edge. She was especially anxious these days. The apartment wasn't selling, their listing agent was nervous, and, at work, there were closed-door meetings and whispers about more downsizing. They'd already had two rounds of layoffs.

She was good at her job but got her degree from Cardozo, not Yale or Columbia or NYU, and did so later in life, at thirty-seven, which made her older than most of her peers. Mitch, her boss, kept reassuring her, "Don't worry, Claire, you're safe." Still, why wasn't she in those meetings? If only they had decided to move the year before! Someone would have snapped up their apartment.

She drove slowly north along Route 145, her wipers lashing back and forth, passing two cemeteries and a pumpkin patch, until she finally came upon the vast flea market. Overhead tarps protected long rows of tables piled with costume jewelry and knickknacks, and large grassy areas crammed with furniture, paintings, and rugs. She headed straight toward the furniture vendors. She knew exactly what she was looking for: a nineteenth-century wrought-iron bed frame and headboard.

The contractor promised he'd have the rooms upstairs finished the following week, and she was counting the days. She hated having to sleep with Sebastian on the living room floor like students. She also hated being apart from him during the week. When she initially proposed the idea, she didn't factor in the emotional toll or how tiring she'd find the constant commute.

What sustained her was her vision of the future: she would find work nearby; he'd start painting again and wean off his meds. They would live a simple life, free of outside pressure, and be able to focus on each other.

The rain subsided. She wandered among the vendors and finally came upon a stack of iron headboards propped against an old sofa back. Rifling through them, she paused at the third headboard, pulling it out for closer inspection. It was a simple bar design with graceful curved corners and fleur-de-lis accents. The matching footboard rested behind it. Both were painted a dirty white enamel, but Sebastian could easily strip that. Otherwise, it was sturdy, unique, an incredible find. Her heart began to pound with hard, erratic thumps that left her almost breathless. This occurred when she was at sample sales and job interviews and networking events. It happened when she first met Sebastian and when her uncle mentioned the house in Caliban.

A large woman in a denim shirt ambled over. "That's a beauty. 1860s. I've got the frame pieces too. You just hammer all the grooves together."

"How much?" Claire asked casually.

The woman scrunched her face, calculating. "I'll take one-twenty. 'Cause of the paint being worn."

Claire knew she could get her lower but was tired of being wet and cold. "Okay. It would be great if someone could help me carry it all to my car." She pulled some twenties from her wallet and, looking up, saw April walking toward her, holding a steaming mug. Their eyes met. For a crazy second, remembering what Sebastian said about her loitering, Claire wondered if she'd been followed—but April looked as shocked as she felt.

Claire stretched her mouth into a smile. "Hi. What a coincidence."

"April!" the vendor cried, leaning in to give her a hug. "You working Connie's table today?"

"Yup, helping out, selling my stuff. She's there—come by and say hi."

"I will in a bit." The vendor turned to Claire. "I'll have my guy come tape these and take 'em to your car." She waved, stuffing the bills inside her shirt pocket, and left.

April spoke first. "Saw Frank Moder's been working on the house."

"Oh!" Claire was momentarily thrown. She didn't expect her to be so forth-coming about her spying. Recovering, she asked pointedly, "So you've been by the house?"

"I have to drive that way sometimes."

Claire couldn't argue with that; the house was right off the highway. "We're putting up insulation and fixing the plaster. We want to make sure it's well taken care of."

"We took good care of it. Best we could."

"Of course, I'm not saying—"

"You all sell your other place yet?"

Really, she was something! But she was obviously tight with the locals. "We have some prospects. And you? Things are good in the new place?"

April let out a harsh, aborted laugh. It seemed directed as much to herself as to Claire. Giving her mug a little shake, she said, "This is getting cold. I'm heading off. Be seeing you." Her last words struck Claire as less friendly than threatening—and also likely to come true.

───────────────

Every Friday, the Eternals hosted a dinner on their farm to observe Shabbat, welcoming the locals to join in the celebration. To Sebastian's surprise, Claire insisted they should go. "Apparently it's quite the event," she said, "sort of a town novelty. We should go and be good neighbors." But the day before, she called to say she couldn't come up until Saturday morning. She got dumped with another last-minute project that had to go out by the end of the week.

"That's twice this week," she hissed over the phone. "And I have to just sit here acting grateful I have a job."

He held the phone, silent, and let her rant. What could he say? That they should be grateful, that otherwise they were screwed? They'd just shaved $20,000 off their apartment listing. Worse, their contractor, Frank, suffered a stroke three days earlier while pulling out old tile in the kitchen. It was a project that should have taken half a day and instead took two.

"Goddamn thing won't *give*," he'd cursed, in a rare show of temper. "I gotta chip out the whole wall."

Sebastian was in the room measuring cabinets when he heard a loud crash. He turned to find the man in a fetal position on the kitchen floor, the live drill he'd dropped lying treacherously close to his stunned, open eye. His symptoms weren't severe, but he had numbness in his face, and the doctors needed a few more days to evaluate him.

In the meantime, work on the house was on hold. The upper rooms and his studio were finished, but the entire wall along the side deck needed replacing, as did the subfloor beneath the downstairs bathroom, rotted from a leaking pipe. Claire was convinced it caused the metallic odor she complained about, even though no one else could smell it. Since Frank's stroke, Sebastian noticed a few locals giving him weird looks, as if he were somehow at fault—likely fueled by Duncan's rumors about him being a jinx. Country locals with their crazy suspicions. This was now his milieu.

Claire asked, "Did you strip the head and footboards yet?" It was the second reminder since she bought the frame ten days ago. The weekend before, they both pushed and dragged the mattress upstairs. She wanted his shoulder to heal, yet she kept piling on these projects.

"No, sorry. I got caught up in something."

He felt her negotiating her response in the long pause. "What are you working on?" she said finally. "Are you ever going to show me?"

"When I'm further along." He felt a strange suspension in his stomach: guilt jumbled with resentment, and the sensation of outright lying. The truth was there was nothing to show. He spent whole chunks of his day poring over articles about religious groups and cults and, now that the workmen were gone, jerking off to images of naked pregnant women he found on health and porn sites. The biological changes in their bodies—their breasts, bellies, and vulvas—at different trimesters were endlessly fascinating to him. He almost felt like an adolescent again, discovering an intoxicating new world, with the same sense of thrill and shame. It was a madness he could never have predicted, brought on, he supposed, by the isolation of the country and being unaccustomed to the size of the house, its quiet and darkness once the sun went down.

Claire knew he wasn't painting because there were no fumes. And though he rarely showed her his work at the beginning of a project, it was unusual for him not to even talk about it.

"I'll work on the bed this weekend," he said, by way of amends.

"That would be nice," she said carefully. "So, I guess you're off the hook for this Friday."

After they hung up, it occurred to him there was no reason he couldn't go to the Eternals' Shabbat alone. He could talk to Anna more comfortably without Claire. She'd been to the café a few times, and Anna even waited on them once, but Claire found it difficult to be around pregnant women and hardly engaged with her.

She did whisper to him, "She sure sticks out. Wonder how she got to be an Eternal."

"You mean 'cause she's Asian? They're pretty open about race, from what I've read, and really into procreation. So I guess she checks that box."

"You've been reading about them?"

"Know thy neighbor," he said with a shrug, before changing the subject.

He thought about the exchange he had with Anna two days ago, something he played over and over in his mind. She had seemed cooler to him and distracted in recent weeks, but that day, after he ordered his second latte, she surprised him by saying, "I know. You always have two, one before and after your breakfast." It was the first remark she ever made to him that was remotely personal.

"Yes," he said, his heart skipping stupidly. "I am utterly predictable."

"I don't think you're predictable at all." The boldness of her statement made him stare in astonishment. Her smile was good-humored, without flirtation or guile. The left side of her mouth curved higher than the other, forming one deep, fleeting dimple. Her dark, straight eyebrows seemed to him like the finest brushstrokes. He shifted his gaze from her face to her smooth white neck, finally allowing himself a furtive glance at her swollen breasts and immense belly. Any day now, she would have her baby. He thought of the words *ripe, fecund, lush*. Silently, he tasted the way they rolled in his mouth.

"Likewise, Anna," he said gently. "You're unlike anyone I've ever met."

She flushed with pleasure, and in that moment, he knew she liked him.

Claire stepped out to get her afternoon coffee on Friday, and when she returned to the office, the receptionist told her, "Mitch wants to see you in the conference room."

She approached the room, feeling numb except for the part of her brain that screamed, *No. No way.* She saw Mitch sitting with Christine from HR, and she knew. The blood drained from her face. Mitch looked up with a tight smile. "Claire, come on in."

She crossed the room slowly and sat opposite from them at the large black marble table. "This is probably not good," she said in a thin voice.

Mitch sighed. "I'm truly sorry. I didn't think things would come to this."

"You told me I was safe," she said, hating how small and plaintive she sounded.

Christine interjected: "This has nothing to do with your performance, Claire. It's about cash flow and overhead. Management, unfortunately, had to make more difficult decisions."

Claire stared at the woman's fake, commiserating smile. Bad enough the worst had happened without having to suffer the corporate jargon of this pert little messenger. She'd never been let go from a job before. It was humbling to realize how unprepared she was to deal with it. There was nothing to be done, she realized now, but act professional.

"What is my package?"

"You'll have twelve weeks' severance and eighteen months' COBRA, starting next week," said Christine, sliding over some papers. "If you could just look these over and sign."

"Next week," Claire said dully. "You mean today is my last day."

Mitch avoided her eyes. "Take your time sorting through what you need. We understand it's an adjustment."

Twenty minutes later, she was on West Forty-Second Street, carrying the contents of her desk in two heavy shopping bags. She looked out at rush hour traffic, stifling the urge to cry. Then she flagged a cab, aware it was now an extravagance. As she got in the back, settling her bags around her, the driver turned and smiled. "Got some good deals?"

She let out a small, derisive snort, and his smile died. Before she could explain, her phone rang. It was Ellen, their listing agent. "Claire, I'm so glad you picked up! The Dixons just made an offer! It's less than the asking, but I think it's fair."

"What's the offer?"

"Six-ten."

"Oh, come on—"

"I know, but hear me out. Their credit is solid, and they'll put down twenty-five percent. They need something fast, and I know your situation. Given all these factors . . . it's less than you want, but is the difference worth risking this sale? My advice is we take it."

Claire suspected she was right, but everything was happening too fast. The cab pulled up to her building. "Let me talk to Sebastian. I'll call you back."

Inside the apartment, it was eerily quiet. The space was half empty, with most of the furniture upstate, aside from a few basic pieces. She called Sebastian, but he didn't pick up. She hung up in exasperation, then immediately redialed to leave a message: "Hi, it's me. A lot's going on, too much to say here. I'm okay, but just . . . call me please when you get this. I really need to talk to you."

It was three thirty. An hour ago, she had a job. Now both she and Sebastian were unemployed. He might never be able to work again, and she'd heard nothing further from the firm in Albany. She stared blankly at the kitchen clock for several minutes. Then she called Ellen.

"Okay. Tell them yes."

"Good! I'll start the paperwork and keep you posted. Congratulations!"

Claire considered the irony of her remark under the circumstances. Or was there something fateful about the timing after all? It could be a sign, the universe pushing her to transition faster into a simpler life. Maybe all her ties to the city had to be yanked away in order for that to happen. She looked around at the apartment, letting the reality of her situation sink in. Then she stood abruptly and went to the bedroom. Grabbing her overnight bag from the closet, she threw in a few clothes and put on her coat again. There was a 4:10 express train to Hudson. She intended to be on it.

Sebastian spent most of the day in the garage, stripping all the bed parts. It was smelly, messy work, but after six hours, finally all the pieces gleamed a uniform gunmetal. He took them upstairs to the bedroom and quickly assembled the frame. Lifting the deadweight of the mattress onto the frame was harder. He winced at the pain in his shoulder, cursing his limited mobility. When it was done, he stood panting and sweating, surveying his work with grim satisfaction.

By the time he showered and dressed in a clean shirt and pants, it was past five, almost sunset. He rushed out the door but, seeing dark clouds, ran back and grabbed an umbrella. As he neared the Eternals' farmhouse, he heard singing and could see several candles flickering through the front windows. The door was ajar and he let himself in. One of the elders greeted him at the entryway.

"Welcome. The others are in the dining room." The elder pointed to a large room past an archway, where about forty people stood in candlelight singing hymns. Most were Eternals and their children, with a few other neighbors Sebastian recognized. He stepped quietly into the room, feeling conspicuous at his late arrival. His eyes adjusted to the light as he got closer, and he saw two long tables set with white tablecloths, more candles, and several covered dishes amid the china and silverware. He was surprised by the elegance, though it was far from ostentatious; in fact, the entire tableau struck him as reverent.

When they finished the last hymn, people began to mill about in the dining room. Some nodded to him politely but, to his relief, did not attempt to converse. He saw Anna across the room, already seated at one of the tables next to Luke. She looked up, saw him, and quickly lowered her eyes. Even in the dim light, he could swear she blushed. He was about to walk over when one of the Eternal women announced, "Everybody, please seat yourselves. Hiram will begin the Kiddush." There was a discreet, but hasty, scramble around the tables, like a polite version of musical chairs. He had no choice but to take the nearest seat, next to an older Eternal couple.

The room went quiet. Two women at each table poured wine into small metal cups and passed them around. Hiram, the elder who sat at the head of Sebastian's table, recited a blessing for several minutes. At the conclusion, everyone said "amen" and sipped from their cups. Hiram blessed and sliced two loaves of challah, passing the bread to each table. Soon after, conversation resumed. The dinner dishes were uncovered, revealing platters of steamed trout and vegetables grown on the farm: green beans, roast potatoes, squash. Sebastian found it incredible they prepared such feasts every week. Still, he found the meal interminable. He tried his best to chat with the Eternal couple, but their mutual reserve produced awkward silences.

Finally, a few young girls began to clear the tables. The Eternal men stood and started to leave the room. Sebastian turned to the couple and asked, "What happens now?"

The man said, "We sing, celebrate, and converse in the parlor. Everyone is welcome to stay—though of course, no one is obligated." He pushed his chair back, and his wife did the same. Sebastian debated what to do. The large clock in the room showed it was six thirty, still early. All the other guests headed toward the parlor, while the Eternal women bustled back and forth to the kitchen, laden with dishes.

He saw Anna raise herself carefully from her chair. One of the Eternal women emerged from the kitchen to give her a brown paper bag. Anna said something to Luke, who nodded, and then she left the room. Luke stayed behind, talking to another Eternal. Sebastian grabbed his jacket and umbrella and followed Anna, who went through a set of double doors leading to the back porch. Weaving through the crowd, he crossed the room and hovered by the doors, checking to make sure no one was watching. Then he stepped outside.

It was dark and misty, almost obscuring the full moon. The wind had picked up, and he could smell rain in the air. Anna was several yards away on the vast lawn, carrying the bag in one hand and a small lantern in the other, heading toward what looked like a large shed. He ran down the porch steps and caught up to her easily. "Anna! Where are you going?"

She whipped her head around. "Oh—Sebastian! You scared me. What are you doing out here?"

"We didn't get to talk before. Let me take those."

He reached for the lantern, but she said, "I'm fine. I have to feed the chickens. You should go back in the house."

"I prefer the company out here."

She gave him a quick sideways glance he couldn't interpret. They got to the henhouse, where he was immediately assaulted by the smell of chickens and damp wood shavings. She tried to lower the lantern to the floor but couldn't keep her balance. He set it down for her next to the coop and took the bag too. "You shouldn't be working. Don't they know that? Let me help. What do you need me to do?"

"Just lift this hatch here, tear the bag open, and toss it in. It's vegetable scraps, they like it. But don't let them out."

He did the task quickly, trying not to let her see his aversion to the clucking, pecking fowl gathering around his hand. From behind, he heard her soft laughter.

"You're not a farmer," she said.

He closed the hatch and stood up with a weak smile. "No, I'm not. I am a gardener, though."

"I thought you were an artist."

"Oh, so you remember," he said teasingly. "I suppose I am, or used to be. I'm trying to be one again."

He bent to pick up the lantern, and she said, "You can leave that here. Just blow the wick out . . . Turn that lever—there."

As soon as he did, he led her outside, anxious to breathe in fresh air. They walked along the far edge of the property line; she seemed in no hurry to get back to the house. She kept her head down, her hands buried in the pockets of her long sweater.

"What do you mean you're trying to be an artist again?"

"Well, I guess you could say I'm trying to make something worthy of my obsessions." He turned to face her full-on. "You might be able to help me, actually."

"How?"

"I'd like to paint you," he blurted out. Her eyes opened wide, as if he'd proposed something indecent. For a moment he worried he'd gone too far. But he was driven by the need to extend this time alone with her.

"Paint—me? Why?" Her voice quavered, and in its tremulous modesty he heard curiosity and that she was flattered.

"I'm not sure why. Discovery is part of the process. I never really know why something compels me until I start the work. You have a quality, Anna. I'm not sure I can capture it, but it would mean so much if you'd let me try."

They had wandered so far across the lawn that they were now near the neighboring property. It began to drizzle. He put on his jacket and opened his umbrella over them, struggling with his good arm to keep it from flipping inside out. He steered her lightly by the elbow toward the road.

"I'd like to help you," she said, "but I don't see how—"

"Would you be willing to sit for me? Just a quick study, it wouldn't take more than a few minutes. We're only two houses down."

"*Now?* Oh, Sebastian, that's impossible. I have to get back. Maybe another time."

He gripped her hand in desperation. It was the first time he'd touched her, and her skin was softer than he could have imagined. He pleaded: "There won't be another time, Anna, once you have your baby. You know that."

Her hand was trembling and he let it go. He couldn't believe his boldness; he half expected her to slap him. But she only sighed and said, "No, you're right. There won't be another time." There was genuine regret in her voice and, he sensed, a deeper sadness from sources unknown to him.

"Please, Anna, no one will miss you for a few more minutes. Look, everyone's inside. Please."

She looked back toward the farmhouse and, after a long pause, seemed to come to an inner decision. "What would you need me to do?"

Moments later, she was crossing the lit threshold of his front door. Her actual presence in his home had the quality of a surreal, suspended fantasy. They had hardly spoken while they walked down the street in the rain, huddled under his umbrella. Now inside they were quiet too, and awkward with each other. He knew he had to be decisive. "Come this way. My studio's in the back." He flicked on the hallway light, apologizing for all the construction. Then he unlocked the door to his studio and led her inside. The room was large and brightly lit, with a rough wooden floor and wide shaded window. A worktable stood in the center of the room flanked by two low wheelie stools. Beyond it, a wall of shelving filled with canvases and a daybed angled in a corner.

"Anna, I'd like you to sit here," he said, helping her to the daybed. "Just face me and hold your hands in your lap, like this."

He barely touched her shoulders but felt an electric thrill. She sat down cautiously and peeled off her sweater, folding it beside her. He grabbed a portable easel from the table and slid onto a stool, moving close to her. Sitting in her strange clothes among all his canvases and materials, she looked as if she'd traveled to him not only from another country but century. His hand trembled as he made several quick strokes with a charcoal nub. He hadn't sketched anyone's portrait in ages and felt like an amateur now, his first strokes so inept they hardly resembled anything human.

A rumble of thunder in the distance startled them both. Soon they heard the heavy pattering of rain. "Are you comfortable?" he asked, to defuse his own nervousness.

She shook her head and began to rise. "I'm sorry, I think I need to—is there . . . ?" She turned pink and he understood.

"Oh, yes. I'll show you the way upstairs. I'm afraid they're still working on the one down here."

Hearing this, she hesitated. Then she said, "All right." At the foot of the stairs, she turned to him, wrinkling her nose. "Do you smell that? It's like . . . rust?"

He stopped in surprise, then sniffed hard and shook his head. "We might have some damaged pipes."

He reached for her arm, but she said with surprising insistence, "Please, I'll find it. Could you just wait for me here?"

"Of course," he said, "it's to your right, past the bedroom."

He watched as she made her way up the stairs, gripping the banister for leverage. For her modesty's sake he turned away, deciding to wait in the living room. A few minutes later, he heard a stifled cry. He ran back to the foot of the stairs.

"Anna? Are you all right?"

She let out a low, prolonged groan.

He raced up the stairs and found her hunched over in the hallway, clutching the bedroom doorframe. There was a large wet pool at the top of the stairwell, staining the braided Craftsman rug Claire found the week they moved in. Anna's water had broken; she hadn't even made it to the bathroom. Looking closer at the stain, he noticed specks of blood. "Jesus Christ."

She groaned again, doubling over, and twisted further in the doorway. He rushed over to hold her up and saw sweat pouring on her brow and cheeks.

"Anna, we need to get you over to the bed. Can you do that?"

She shook her head, making pained animal sounds. He half carried, half dragged her over to the bed, with only the bare mattress on the frame. Clumsily, he lowered the unwieldy weight of her body onto the mattress. She lay across it sideways, her legs hanging off the edge. He tried to lift her legs to straighten her, but his shoulder pulled painfully and he had to stop.

Her eyes were glazed; spittle leaked from a corner of her open mouth. He grabbed a handkerchief from the dresser to wipe it off. Then he noticed the dark stain on the front of her skirt. Soon it would seep into the mattress. His shirtsleeve was soaked in blood; there were also several large spots smeared across the newly finished floor. Everything up to this point had passed in a dreamlike haze, but now he saw each detail with heightened clarity. He stared down at her in growing panic. She covered her eyes with the handkerchief, whimpering in fear and shame; her other hand clutched at her abdomen.

"I'm going to call for help," he said, reaching in his pocket for his phone. It wasn't there. "I'll be right back."

He raced downstairs to look, but it wasn't in any of the usual places. "Goddamn it!" he screamed. He thought about the Eternals a few doors down . . . but would she be okay if he left her? He stood frozen with indecision. Outside, the wind howled and rain poured down with increasing force. From above, she let out another cry, this one more high-pitched and desperate. Then he heard her scream out his name.

———————————

Mackey's Grill was a pub in Hudson just two blocks away from the train station, which made it a popular stop for commuters and locals alike. Most Friday nights it was packed, and tonight was no different. All the tables were occupied and even the bar was full up.

April had gotten there early enough to snag a stool. She'd changed her outfit at the last house she cleaned for the day and did her hair and makeup in the truck. Checking herself in the bar mirror, she thought she looked pretty good. Her blond hair was moussed and tousled, her eyes smudged and sexy; she wore her best skinny jeans, and her black tank top showed just enough cleavage. She hadn't had a Friday off in over a month and was ready for a good time. This plan got hijacked when Cliff, another regular, slid onto the stool next to her. *Oh Christ.*

He was a slack-bellied man in his late fifties who wore the same wrinkled suit each time she saw him. He lived in Yonkers but worked at an accounting firm nearby, and he always bought her rounds and offered to do her taxes for free. He was mostly harmless, never pushed that hard, and was occasionally funny, so she let him put her beers on his tab while she looked around for better prospects.

After the first beer, she didn't mind his company so much. By the third, she was bored as fuck and desperate to get rid of him. She scanned the place, which was now so crowded it was hard to even tell who was attractive. The last time she was there, she flirted with an electrician named Doug, letting him get a little handsy at the bar. She might have gone home with him, except her daughter Cara called to say she was sick and throwing up. April had hoped he might be back tonight, but no luck.

And then, by the door, she saw the woman who'd bought her house. Claire. She looked tired and irritable; her eyes seeming dazed as they took in the room. *Well, whattaya know,* April thought. She stood abruptly and told Cliff, "Hey, save my seat. I see someone I know." As she squeezed through the crowd, teetering slightly in her heels, she welcomed the tipsy buzz that went with her.

Claire was looking in the opposite direction when April bumped into her, hard. "Told ya I'd see you again."

Claire yelped and whirled around. After a frozen second, she sputtered, "You!"

"Jesus, your face!" April said, laughing. "You look like you're about to piss!"

"It's not funny," Claire said. "You really scared me."

"That's what I meant to do! What're you *doing* here? Why're we always running into each other?" She suddenly found the whole situation hilarious.

"I'm waiting for my husband."

"You're always waiting on him! Have a drink meantime." She grabbed Claire by the arm and pulled her toward the bar. "Cliff, scoot off and let my friend here sit. Come on, be a sport."

He didn't look happy about it but said, "Sure." For a few minutes he tried to talk to April with Claire in between them. Finally, he turned to the woman on his other side.

April leaned into Claire and whispered, "Phew! Thought I'd never get rid of him."

"Oh," she said. "I thought at first you were together."

"What?" April said, taken aback and offended. "*Please.* If he wants to buy me a beer, fine, but otherwise . . . huh! The day I'm that desperate, shoot me. I'm good on my own with my kids, thanks."

"Where are they now?" Claire asked.

April shrugged. "At home. Maddy can watch 'em for a while. Gives me a chance to have a life too—which doesn't mean hanging out with him all night," she said, jabbing her thumb in Cliff's direction.

"I see." Claire reached for one of the laminated menus on the bar and began to look it over. "Glad I could be useful."

April squinted, unsure if she was being sarcastic. "Yeah, well, you got a seat, right? Worked out for us both. Your husband might have to stand, though. Unless I take off. I might, I dunno. It's still kinda early."

"Sebastian won't stay. I left him a message to pick me up, and I'm just waiting to hear back. We'll leave once he gets here."

April was relieved to hear it. When she met him at her house, she thought he was kind of a dick—snotty and above it all, like his shit slid out in perfumed baggies. People in town thought so too. Duncan McAuley was spreading rumors about him being bad luck because of his broken knee and Frank Moder's stroke. Duncan was a loser, but April had felt some glee. She'd resented the new owners for the sneaky, back-channel way they got her house in foreclosure, swooping in like buzzards. If Karl hadn't been her father's friend she would have pushed for a higher price. Her brother, Mark, told her not to be stupid, but she didn't listen and, later on, felt exploited. As payback, she left the house in the most disgusting condition possible. She felt a little bad about it now, sitting next to Claire. But fuck it, it was done.

The bartender came and topped off April's beer without asking. Claire ordered a red wine and a chicken sandwich.

"You're eating?" April asked. The bar food was so overpriced.

"Yes," Claire said, looking sheepish. "I shouldn't have gluten, but I'm starving."

April shrugged. But when the food came, she felt her stomach rumbling. She hadn't eaten since one thirty, and it was past seven. She normally didn't get hungry when she drank beer, but now, with someone sitting right there with a plate of food . . .

"Why don't you have the other half of my sandwich?" Claire offered, pushing her plate over. "It's huge, I can't eat it all."

April was surprised by the gesture. She looked at Claire warily, suspicious of charity. "Nah, I don't love chicken. But maybe I'll pick at your fries."

"Take them all, seriously. I don't need the extra carbs."

"Ha," said April dryly, but she reached over and grabbed a few fries, dunking them in the little ramekin of ketchup. They were crinkly and salty and hit the spot. She finished them before Claire had eaten half her sandwich. April exhaled loudly. "Thanks. I'm stuffed. Shit, I think I'm even sober."

Claire smiled at her, then tilted her head back and closed her eyes with a sigh. "I'm the opposite . . . finally feeling the wine. God, what a long, bizarre day it's been. Oh, shit." With a jolt, she opened her eyes and reached for her phone, which still hadn't rung. She checked it to make sure there was no message.

"No word from your man?" April asked.

"No—I'm starting to get worried. I've left four messages, and I don't know if he's not checking his phone or if something's happened. I guess I won't know until I get home, except I can't *go* home until he comes and gets me." Claire stopped, looking embarrassed.

April hesitated. Then she said, "If you want, I can give you a lift. I mean, I know where you live and all."

Claire looked genuinely startled. "That's awfully—well, but I don't want to rush you."

"Oh hell," she said, giving the room one last look around. "I've been here since four thirty. Not much worth staying for."

"Well, if you're sure . . . I'd really appreciate it. At least let me get this, then." After she paid the check, she texted Sebastian one more time.

When April opened the door to step outside, it was pouring rain.

"Dammit," Claire said. "I don't have my umbrella."

April zipped up her hoodie. "We'll have to make a run for it. Come on!" She sprinted through the parking lot in her heels, and a second later Claire followed. The truck wasn't far, but even so, by the time April unlocked the doors and they clambered in, they were both soaked.

"Jesus!" she yelled. "It's fucking cold!" She turned on the lights and wipers and blasted the heat.

Claire nodded, her teeth chattering. "Sh-shit."

April looked at her, eyes agog and shivering, and they both burst out laughing. It was hard for her to remember why she'd hated Claire so much. The woman wasn't so bad, once you scratched below the uptight surface. She knew the moment meant nothing, that it would be gone as quickly as it came, but for now, she was okay with this truce.

When the windows were defogged, April pulled out slowly onto the dark, wet street. For a long time, there was nothing but the fast, steady squeak of the windshield wipers. Then she heard a deep crackle of thunder in the distance.

"Wow," Claire whispered.

April nodded, turning the radio up, and Steely Dan came through the speakers. As she steered onto the two-lane highway, the rain began to pound, hard pellets lashing against the windshield. They could barely see beyond their own headlights. April had the sensation of being in a small boat at sea. It was exciting and frightening but also soothing in a strange, insular way. She looked over at Claire as the woman's eyes fluttered closed. A few moments later, she was asleep. April didn't mind; in fact, now that she was sobering up, she was relieved not to have to make conversation.

She drove the rest of the way cautiously, still a little buzzed, listening to soft rock on the radio. When she got to her old house, she pulled into the driveway and shook Claire's shoulder. She woke up with a start and blinked at April.

"Hey. You knocked out. We're here."

At first, Claire was too relieved at the sight of the lit hallway to notice anything unusual. Still foggy with sleep, she watched April's truck pull away and then called out to Sebastian. She grabbed a hand towel from the small bathroom to dry herself and was about to go upstairs when she noticed the door to his studio was open and that the light was on in there too. Whenever she was home, he kept that door closed. In all their years together, she never went through his private things, his files or mail or computer. Her curiosity never exceeded her fear of what she might discover, or his contempt if he ever caught her.

She went down the hallway and paused outside the doorway. "Sebastian?" she said softly, poking her head in. No one was there. She walked in and saw one of the stools over by the daybed and a rough, abstract sketch on the table. Then she noticed the sweater. She knew even before picking it up it didn't belong to her husband, nor any man; something about its careful folding, its marled natural yarn and crochet stitch. She'd hardly absorbed the shock of it when she heard a woman's cries coming from upstairs.

"Oh my god," she said, dropping the sweater. She ran down the hall and up the stairs, her heart banging against her chest. At the top of the stairs, she heard Sebastian's voice, low and pleading: "Hold on, hold on . . ."

She rushed past the dark wet stain on the floor and into their bedroom. Just past the doorway she stopped short.

Sebastian, his back toward her, was kneeling in front of the bed—her bed—where a woman lay writhing and moaning. Her legs were splayed open, her skirt hoisted above her massive belly. Claire could not see her face, but she registered with dull shock the blood on the floor and on her husband's hands that were cupping the woman's knees. He was saying to her, "Something's coming, I see it . . ."

"Sebastian, my god—what are you doing?"

He whirled around. "Claire," he said slowly, as if he were testing the sound of her name. She had never seen his face so contorted. "Help me. You have to help me."

Between the woman's legs, something was pushing through . . . it didn't seem like a head, and then, indeed, she saw it was not when the shape unfolded into two tiny legs. The woman screamed, digging her fingers into the mattress. "Get it out, oh please, *get it out*!"

Sebastian yelled, "Call 911! Or get the Eternals! Please, Claire, I can't leave her." He turned back to the woman. "Come on, Anna, *push*. It's coming out but it's—I see the legs . . ."

Claire heard herself say coldly, "It's breech."

"No, no," the woman moaned, "please, God, don't curse my baby, it's my fault, it's all my—"

Her voice broke off into another anguished scream, and as she twisted her head from side to side, Claire could see who she was: the young Asian girl from the café. "My god," she moaned, clamping her hand over her mouth. She was going to be sick. She backed away but could not tear her eyes from the sight of her husband reaching into the girl to pull out her baby, holding on to the legs while the small torso and finally its head emerged, the umbilical cord looped around its neck. With a gush, more blood and viscera spilled out.

Sebastian unwound the cord and wiped at the baby with his bare hands. It was limp, unmoving. The girl panted and groaned, trying to lift her head to see. "Is it okay? Is it a boy?"

"Yes, it's a boy," he said. Claire watched as he lightly slapped the baby's bottom, waiting for the sound of its wail. But it never came, and all she heard was her own.

2
PENANCE

The man leaning against April's truck had a dark, chiseled face and was almost seven feet tall. She would have recognized him anywhere, but still couldn't believe he was actually in front of her, standing a few yards away instead of locked up. Her knees almost buckled from the shock. He used to make her go weak for other reasons, and maybe that old pull was still there, but mostly what she felt now was panic. No one else was on the narrow road where the mobile home she rented stood alongside two others, all equally ugly. She saw a small blue Nissan parked a few feet away from her truck.

"Eli. What the hell?"

"Heard you lost the house. That's too bad. And the new owners split 'cause the guy was fucking around?" He clicked his tongue, shaking his head.

April's breath caught. That he'd been in town long enough to catch up on gossip was a bad sign. "Yeah, well, it happens. You'd know."

He flinched but recovered quickly. "Anyway, been a long time. You look good."

So he was still a liar; that hadn't changed in the last nine years. There was gray in his hair now and lines around his eyes and mouth. He was thirty-five, seven years younger than her, but prison had made him catch up, which left her feeling both gratified and sad.

"What do you want? How'd you find me?"

He blew out a short gust of air, as if her question was too stupid to warrant an answer. He'd always had the uncanny ability, even with his height, to spy on people unnoticed—what he jokingly called his "Indian stealth," though he was only half Seneca. "Anyway, I'm sorry. I know what that house meant to you."

"Right." She'd been gripping her car keys, and now she shook them in his face. "Can you move, please? I'm late."

He smiled. "Damn, girl, you got all tough. Where you going?"

"None of your business. When'd you get out anyway?"

"About a month ago. Finally found a lawyer who knows what she's doing. Got me an appeal on that burglary charge, and the judge waived my sentence. So, I'm out. I'm free." His face got that rueful expression she used to find charming, one that said, *Shit, can you believe my luck?*

This time, she really couldn't. He'd been sentenced to twenty-three years. She never imagined he'd get out so soon. She itched for a cigarette but had sworn to quit for good. "Well, good for you. Now what do you *want*?"

He leaned in suddenly—too quick for her to pull away—and pressed a kiss on the side of her mouth. "Maybe I just wanted to see you." He pulled away, and the brief moist warmth on her skin turned cool. The bastard. He wasn't going to tell her anything. "How're the girls?"

She laughed. "Well, Maddy still hates your guts. And Cara doesn't remember you."

His face lost its confident smirk. "You never gave them a choice, or me—just cut me off. What did I do to you?"

"What didn't you do? You lied, you cheated, you stole. And I don't owe you shit. They're my kids."

"Not all of them. I mean, they're not all just yours. I've seen the boy. His name's Justin, right?"

She felt herself go cold. "Stay away from him, or I'll call the cops, I swear!"

"Hold on. I'm not looking for trouble. I just—he's my son," he said pleadingly. "I knew it the first time I saw him."

"He's *not*. Sorry, but you weren't the only guy I fucked."

"Maybe. He's still my kid. Look, I know you're pissed. But you couldn't have hated me that much. Not if you decided to keep him."

She punched his face, hard. They were both stunned. For a second, she thought he might hit her back. But he didn't—and she remembered the one thing he never did was put a hand on her.

"Shit," he said, rubbing his jaw. "That hurt." He stepped away from the truck. "All right, I didn't come here to upset you. We can talk another time, maybe, when you're feeling more friendly. So just . . . go on about your business."

"You go first. And don't you dare come back. I will fucking get a restraining order."

He stared at her in disbelief. "Jesus, April, don't do that. I'm living straight now. I'm dry, I'm going to treatment. I got a job. Remember Charlie? I'm working at his body shop. You change your mind, you can reach me there or at my sister's. She's still at the old number."

At your sister's, right, she felt tempted to say but didn't. Driving away, he stuck his hand out the window to wave—and as usual with him, she couldn't tell if he was being sincere or ironic.

———————————

Eleven years ago, Eli came up to her in the hardware store she worked at and said, "You look like a girl I had a crush on once."

Back then she was used to getting hit on, but he was so tall and striking, she actually felt tongue-tied. After a beat she managed to say, "Really."

"Yup, when I was a kid. She lived next door. I think she molested me."

"Okay."

He burst out laughing. "I'm kidding! She didn't! Just wishful thinking."

"So you were some perverted little kid."

"Not perverted," he said, locking his eyes on hers. "Just curious. Still am."

She never thought it would amount to much. But he was straight up the sexiest man she'd ever seen. He worked for a contractor doing a job nearby. The day he met April, his drill crapped out, and he liked to say how that was typical of his bad luck turning to good.

Eli wasn't fazed by the fact that she was older and had kids. He came on strong and she was flattered, but she still saw other men and made sure he knew it. They'd cross paths in bars in Freehold and Medusa, both with other people, feigning nonchalance through peripheral surveillance. Twice they had quick, drunken sex in public bathrooms. She'd emerge feeling dazed, self-satisfied, kinder to her date.

"Why don't we cut this crap," he said finally, "and really be with each other?"

It was what she wanted, and it scared her shitless. But the early days were thrilling. They partied almost every weekend with friends he'd known in Oneida County, some fully enrolled Natives and others, like him, who'd never lived on a reservation. The men gave April frank, appraising looks; the women were polite and distant. Everyone was a lot nicer wasted. They smoked weed so potent her limbs went numb while her mind traveled galaxies . . . then a bump of coke to clear the head and whiskey to get them back to where they started. In the morning, when they picked the girls up from his sister Aiyana's, April could see the indictment in her eyes and in Maddy's too. She'd think, *I'm getting old for this*, and keep doing it anyway.

Within a year, Eli moved into her house in Caliban. To her surprise, he gave her money toward expenses. She'd never known a man to do that freely before, except her brother, Mark, who helped out when he could. Her ex-husband, Keith, was a tightfisted drummer for hire, only making money when he toured. At first, she was grateful to Eli. Then there was a flat-screen TV and DVD player, twelfth-row tickets to Foo Fighters.

"Since when does contracting pay so good?" she asked.

He shrugged. "I do other odd jobs here and there."

Her face got hard. "Don't treat me like I'm stupid. Where are you getting all this money?"

So, he told her. He was part of a crew that looted homes and businesses they had access to. They waited months before they hit and only at sites the others had worked at. "It's just once in a while, and trust me, these assholes are insured. I'm not going to tell you anything else, for your own protection."

"For my *protection*?" she yelled. "Chrissake, we live together, I'm taking your money . . . I'm a fucking accomplice!"

They ended up in a screaming fight that stopped abruptly when he stomped out. He didn't come home for twelve days. She walked around feeling gutted, his absence a physical pain in her body, wondering if she overreacted. Then he came back, humble and repentant, and told her he was going to stop. She had few reasons to believe him but plenty for wanting to.

They had a tender few weeks of reconciliation. Two months after Eli said he stopped stealing, the Albany police arrested him along with a coworker at their latest job site. A former coworker had given them up to plea-bargain a weapons possession charge. The police also found a bag of weed and two grams of cocaine in Eli's car. When he called her from jail later that night, his fear was so palpable she almost forgot her fury. Then he told her the amount of his bail.

"Twenty-five thousand dollars?" she cried. "Who the hell has that kind of money?"

"I do," he said in a tight, clipped voice. "Ask Aiyana. She knows where to find it."

"Really," she said coldly. "Why didn't you call her first?"

There was a moment's dead pause. "Because you're my woman. Or aren't you?"

"I don't know anymore," she said, her voice breaking, and hung up.

She called Aiyana next. "You knew what he was doing, didn't you?"

"Yes."

"And you never tried to stop him?"

"There are many things my brother does that I don't approve of and can't change."

April let the dig pass. "Well, you better get the money and call his attorney."

"If I put up the bail, they'll ask where it came from. It's a lot of money."

April hadn't considered that—nor, obviously, had Eli. "Talk to him. Maybe he'll listen. He sure doesn't take my advice."

She was about to hang up when Aiyana said, "Wait—are you going to stand by him?"

"That's really none of your business."

"Maybe. But there's something I should tell you. Believe it or not, it's for your own good."

April felt her stomach drop. When Aiyana spoke again, it was like she already knew: "He's got another woman. He always has. She's a full-blood Iroquois and she lives downstairs, on the first floor."

———

She saw the woman once, from a distance. For two days in a row, she went to Aiyana's building to press buzzer #1, hiding quickly behind a parked car. She thought of the many times she brought the girls over—at Eli's prompting—and wondered what type of person would put up with such disrespect. The first time she pressed the buzzer, nothing happened. But the second time, a dark-haired woman came out of the building and onto the sidewalk. She had a narrow face with long, darting eyes. She wasn't sexy or pretty. If anything, she looked tired and older than April. Somehow it hurt worse, seeing she was nobody special, just a skinny woman in a loose, ugly T-shirt, squinting up at the street like she was lost.

———

The drive from April's house to Cornwallville, a wealthy hamlet eight miles west, took her through winding country roads dotted with large farmhouses, converted barns, and Colonial estates with neat yards and filtered ponds. The views were picturesque, but as she kept checking her rearview mirror, all she looked for was Eli's blue car. It was a few days after his surprise visit and she was on high alert, expecting to see him whenever she walked out of the house. So far, she hadn't.

Aside from two friends, the only person she told about his return was Maddy. Her daughter had figured things out by the time she was ten. One day, she found April in the garage, staring into Eli's old toolbox, and said, "Justin's his, isn't he?"

The boy started asking questions six years ago, when he realized Keith wasn't his father.

"You have a different daddy," April told him, "but he left a long time ago. Not everybody's mom and dad live with them."

"Is he dead?"

"No, baby. But that doesn't mean he's going to come back." At the time, she believed it.

The morning traffic was light. Soon she pulled up to a sprawling nineteenth-century farmhouse with a pebbled driveway owned by the Burnetts. Michael was a contract lawyer, and Laurie, a financial analyst on the last few weeks of her maternity leave. April walked into the kitchen through the side door and saw Laurie at the island counter, frowning at her laptop screen. The new baby lay on a bassinet nearby while Mikey J., a hyper four-year-old, ran around with a toy missile.

Laurie saw April and jumped up. "Oh my god, I totally lost track of time. Should we move?"

"That's okay, I can start upstairs." April cleaned on average five houses a week on top of working four shifts at CVS and, on most Saturdays, her friend's booth at the flea market. She was heading out of the kitchen when a young Asian girl walked in, holding a box of wet wipes.

Laurie said, "April, this is our new nanny, Anna. She's in the guest room behind the laundry, so go ahead and change those sheets too." To Anna she said, "April comes by every Thursday and makes the house livable."

"Nice to meet you," April said, smiling—and then, looking at the girl again, she knew who she was. Her mouth dropped and quickly clamped shut. After all, it was none of her business. But the girl saw and flushed a deep red.

April left the room and went upstairs, thinking, *Holy shit.* She'd never officially met the girl before but heard about the Chinese cult bride and saw her months ago near the Horizon Café. Back then, Anna wore long gowns and plaited her hair like all the other Eternal women, but her different features and obvious pregnancy made her stand out. Now she was pale and slight, dressed like a schoolgirl in a plain blouse and calf-length skirt, her hair shorn like a boy's. April heard the girl was shunned by the group and her husband. That her baby died in her old house connected them in a way she found unsettling.

As for the Pedersens, they left town right after the incident, no one knew where to. Their house was unoccupied and still only partially renovated. All those rumors about Sebastian's bad karma, it seemed, turned out to be true. April still thought he was a creep, but Claire wasn't so bad in the end. You had to feel sorry for her, with her man going after a girl so young, not to mention married and pregnant.

She was emptying the trash in the upstairs bathroom when something bright caught her eye. Sifting through the large plastic bag, she pulled out a floral-printed cotton handkerchief, crumpled and frayed in one corner but still pretty. It wasn't her style, but maybe one of the girls might like it. She made sure no one was around and stuffed it in her back pocket, amazed how casually people tossed away good things.

Walking out of the bathroom, she saw Anna hovering in the hallway outside the nursery, the baby asleep in her arms. "I was going to put him down," the girl said, "unless we'll be in your way?"

"No, I'm finished up here." April couldn't help staring at her holding the baby—and then she had a horrible thought.

Anna approached her and pleaded, "Please don't tell her about me. I know she'd ask me to leave, and I have nowhere else to go."

"You're not planning on stealing him, are you?"

The girl's expression was so appalled it had to be genuine. "No! I can't be a mother. But I can be a good nanny. I took care of children, before. All that part I told her was true."

"But taking care of him right after your—I mean . . . isn't it hard?"

The girl looked down and whispered, "Yes. That is my penance."

God, April thought, *these people.* Life was cruel enough without inventing more punishment. "Do they know about your religion?"

"They think I'm Christian. They don't mind how I worship as long as I stay private about it."

So they didn't know she was an Eternal—or, anyway, used to be. For a moment, April considered whether she owed Laurie this information. She decided she didn't.

"Also," Anna said, "could you please not tell anyone in Caliban you've seen me? They wouldn't like it at all that I'm nearby."

"Are you hiding from them? Is that why you cut your hair?"

She blushed. "No, they did that. To mark my dishonor."

April gaped. It sounded so barbaric. "Okay. I won't say anything."

Anna reached out and pressed April's hand. "Thank you." She could feel the girl's gratitude shoot through her warm palm and felt immediately discomfited. It was enough of a burden having her own secrets. She didn't like being the keeper of others'.

───────────

That weekend at the flea market, Harlan, another vendor, stopped by her table. "Hey. Saw your old flame the other day. That half-breed ex-con? Took my car in to Charlie Huckster's, and whoa! Surprised the hell outta me." Years ago, Harlan was one of the men she tossed aside to be with Eli. He'd found someone else—there she was three feet away, giving her the stink-eye—but he still held a grudge.

April leveled him with a flat stare. "So?"

"Nothing. Just curious if you knew. Folks around here better start locking their doors."

When the flea market closed, she picked Justin up from a friend's house before heading home. "Home"—by now she'd gotten used to calling it that, but part of her still winced whenever she pulled up to the lot and saw the sad trio of mobile units, all raised on short stilts with two wooden steps leading to the front door. Her landlords, Ed and Delia, lived in the largest unit, and Delia's mother, in the smallest one set farther back. Ed was Black and Delia was white; they were one of the few interracial couples to live in the area besides April and Eli and, until recently, Anna and her husband.

She turned off the ignition and Justin undid his seat belt. "Hold on, little man," she said, taking him by the hand. "We need to have a chitchat."

He turned in surprise, and then his face got serious. He had Eli's dark eyes and wide, strong nose, and at nine years old, he already towered over his classmates.

"Relax, you're not in trouble." She tried to smile, but her heart was racing. "Justin, remember what I told you about your dad, how he went away before you were born and I didn't think he was ever coming back?"

"Yeah."

"Well, people are saying lately they've seen him around. I wanted you to know, in case . . . You might hear stuff about him, like he's a bad man. He's not a bad man. But he did some bad things." She paused but he was silent, watching her with big eyes. "He stole things. And he went to jail. That's where he's been all this time. But now he's out."

"Will I get to see him?"

It was the question she'd dreaded. "I don't know. First, I have to talk to him, make sure he's not going to do any more bad things. The point is, if he or anyone else comes up to hassle you, I don't want you talking to them. Okay?"

He frowned. "Do a lot of people know about him?"

"Not as much as they think. But people talk, you know, and make things up. Most of what people say isn't the whole truth."

"Did you know where he was all this time?" Throwing her words right back at her.

"Yes. I didn't tell you because . . . it wasn't a very nice place, where he was. And I thought he would be there a long, long time. Sorry. I was going to wait till you were a little older."

After a while he said, "Okay. Can I go inside now?"

"Sure. You all right?"

"Yeah."

She leaned over to hug him, but he slid away and got out of the truck. She watched him walk into the house. Then she groped in the glove compartment for the emergency cigarette she'd stashed.

When April went back to the Burnetts', Laurie had returned to work, leaving Anna alone with the children. April was in the laundry room, folding towels and bedding, when she felt a presence behind her. Turning, she saw Anna standing in the doorway.

"I didn't mean to startle you," the girl said. "Laurie wanted to make sure I gave you this." She handed over a sealed envelope containing, April knew, seventy-five dollars in cash.

"Thanks." She stuck the envelope in her back pocket and reached into the dryer to pull out a big flat sheet.

"Let me help," Anna said, taking a corner.

April said firmly, "That's okay, I've got it." She didn't want Mikey J. seeing them and tattling that Anna was helping her do her job. Over the years, she learned that employers got touchy over the smallest things. It was pointless to get defensive and lose clients. She knew that for these rich professional women she was the perfect help: white, efficient, not too young or pretty.

"All right. I don't want to interfere." Anna stepped back but still lingered at the door. "It's just that the children are napping, and I'm not very good with idle time."

Huh, thought April, *I should have that problem.* Then, remembering Anna's recent tragedy, she realized she probably needed distraction. She wondered what the Eternals did for fun besides sing and talk to each other. They weren't allowed to watch TV, she heard, or use the phone and computers except for business or emergencies. Their rules were inexplicable to her, and she wondered if Anna still followed them, now that they'd ousted her.

"How old are you anyway?" she asked.

Anna seemed startled by the question. "Twenty-four. I know people think I'm younger."

No fucking shit, thought April. The girl barely looked older than Maddy.

"I wanted to ask: How did you know me? Did you come to the café? I don't remember ever serving you."

"No, I never ate there. But I passed by all the time." April hesitated, then said, "Look, this is a weird coincidence, but the house the Pedersens owned— that used to be my house."

Anna looked stricken. She whispered what was already obvious: "I didn't know."

"Yeah. Sorry to shock you. Like I said, it's weird. Freaked me out too."

Anna put her hand slowly up to her cheek, as if she'd been struck. "Maybe it's not such a coincidence. Maybe it's God's way of reminding me."

"Reminding? Like you'd ever forget?"

"No, not that I would. But that *He* hasn't. It's a sign I'm on the right path."

For the first time, it occurred to April that the girl might be a little unhinged. "I don't get it. Haven't you suffered enough?"

"We Eternals believe there can be redemption in suffering, in being broken."

"How?"

"We become humble. Emptied of pride. Pride is the greatest barrier to salvation. Without it, we're more receptive to God's grace. Besides, what I've suffered is nothing compared to the injury I've caused."

"You got married too young. So did I. Nobody plans on breaking their vows or whatever, but it happens."

Anna's cheeks reddened as she lowered her head. "I dishonored my husband, but not in the way people think. Sebastian . . . what he corrupted was my mind. The night I went with him to the house, it was like I was under a spell. He made me feel things, things that make me so ashamed, and it killed my baby. *I* killed my baby—they were *my* feelings. But it started with him." Tears filled her eyes as she said softly, "I think sometimes I make bad things happen."

April could only stare with pity and impatience. Why was she confiding all this to her? Did she need someone to confess to, now that her people had shunned her? "Well," she said, folding up the last towel, "all I can say is you're awfully hard on yourself."

Anna shook her head. "Haven't you ever done something so terrible you wished with all your heart you could take it back?"

April let out a short, bitter laugh. "Yeah. Plenty."

"We Eternals believe when we've sinned, we can only regain God's grace through repenting. He provides the path by reminding us of how we strayed. It means that, despite our trespasses, we haven't been forgotten."

Her god sounded to April like a sadistic asshole, even worse than the Catholic version she feared as a child and later rejected. "So, when do you know you've repented enough?"

"When the ones you've wronged forgive you."

"And what if they never do?"

"Then, if you continue a life of penance, when you leave this earth God will forgive you."

What if you don't believe in God? would have been her next question, but there was no point in asking it. It was all good and fine for people like Anna, but nonbelievers like her had no afterlife to bank on. They had only this one to square away their mistakes, or else die knowing they hadn't.

———

Just on the outskirts of town, a wide, shallow creek flowed beneath an overpass, with birch trees lined along the bank and a gentle slope of shale rocks leading to the water. It was a strange place to meet Eli, but when he suggested it, she couldn't think offhand of a better idea. Bars were out of the question, now that he was dry, and meeting him in a restaurant felt too much like a date. But as she waited for him, parked by the overpass, it occurred to her the creek could also be considered romantic.

There was only one other person farther down on the bank, walking his dog. Right at the appointed time, Eli's blue car approached the overpass. He parked behind her truck and got out, wearing mechanic's overalls and work boots. She rolled down her window as he approached.

"You came from work? We could have met near there instead."

"This is fine. I've got an hour. You want to sit on that rock there, or is it too cold?"

She shrugged, grabbed her coat and hat from the passenger seat, and followed him over to a large, flat boulder. They sat side by side, a foot of space between them. "Anyway, this won't take long," she started, and then found herself at a loss for words. He waited until she spoke again: "You were right. He is your son."

He inhaled sharply. "Does he know about me?"

"He knows you had to go away for a long time and that we weren't sure if you were ever coming back."

He stood abruptly and walked a few feet away. She could tell by his coiled, rigid posture he was angry. With his back to her he asked, "Why'd you keep him a secret for so long?"

"I didn't even know I was pregnant till you got sentenced. By then it seemed pointless. And I was pissed. You told me so many lies—"

He whirled around. "That's why you cut me off like I never existed? I was in fucking prison, April. I lied about stealing, okay, but it's not like I was stealing from you."

She laughed. "No, you were just cheating. You want to talk about secrets, how about Aiyana's little neighbor downstairs?"

He flushed. "All that stuff got blown way out of hand. That was years ago. By the time I met you we were just friends."

He was still trying to bullshit her! "Whatever," April said crossly. Why was she picking at these old wounds? "It was probably all for the best anyway."

"Maybe for you, if it makes you feel better. How do you know it was the best thing for me, or for Justin?"

"Who knew you were so into being a dad? You sure weren't with the girls. Besides, you don't think it would've made you crazier if you'd known about him? You were sentenced to twenty-three years, Eli."

"It could've given me something to look forward to."

"What about him? At least this way he never missed what he didn't know."

"Bullshit. My dad kept me away from my mom and I missed her plenty, even if I never knew her." He came back to the rock and sat down. "So, why'd you decide to tell me now?"

"There's been talk since you've been back. It's a small town, people remember. Sooner or later, he'll find out, so I don't really have a choice. The thing I want to know is, are you planning to stay here or move on?"

"I can't break parole. And I should stick with the job for a while. Why?"

"If you stay, are you gonna keep out of trouble? 'Cause I can't have whatever mess you get into come back on him."

"Thanks for the vote of confidence. Who cares what people say? Why don't you let him judge me for himself?"

"I don't know. I need some time to think about it. A lot depends on you too."

He cursed and stood up again, pressing his palms against his temples. "Okay. Like I said, I'm not going anywhere. You know how to reach me. But don't drag this out too long. Don't punish him along with me."

Punish? Was that what she was doing? It annoyed her that he thought so. She was about to say something in her defense, but he was already walking back to his car. She watched him fold his long limbs awkwardly into the driver's seat. After he drove off, she stayed by the creek, listening to its thin gurgling echo. The wind had picked up and she shivered, suddenly aware she was completely alone. Her surroundings now seemed bleak, holding neither the threat nor promise of romance. Ten years ago, she'd cut him out of her heart. But it seemed only today they both acknowledged it.

April sensed Anna was lonely and had developed an odd attachment to her. Over the next few weeks, she learned that she wasn't Chinese but Korean, adopted by a white mother and Korean father who joined the Eternals when she was a baby. She'd known her husband, Luke, since childhood and considered herself lucky she was "chosen" for him; some girls had to marry much older men.

April was horrified. "So did you—were you even attracted to him?"
Anna colored. "Of course. He's my husband."

When April asked if she was curious about her real parents, Anna said, "It's enough that I know my immortal Father. Parents can only guide us through our earthly journey. I can't imagine my birth parents could have done that any better than my adoptive ones did."

"Do they know where you are now? Why can't they help you?"

She shook her head. "It's best to stay away. I've brought so much shame upon them as it is."

April found it all creepy and fascinating. Sometimes she wanted badly to tell someone, anyone, about Anna and the details of the cult. But telling one person meant telling everybody. She was all too familiar with the wildfire nature of small-town gossip, having been its target often enough.

And then, just before Christmas, their amiable acquaintance came to an unexpected halt. When she entered the Burnetts' house, Anna rushed up to her in distress. "I need to talk to you. Please, it's urgent. She's going to let you go, after the holidays, and it's all my fault."

"What are you talking about?" April said, alarmed.

"Laurie. She asked me the other night if I was happy here, and I said of course. Then she asked if I would mind, for a little extra money, doing some of the cleaning too, in my spare time. I asked what about you, and she told me with the baby they have to budget. She said since I already cook and care for the boys, it would really help them out if I took on the cleaning too. I'm supposed to think about it and let her know." She finished, breathless.

April gaped at her in shock. She'd been with the Burnetts for almost five years. They were one of her best clients, paying $300 in cash each month. How would she make up for it?

"I never meant for this to happen," Anna said, nearly in tears. "Please believe me. I feel terrible because you could've told her about me and didn't. I should be the one to leave. Then they would keep you."

April was amazed that after everything she went through, the girl could still be so naive. She saw how easy it must have been for Sebastian to manipulate her, how the Burnetts were manipulating her now—and how tempting it would be for her to do the same.

"Don't be stupid. Keep your job. One of us might as well. They need a nanny. If it's not you it'll be someone else. And they'll ask her the same thing."

Anna was silent as she considered the logic of this argument. "What will happen to you?"

"I'll be okay." But April's head was spinning, thinking of ways she could stave off disaster: request more shifts at CVS; beg Keith or Mark for a loan; guilt Laurie into a reduced schedule. She had $12,000 put away in a savings account—all she got from her house after liens, taxes, other expenses—but that was for the kids, and she was loathe to touch it.

Anna said, "Can I—would you let me give you some of my earnings?"

April was touched. But taking charity from Anna would be truly pathetic. She shook her head and said again, "I'll be okay."

To her surprise, Anna gave her a quick, fierce embrace. "I can't tell you how much your kindness has meant to me. You are a truly benevolent person."

April flushed. "Believe me, I'm not."

"You are. I'll keep you in my prayers. And I know God will provide."

———————————

On New Year's Eve, the owners of the Gifford B&B organized a potluck followed by fireworks on their huge back lawn. All the nearby townspeople were invited. April wasn't much in the mood for celebrating, but she hoped the outing would perk up Justin. The girls had left right after Christmas to visit Keith and his parents in Philadelphia. Justin moped around, feeling abandoned. When he asked again about seeing his dad, April gave a noncommittal answer. But she knew she couldn't stall forever.

Ed and Delia offered them a ride. By the time they pulled up to the Gifford, the parking lot and streets on either side were packed, and a sizable crowd had assembled inside. They walked toward long tables where food was set up in the big dining room. April put down the six-pack and corn casserole she'd brought, popping open a beer for herself. As they filled their plates, she saw a group of the Eternals sitting at a table several yards away. She felt the urge to go up to them and say, *Hey, lighten up—she never even fucked him.*

While they sat eating, April's friends Jody and Brian walked by with their two boys. She was godmother to their youngest, Patrick, who was Justin's friend. "Hey, little brat," April said, ruffling Patrick's hair. "I didn't know you were all gonna be here!" The boys ran outside to join other kids gathering branches for the firepit.

Jody said, "Guess what? I ran into Karl Udall the other day and got some scoop on the Pedersens. They split up—he hopes for good—and she might come back on her own next year. Takes some balls, that's for sure."

April absorbed the news in silence. For months, the house had stood half renovated, dark and unoccupied, a grim reminder of tragic events. People even talked about it as if it were cursed. In the beginning, when she first moved, she drove by often just to stare. But lately she found it too depressing. "I guess it's better than it being empty," she said.

When it was pitch-dark, everyone put on their coats and went outside to watch the fireworks, gathering around a huge crackling pile of wood. April noticed the Eternals leaving and rolled her eyes. *God forbid they have some fun.* She stood behind Justin, wrapping her arms around his shoulders. After a moment, she felt him lean into her. She was on her third beer, feeling buzzed and grateful they decided to come out. For twenty minutes they looked up at the colorful spectacle, gasping with intermittent delight. The show was reaching its finale, an avalanche of white streaks arching over them, when she saw Eli's face illuminated less than twenty feet away. Looking in their direction.

She froze. The sky went dark again, and when the next bright burst appeared, he was gone.

"Be right back," she whispered to Justin. He barely nodded, rapt with the pyrotechnics, as she walked toward the spot where she thought she saw Eli. Another deafening, final volley of fireworks, and there he was again, his height unmistakable, leaning against a large cedar tree. She stalked toward him and shouted, "What the hell are you doing here? Did you follow us?"

The fireworks ended and everyone clapped and hooted. People with children started to leave, while others went back inside for more celebrating.

"I wasn't, I swear. I was just driving around and saw the fireworks, so I came here. Swear to god," he said, thumping his chest. All he wore was a flannel shirt, jeans, and boots. She saw the bottle he held and smelled his breath in the same shocked instant.

"Oh Christ, are you out of your fucking mind? Is this how you want him to see you?" She whirled around in a panic, grateful for the darkness concealing them. "Stay here. I'm coming right back, and then we'll talk. Eli!"

"Sure," he said, waving her off. "You call the shots like always."

She rushed up to Delia and told her she ran into someone she had to talk to, asking if she and Ed could take Justin home.

"Of course," said Delia. "Everything okay? You want us to wait?"

"I'm fine. Justin, you go on ahead with them. I'll be home real soon, promise." She kissed his forehead over his protests and pushed him toward Delia. When they started walking away, she turned and ran back to the cedar tree. Eli was still there but sitting down, a large, almost empty bottle of whiskey resting against his thigh.

He looked up and said, "Whattaya know—she's back. Where's Justin?"

She snorted. "Not here." Squatting next to him, she snuck the whiskey carefully into her bag. The night air was frigid and hazy, smelling vaguely of cordite. It was later than she expected, past ten, and the crowd of people leaving was starting to thin out. "Eli, get up. Come on, where's your car?" She helped him to his feet and he leaned on her heavily, squashing his shoulder against her head. "Where's the car? Can you remember?"

He looked around for a minute. "Yeah, this way." They started walking down the street. "He's a beautiful kid, that Justin. I saw him and you . . . Hey, where're the girls?"

"With Keith, thank god."

"That prick."

"Yeah, well, you're one to talk."

They finally reached his car. He fumbled around in his jeans for the keys. As he opened the driver's side, she grabbed them. "Oh, no no no. You get on the other side."

It took them a minute to adjust their seats, the difference in their heights almost comical. He felt around and asked, "Where's the bottle?"

"It's gone. I threw it out."

He looked at her in stupefaction. "What the hell'd you do that for?"

She turned to him and hissed, "You are a complete fucking *idiot*. You'll never get your shit together, will you? What happened? Why'd you start drinking again?"

He laughed bitterly. "It's the only thing I still can do, legally. 'Side from that it's just piss into a cup, go to work, pretend I don't see or hear shit." He leaned away and stared out his window. When he spoke again his voice sounded thin and far away: "You know my mom was an alcoholic. That's how she died. Something to look forward to, huh?"

"Don't say that. *Hey.*" She shook his shoulder to get his attention. "Eli, you can't do this. You're gonna fuck up and end up right back in prison. I just know it."

"I know it too," he said, his face crumbling. To her shock, he began to weep. The sounds started out as small, strangled gulps and escalated into a series of howls. "Fuck, *fuck!*" he wailed. He thumped his legs and pounded the dashboard so hard she could feel the car vibrate. She had never seen him cry. The closest he came to it was the night he called her from jail—and even then, it was only his voice that quavered. She watched him now with a mixture of pity and horror, unable to let out a single breath. Finally, he stopped. He kept his head down for a while. Then he blew his nose into the front of his shirt, honking loudly several times. He looked at her, his eyes still wet, and gave her his old sheepish smile.

"Well . . . wanna make out?"

Tears sprang to her eyes as she laughed. "No," she said, punching his arm. "Let's get you somewhere to shake this off."

He nodded, docile as a child, and closed his eyes, tilting back against the headrest. He looked spent but unburdened. She had a sudden, vivid recollection of herself as a girl during confession, how absolved she felt after the priest forgave her. It seemed a miracle to her now, that someone could grant such peace of mind so easily. *Shit, I've let Anna get under my skin.* Easing forward, she drove slowly, feeling unfamiliar with his car and still a little buzzed herself.

When she pulled into her lot, she could see Delia had left her front light on. She parked the car and killed the engine. Eli was dozing. April eased out of the car and entered her house quietly. The hallway was lit, and she could see the door to the bedroom she shared with Justin was open. Tiptoeing to the doorway, she peered in. He was in his bed sound asleep, one arm flung above his head. She longed for sleep too, but it would have to wait. Closing the door, she retreated, turning off the hallway light, and flicked on a lamp in the living room.

She went back outside and saw Eli stepping out of the car. He rubbed his eyes and blinked. "Where are we?"

"My house. And don't think you're getting lucky 'cause you're not. Those days are over." She'd said this before, to herself and to him, but never with the conviction she felt now. It wasn't because he was broken and no longer beautiful. It was because looking at him too hard was like looking at a self-inflicted scar. Because he was a fucking mess and probably always would be. And because she was too old and tired to take care of him on top of her kids. Then she almost laughed out loud—because that was exactly what she was about to do. Just this one time more.

"We have to be quiet," she whispered, as they walked through the front door. She took off her coat, led him to the kitchen, and pulled out a chair. He sat and watched her silently as she began to brew some coffee. Then she cracked some eggs into a skillet.

He looked at her with puzzled, bloodshot eyes. "What're you doing?"

She poured the coffee into a large mug and placed it in front of him. "Shut up and drink. You've got about six hours."

"To do what?"

"To get sober before your kid wakes up."

3
RENOVATION

The first thing Claire noticed going back to the house was that the weather-vane was off-kilter again. The second was that while it was pleasant outside, the house was cold. It seemed impossible; they'd spent so much on new insulation. She pulled out space heaters but still shivered as she walked through the rooms, making lists of what needed to be fixed, kept, and thrown out. She dreaded seeing the master bedroom and Sebastian's studio again, though most of his things were put away in the basement: his paints and brushes, all his empty canvases and paintings—including the ones they'd hung on the walls. The bedroom was scrubbed clean, the wooden floor stripped or replaced where the blood would not come out. Her uncle oversaw that part of the work in her absence, using the contractor from before. Now that she was back, she would handle the rest.

Claire debated, then decided to keep the antique bed. Of course, the mattress was unsalvageable, stained with blood and afterbirth. She would never forget seeing that girl lying there with her legs splayed open, Sebastian on his knees pulling out her dead baby. He admitted to having a "fascination" but swore he never touched the girl, and that she came to the house only to pose for him. It was a temporary moment of insanity, he said.

She tried to move past it. Technically, he wasn't unfaithful. They fled Caliban and went back to Hell's Kitchen. They had six weeks to vacate the apartment for the new owners and figure out their next move. She suggested they go somewhere warm for the winter—Mexico maybe, where it was cheap and no one knew them. They were both free, without jobs. They could float for a season, let the scandal die down, then brave the gossips when they returned in the summer.

He let her talk and said little. It was only when she started looking into Oaxaca rentals that he told her to stop—that none of it was any good.

"What do you mean?" she said irritably. "Then where do you suggest we go?"

He shook his head. "We can't go anywhere. Not together. I think I need some time by myself."

"What do you mean, 'you think'? Like a trip somewhere?"

"Yes, away—separately."

Hearing that word, her whole body went cold. "Do you know what you're saying?" she finally whispered. "Because you can't . . . you can't say something like that and take it back later. You can't do that to me."

"I know." He spoke to her with a gentleness that ratcheted her fear. "You hate my guts right now. I wish I could make you less angry, but I can't even—I don't *feel* anything, Claire. It's like I'm watching my life, like it's all happening outside of me."

"Aren't you lucky." She forced herself to be calm. "Okay. Maybe we talk to your doctor about switching med—"

"*No.* I'm sick of it. They make it worse. I'm asking you to please, please, listen to me. I can't go to Mexico. I need time on my own. And I'm not going back to that house."

She felt a slow-burning rage. After all she sacrificed. "Sebastian, we own it. We moved there for you."

"That's not true and you know it. You keep it, then. Keep it all."

She didn't think he was serious until he booked a flight to Houston, where his brother, Lars, lived. Lars was nine years older and a conservative, wealthy cardiologist. The brothers weren't close. His asking for Lars's help brought his decision into sharp reality. All her pleas and suggestions only evoked from him a sad, pained refusal.

The morning he left she stood in the bathroom doorway watching him pack up his toiletries. "Sebastian?"

"Yes?"

"How much time do you think you'll need?"

"I don't know."

She watched him in silence for a few minutes. Then she said in a small voice, "Why won't you let me help you?"

"You can't." He shook his head and sighed. "But that's the thing, Claire. You keep trying."

At first, he would check in every week or so. Then he left Houston, and his calls stopped entirely. After that, only the occasional text. As if they were casual friends. It seemed impossible that eighteen years together could end like this. "Divorce him," everyone insisted. But something in her couldn't, because he hadn't quite asked for it.

She went to a friend's empty guesthouse in Tampa for the holidays. Her friend told her to stay on, and having nowhere to go, she gratefully accepted. Somehow the months passed, and winter turned to spring. She channeled her anguish into punishing workouts and starvation diets, noting with grim satisfaction her hard-won results. She had no fantasies about luring Sebastian back with a slimmer body, nor any interest in dating. It was simply gratifying to know that certain achievements were still possible through sheer self-discipline.

Finding a job was more challenging. First, she had to decide where to live. She had friends in Tampa, but the sticky summers were unbearable. And she could no longer avoid the fact she owned a vacant, unfinished house in Caliban. It was stupid not to go back, especially since her aunt told her Anna had been banished. But there were no jobs in the area comparable with her old position. Finally, a former colleague connected her to a paralegal job with a law firm in Hudson. It paid only two-thirds her previous salary, but she got health insurance and could work part of the time remotely. She figured it would do for the time being, and once the economy improved, she'd look for something better.

Her return made Karl and her aunt Evelyn happy. There was no one else she cared to see. She never had the chance to make real friends before Sebastian ruined everything. This time, she lacked the energy for social overtures. She wanted people only to leave her alone and, if they couldn't be kind, to at least show discretion.

Frank Moder, the contractor, renovated most of the house under Sebastian's supervision; now he went out of his way never to even mention his name. "When I was here before . . ." he'd say, avoiding her eyes, or "Last time we talked about it . . ." She gritted through these awkward exchanges because of his low estimate, which her uncle helped negotiate.

Frank was surprisingly fit, with a tall, ropy body and muscular chest and arms, but his face and neck were lined and leathery, far more aged than the rest of him. He was a strange, taciturn man, communicating only when necessary. She wondered if he was self-conscious about the slight drag in his speech from the stroke he suffered while gutting their kitchen.

"I'd really like everything to be finished this month," she told him the first day he and his men came back on the job. "It's just the bathroom down here, the hallway, and the kitchen, right?"

"There's them panels in the side deck too, needs replacing."

"Right, those carpenter bees. You talked about the nest with—before." *Now I'm doing it,* she thought with annoyance. "Let's focus on the kitchen first, then the bathroom. I still smell something rusty and it's driving me nuts. And if you could fix that weathervane. So, a month . . . is that possible?"

"It's possible. Sure." His shrug seemed to suggest otherwise.

"Good. I'll be working upstairs this week if you need me."

"Might get loud sometimes. Just letting you know in advance." The way he said it made her feel he didn't want her around.

"I appreciate the warning," she said dryly. "I'll leave you to it, then." And for the most part, she did. But even when she gave what she considered cursory supervision, his whole body stiffened. She got the distinct sense he didn't like taking direction from a woman. He often looked past her shoulder, as if she weren't there.

The next time she called her uncle, she asked about Frank, careful not to sound like she was complaining. "He seems, I don't know, less friendly than before. He hardly makes eye contact. I have no idea what people are saying about me, but could that have something to do with it?"

"That's just Frank. Don't take it personally. He's had a rough couple of years, losing his wife, and then that stroke."

"I didn't know he had a wife." It was hard to imagine. He seemed so insular and impenetrable. "What happened?"

"Breast cancer, four years ago. Nice lady, taught at the junior high. They have a son somewhere, but he's estranged, so basically, Frank's alone now. Some men aren't so good on their own."

Hearing of Frank's loss softened her judgment. She wondered how he would respond if she expressed sympathy or told him about her mother. Probably with horror. He hardly seemed the type to discuss anything personal. He could barely stand to talk to her about plumbing.

One night, she sat in the dusty, tarp-covered dining room, sipping her third glass of red wine, and said out loud, "I lost my mother to cancer, you know." She imagined Frank across the table, his stoic expression changing, and maybe his opinion of her too.

I'm sorry, he would say, *though it's not the same as losing a spouse.*

Oh, she'd tell him, *but I lost that too.*

The next morning, recalling her tipsy, momentary reverie, she felt mortified. When would she outgrow her disgusting need to win people over? All those years of therapy, antidepressants, hypnosis, and yoga failed to dispel her persistent anxiety. Sebastian obviously found it tiresome. Still, she couldn't understand why he channeled so much bitterness toward her, nor why he turned to the Eternals, and Anna, for solace.

He never expressed much interest before in theology, was in fact appalled by her brief flirtation with Kabbalah several years ago. But in his file cabinets she found all the Eternals' pamphlets decrying the sins of modern life to promote their simple, penitent ways as the holy path. She also found copies of research on their cult and others, along with vivid printouts of naked pregnant women that were alternately forensic and pornographic. She forced herself to examine each one, her hands trembling, as if looking for clues to a crime. Did he find the girl exotic, or was it her pregnancy that drew him in? He'd never expressed the desire for children before. If anything, she sensed the opposite. When did he change from the person she knew best to the silent stranger who walked out on her?

These questions tore at her, especially at night. She imagined them as actual demons clawing through her heart and head. Useless to go down that rabbit hole. She needed to get out of the house more, drink less, start exercising again. Since her return to Caliban, she'd gained back three pounds. Working most of the week remotely was not the advantage she'd expected. At home, she felt sedentary and distracted, and when she went to the office, superfluous and invisible. It was demeaning doing the grunt work for these DAs who were younger and less experienced, and to feel peripheral to the office culture. *Well, it's a job. God knows I need it.*

That week the work in the house turned especially disruptive, with the men using sanding machines and drilling cabinets into the kitchen. One afternoon, the noise was so relentless she couldn't think. She let her office know that for the next two hours she would have no internet. Then she put on her running clothes and trainers. On her way out, she passed Frank in the hallway. He did a double take at her spandex attire, then nodded once in acknowledgment and went into the living room.

Good day to you too, she thought with annoyance. Out loud she yelled, "I'll be back soon!" just so he wouldn't expect otherwise. From now on, she would be more assertive, and if he thought she was a bitch, then so be it. She'd been called that and worse.

―――――――――――

The night before Claire left Tampa, her friends Vincent and Marcus took her to a club downtown for a last "girls' night out." She hadn't been to a club in years and at first felt old and out of place. Three shots later, she didn't care. Some blurry time past midnight, a man approached her at the bar. "You look like a real bitch," he said with a slight Aussie accent. He had a cocky smile and looked to be in his mid-thirties. "It's a huge turn-on," he added. Something about him reminded her of Sebastian: the wiry build and coiled confidence, the provocation as flirtation. From across the bar, Vincent gave her a wink. She decided to go with it and let the man pull her onto the dance floor.

Within minutes, they were groping each other. She was very drunk and had to lean on him for balance. Part of her mind was elsewhere, lost in the fog of music and lights. But the other part accepted his tongue in her mouth and his hands on her ass, her breasts, each of these things jolting her with an electric shock. It took her back to bygone days of heedless abandon: partying in Miami clubs and frat houses, tanned boys with beautiful lean torsos, the power of feeling wanted.

Then they were outside in the parking lot, pressing against his car. Under the streetlight his face looked feral, older. She remembered the night air was cool, and that she came to her senses a bit. "I don't know . . ." she started to say. He lifted her dress and pressed his hand between her legs. "Yes, you do." They never even got in the car. He turned her around, bent her over the hood, and pulled her panties down from behind. She told herself it was better that way, less personal. As he pumped away, she kept thinking, inanely, *Live a little*, the words going through her head like a tape loop. Laughter bubbled in her throat until she heard someone from a distance yell out, "YE-AH, baby, take it!"

Jesus Christ, I'm fucking a stranger in a parking lot. Shame coursed through her—and then a perverse excitement. She imagined herself on a spotlit stage, men cheering while Sebastian watched her getting humped by his doppelgänger. Her hips spasmed and she cried out, reaching behind to clutch his ass. After a moment, her heartbeat subsided. A trickle of drool slid down the side of her mouth. She twisted away and pushed him off. He said, "Hey, what—?" Turning, she saw his indignant, ridiculous face, no longer like Sebastian's so much as a schoolyard bully's. She felt a wave of disgust for him and herself. Yanking her dress down, she said, "I have to go," first walking, then running back toward the club. She heard him scream after her: "Are you kidding? You *bitch*! *Fuck* you, you dry old cunt! Stupid whore!"

———

Two weeks later, the kitchen was finished. Claire was preparing an omelet for dinner on her new stove when she saw a large rat shoot across the floor from the pantry, disappearing beneath a gap under the oven. In quick succession, two smaller ones followed. She let out a high shriek, sending her spatula flying across the counter. Mice would have been bad enough, but rats! And not just one but a whole family!

She spent the next half hour fearfully sorting through the contents of the pantry. Grimly, she noticed large droppings on the shelves and signs of gnawing all over her newly organized boxes of oatmeal and brown rice, her expensive loaf of gluten-free bread. She tossed everything into a large trash bag and stuffed them in the bins in the garage. Back in the kitchen, she saw her half-cooked omelet cooling in the pan, a huge fly busily feeding in the middle. Her stomach heaved. She barely made it to the sink, vomiting flecks of greens and carrots from the salad she had for lunch.

The nausea abated as quickly as it came, but she lost her appetite completely. She poured herself a glass of wine and went upstairs, barricading the space between her bedroom door and floor with a thick towel. She tossed in her bed fitfully, imagining creaks and scratching behind the walls, before finally nodding off.

Sometime during the night, she jerked awake and sat up. Seconds later she heard a loud, steady scratching. She turned on the nightstand lamp and stood on the bed, looking all around the room. There was nothing. After some time, she turned the lamp off and lay down again. On the wall to her right, she saw a large, rounded shadow cast against the streetlight from the window opposite. As she continued to stare, the shadow began to rise toward the ceiling and un-dulate slowly, as if it had a pulse. She held her breath, eyes widening, as it moved across the room, then in front of her, before disappearing out the window. She got up and went to the window. Across the road, she saw what looked like two figures in long dresses walking down the highway, but when she peered closer, they were gone. She opened the window and stuck her head out. There was no sound or sign of activity, only the same dimly lit highway and darkened houses of her neighbors.

The next day, as soon as Frank and his workers showed up, she told him, "We have a big problem. I saw *rats* in the kitchen last night—three of them! They got to everything I put in the pantry. And I heard scratching in my room upstairs too. Something must have opened up with all this construction."

Frank's brow furrowed. "Rats? You sure they weren't mice?"

"They had tails, like this!" She spread her hands a foot apart and shook them in his face.

He looked at his two men, then back at her. "Okay."

"*Okay?* That's all you have to say? They're in my house. I can't live like this!"

He looked alarmed at her outburst and actually took a step back. "Well . . . I don't see how this is our fault. I mean, it's the country."

"I don't care! Living with a colony of rats is not acceptable! Look," she said, forcibly calming herself, "I'm not saying it's your fault. I'm just asking you to help. Can you do that?"

He shrugged. "We can set some traps. I'll have to send Jim to the hardware store. Back and forth, that's almost an hour. Then setting out the traps. What I'm saying is it's gonna delay us. We won't finish plastering the bathroom and hallway today. It's up to you." It was the longest string of words he'd ever uttered in her presence. She wondered how much this delay would cost her. She was certain he was exaggerating. But it seemed she had no choice.

Every day, she had Jim check the traps. He was resistant until she pressed a twenty in his hand. By the end of the week, the two smaller vermin were caught.

"There's still that big one," she fretted.

"It'll show up," Jim said, "or else it's figured out this place ain't friendly."

Finally, all the inside work was complete. When she had more money, she'd deal with the landscaping and the pool. A sweet, moldy smell rose from the roots of the maple tree, likely caused by some fungus, but finding an arborist was low on her list of priorities. She tried to garden but didn't have Sebastian's touch. The one time she dug around in the neglected vegetable bed, the soil was full of strange-looking tubers and a writhing colony of slugs, making her reel back in disgust. At least the house was almost done, except for the exterior, which still had to be painted. Frank said he'd come back in a few weeks, when his schedule was more open. "See you," he mumbled, and then, without so much as a wave, he and his men were gone.

It took several days for her to clean and set up everything the way she wanted. There were so many rooms, most of them barely furnished. She was perturbed that, despite the upgrades to the downstairs bathroom, the rusty odor lingered. And her smooth new walls and refinished floors only emphasized the meagerness of her furnishings, making the candelabra dominate the living room. Her older pieces looked especially shabby. It would be a while before she could afford to buy more, even if they were secondhand. There was a time when she would have welcomed such a long-term project. Now it just felt onerous. More and more, it seemed the only easy thing about the house was getting it. She was relieved the renovation was nearly over, but as she walked through the spartan rooms, her lone footsteps making hollow echoes, she couldn't help wishing she felt more satisfaction.

Later that night, she woke again to the sound of scratching. It disappeared as soon as she sat up, but there on the wall was the same strange shadow. Seeing it for the second time, she felt even more frightened. It appeared to have grown in size and density, as if it were now *embedded* in the wall instead of projected—and in that instant it struck her as ratlike, monstrous. Her heart thumped with terror. As she stared, its curved edge began to expand and contract in rhythm with her quickened breathing, as if it were breathing too. She sensed a malevolent energy in the room. "What do you want?" she whimpered. The shadow began to pulse and rise toward the ceiling, growing rounder and larger . . . and now she saw that its shape did not resemble a rat at all but an enormous, distended belly. She clamped her hand over her mouth in horror. *My god,* she thought, *it's a baby—it's that girl's dead baby.*

The smell of meat roasting in the oven almost made her sick, but beneath the revulsion, Claire's appetite stirred like a deadened nerve brought back to life. It had been more than twelve years since she tasted red meat and almost five since she last cooked it, for Sebastian on his fortieth birthday. Tonight was an occasion of sorts. She'd invited Karl and Evelyn over for dinner and wanted the meal to be impressive, as thanks for all their help over the last year. It would also be the first time they saw the house since the renovation was completed. She wanted the evening to be celebratory, but something happened earlier in the week that upset her.

She got an El Paso postcard from Sebastian. She hadn't heard from him in almost two months, not even after she let him know she was returning to Caliban. The postcard was addressed to the house, so he clearly got her text. But all he wrote was: *Hot as Lucifer's balls out here. Off to more temperate climes. ~S.* Nothing personal; only letting her know where he was or had been. Was this to be his new form of torment, dropping these small detonations into her life at his whim? Shaking with fury, she texted him: *Please don't send any more postcards. If you can't communicate with me like a normal person, I'd rather not hear from you at all.* Later that night, a short reply back: *Understood. Sorry.* She felt a tiny measure of self-dignity return.

But it still weighed on her mind. She forced herself to focus on the menu she'd planned: an elaborate meal of pot roast with glazed carrots, gratin potatoes, a kale and quinoa salad, and blueberry crumble with ice cream for dessert. She would eat only the salad, but she spent all day in the kitchen carefully following recipes for these hearty dishes.

Promptly at five thirty, her aunt and uncle arrived. Both in their late sixties, they were an inseparable if odd-looking pair. Karl was tall and big-boned, while Evelyn was tiny and birdlike, with a mass of ginger-red hair. Karl held a bottle of champagne in one hand and a gift-wrapped box in the other. "Oh no!" Claire exclaimed, letting them in. "You didn't have to do this, Karl, you already got me that dresser!"

"It's just a little something." The box contained six elegant crystal flutes. She gasped with delight as he popped open the champagne. While they sipped, she walked them through the house, pointing out all the improvements. Opening the new French doors leading to the backyard, she said, "Frank still has to paint the exterior, and I need more furniture, obviously. But it's come a long way."

"It seems so much bigger!" Evelyn said. "I could hear us echoing."

"Some rugs would help with that," Karl suggested, and then, seeing Claire's hurt expression, "but all in good time."

"You don't get spooked sometimes?" Evelyn asked.

For a moment, Claire considered telling them about the strange scratching noises at night and the bizarre shadow on her wall. But it would sound crazy, and besides, it was hard to describe something she barely understood herself. She hadn't seen it again, and now she wondered if it really had been Anna's baby or maybe the restless spirit of some other poor infant. "It is an old house. Have you ever heard of it being haunted?"

Karl laughed. "If I did, I wouldn't have paid any mind. Don't listen to idle gossip, honey. This is a fine home you've got. You and Frank did a great job."

During dinner, Karl and Evelyn ate everything with unfeigned pleasure. It was gratifying for Claire after all her hard work, except that Evelyn kept nagging at her. "The roast is so tender. You won't even have a bite?"

"I'm fine, really."

"You can indulge a little, honey. You're practically wasting away."

"Evelyn, please! Just enjoy your meal and let me enjoy mine!" There was a strained, frozen moment, which Claire broke by asking, "More wine?" She poured them all generous refills, upset with herself for snapping. After all, they were her only family now. Claire's father was diagnosed with Alzheimer's five years ago, and ever since, his wife kept him away from "people who upset him"—her way of ensuring, as she had for most of Claire's life, that they not have a relationship.

Karl was her mother's younger brother, and after she died, he became more doting and protective of Claire. He and Evelyn met later in life and had no children. Evelyn once tried to list the benefits of their situation, but Claire said, "The difference is, Evelyn, that was your choice. It wasn't mine." Though that wasn't entirely true, and she often regretted the fear that propelled her to make such a hasty decision. She'd just had her first lumpectomy, and her BRCA1 test came back positive. Her mother let her disease progress with the same defeatist acceptance she showed toward every bad thing in her life. Claire would not be so passive. And Sebastian was adamant: "I don't want you to risk it. You're more important than a baby. We can always adopt." But somehow that never happened.

Over dessert, Karl asked Claire whether she'd socialized with any of the locals yet. When she said no, Evelyn mentioned an upcoming cookout later in the month. "The Erikssons are hosting it in their barn, just over in East Durham. Why don't you come with us? It would be a good way to see everyone and, you know, get all that business over with." Claire made a face, and Evelyn said, "Now, honey, you can't spend your whole time here avoiding people. Sooner or later, you'll need more company than just us."

Claire drew herself up stiffly. "I'm sorry if my being here puts you both in an awkward position. I don't want to monopolize all your time."

Evelyn flashed Karl a look of helpless frustration. "That's not what she means," he said. "We don't give a hooey about what people say. And neither should you. It's all yesterday's news, so just come out and enjoy yourself."

"It's not yesterday's news if they're still talking about it," Claire muttered. But she saw their point. She couldn't hide forever, and if "everyone" was going to be at this cookout, better to face them with some support instead of alone.

A few weeks later, Frank came back to paint the exterior of the house, warning her again of noise and disruption. "We'll have to scrape, sand, and prime before we even put on the color. Plus all those shutters."

She knew this was his way of cushioning the time to do the job. "So how long do you think to finish everything?"

"With me and Jim it'll take about two, three weeks. Two more guys and I can cut that time in half. Cost a little extra."

"How much extra?"

"Uh . . . two thousand. So seven total."

"What do you mean? We agreed on four before, not five!" God, she was so tired of all this negotiating. She was already stretched beyond her budget. "We had this conversation last month and you distinctly told me four."

"Did I? Oh . . . okay." He capitulated so easily, she wondered if he actually forgot his quote or was tired of quibbling over money too. He was the oddest man she'd ever encountered, the epitome of everything she found irksome in these old-time country locals: stubborn, touchy, suspicious. Physically, he was odd as well, with his young-man body and old-man face. She found herself constantly looking back and forth between the two, repulsed and fascinated.

"So, it'll be just me and Jim then," he said, "if you're okay with the timing."

"I guess I'll have to be. You got the colors, right? Buttercup walls and Cypress shutters?"

He grunted affirmation and walked away. She told herself she would have to put up with his bad manners for only a few more weeks. At least they wouldn't run into each other that much, since he'd be working outside. But on the days she was home, she'd look up from her desk or walk through the house and see some part of him framed in one of the windows: long legs perched on a ladder, a splice of torso and outstretched arm, and once, from her bedroom upstairs, the top half of his head, eyes meeting hers through the pane briefly before ducking out of sight. She never caught these disembodied glimpses of Jim—only Frank.

She'd used the shutters before to block out light, but he took them all down to be primed. She thought about tacking up bedsheets for makeshift curtains but didn't want to mark up her new windowsills. Nor did she want to appear paranoid or prudish. It would be like suggesting he was trying to peep in. She considered that possibility, then dismissed it. He clearly had no interest in her that way. She couldn't imagine him having sexual interest in anyone. Yet he obviously took care of his body. Those lean muscles couldn't be just from carpentry—and for what? Though she could ask herself the same question.

Why was she working so hard to stay fit, running thirty miles a week and consuming less than eighteen hundred calories a day? Why did she bother styling her hair and dyeing her roots every month, applying sunscreen in the morning and moisturizing cream at night? Was it positive or pathetic that she still had some vanity?

One night, after the men left, she stripped in front of the full-length mirror in the upstairs bathroom. Though she got on the scale unclothed every morning, she couldn't recall the last time she truly *looked* at herself naked. Now she turned on the lights to their brightest setting and examined herself pitilessly from top to bottom:

Wavy hair showing gray at the roots beneath the auburn dye. Dark blue eyes, once her best feature, now overly large in her small face. Wiry arms, bony chest. Full, drooping breasts with large nipples, two barely visible scars on each side from separate lumpectomies. Stubborn pouch of lower belly. Thick dark thatch of pubic hair. Hips that would always be wide, no matter her weight. Child-bearing hips, her friend Ruben used to tease, until she had her ovaries removed. Turning around, she twisted her neck to survey her once cushy, heart-shaped ass, now tighter, smaller, with cellulite above the crease and on the backs of her thighs.

She dimmed the lights to a soft glow and faced her body again from the front, looking at it this time the way a lover might. Cocking her hip to one side, she tilted her head back and lowered her eyelids, trying to envision a seductive situation . . .

"Dry old cunt!"

She squeezed her eyes shut. That episode, encounter, whatever it was, could hardly be called a seduction. But was it an assault? The question was too disturbing. It was a sloppy drunken sequence out of time, much of it already obliterated. Someday, she hoped, she would forget it entirely.

In her youth, before Sebastian, she'd been with several young men; some were tender, others callous. All those boys she'd known with their athletic physiques—she wondered what they looked like now, if they'd gone paunchy and gray with middle age. Although Sebastian hadn't. Nor Frank—and he was almost her uncle's age. Not that she was interested in seniors.

Would men still find her desirable? She placed her hands under her breasts, moving them down the length of her flanks and across her midriff, palms flat against her skin. As she pressed against her lower belly, her right hand froze in surprise. Beneath the soft cushion of fat, she felt something hard, like a small knot. She pressed again, found nothing, and then—there it was, almost level to her hip. Probing the area further, she realized the knot was in fact nearly two inches long, like a piece of cartilage inserted into her flesh.

She felt the cold familiar fear that seized her whenever she discovered any strange new lumps. With her mother's history, she could never be too careful.

She'd had tumors and cysts over the years; two were internal and seemed like menstrual bleeding. Some went away on their own, while others were removed through minor surgeries. This one was likely another benign growth of some kind, nothing to panic over.

"You're fine," she said out loud to her reflection. She said it again, more emphatically, and then remembered this was exactly what she once told her mother.

———

On the day of the Erikssons' party, the weather was unusually warm and muggy, hitting ninety-two degrees by noon. Karl and Evelyn picked Claire up shortly after. She'd planned her outfit carefully: a sleeveless chambray dress with new sandals and a straw fedora. Evelyn said, "Oh, you look so nice and fresh."

"Believe me, I don't feel it," Claire said, getting into their car. The rooms in her house, normally shuttered from the sun, were now exposed and stifling, with only ceiling fans to cool them off. She couldn't afford to install central air for at least another year, and it seemed wasteful to invest in temporary window units.

"Such unfortunate weather for the cookout," said Evelyn. "I hope people will show up—and that it doesn't rain."

It was a short drive to the Erikssons' home, an imposing brick Colonial on a long grassy slope, the only residence visible for several acres. The road leading to the house was already lined back to back with vehicles.

"So much for the poor turnout," Claire said, suddenly nervous. "This AC feels so nice. Can't we just stay in here?"

Karl said, "Come on, it'll be a good time."

He got out of the car and they followed, the wall of heat hitting them instantly. They walked past the house to the large red barn behind it. Both its double doors, front and back, were flung open. Claire could see clear through to a vista of wildflowers and lush green meadow, breathing in the sweet smell of freshly cut grass. She had never seen anything so bucolic.

"Jesus, what do these people do?"

"Jakob's a contract attorney and Lena's an artist—quite renowned, in fact," said Evelyn. "See? We're not just some upcountry bumpkins. And if you think this is nice, you should see some of the houses in Rensselaerville!"

Entering the barn, Claire saw several tables covered with assorted dishes: burgers and sausages with buns stacked beside them; platters of barbecued ribs; corn on the cob, coleslaw, and salad; crudité with dip and hummus; cheese, bread, and crackers. An entire table was devoted to desserts alone, including cakes, pies, cookies, and brownies. There was so much food. The sheer gluttony of it all was obscene, but she found herself salivating. The smell of meat grilling wafted from outside. She turned away from the food and noticed another table nearby that served as a makeshift bar, with an array of wine and hard liquor and, below, an ice chest full of beer and bottled water.

"Look at that spread," said Karl.

As they served themselves, several people greeted him and Evelyn with hugs and happy cries. Evelyn kept saying, "Do you remember Karl's niece?" until Claire's jaw ached from smiling. Everyone was cordial, but after a while she excused herself to make her way over to the bar. Balancing her paper plate of crudité, she poured white wine into a large plastic cup and headed toward the back of the barn. She leaned against the doorframe, sipping her drink while she took in her surroundings. Around thirty people were milling about in the barn, while others wandered out to the meadow, where chairs and picnic tables were scattered. Outside, the sun beat down without mercy, but there were patches of shade beneath some crabapple trees, and two misting sprinklers to provide relief.

Across the meadow was a large pond surrounded by cattails with a wooden dock jutting out at one end. Several children in swimsuits stood on the dock single file, waiting to dive in, while others splashed around in the water. Their laughter and squeals rang throughout the yard.

Evelyn came and stood next to her. "Okay so far?"

"What? Yes, thanks. I didn't know there'd be so many children."

"Of course, everyone comes. Look, go stake out those chairs while I get Karl. It's so awkward to eat standing up."

As she crossed the lawn, Claire heard someone call out her name. She turned
to see Jan Strauss waving and heading in her direction, two other women trailing behind her. The year before, Claire met her for coffee twice and found her a
pleasant, acerbic gossip.

"You're back!" Jan said, giving her a big hug. "Wonderful! Have you met
Paula and Becky?"

As she shook hands, the women spoke over one another: "Nice to meet you."
"Welcome back!" "I hear you're up here full-time now."

Karl and Evelyn came up, and they all went together to find chairs. As Jan's
friends circled around, Claire braced herself for a barrage of intrusive questions. But they were polite, asking only about the renovation and her job,
telling her how great she looked. No one brought up the past. They'd talk
about it behind her back, no doubt, but in her company, they maintained
a facade of obliviousness. It wasn't just Frank. There seemed to be a code
out here, a tacit understanding behind the friendly smiles and quick glances.
Claire found herself beginning to relax. She could handle this kind of casual,
complimentary banter.

More people showed up. The crowd and heat, along with the wine, made her
feel light-headed, but when her cup was empty, she stood to get a refill, stum-
bling out of her low chair. "Oops," she said, blushing. "I'll be back. Anyone
want anything?"

They all shook their heads, smiling brightly. She noticed most of them had
bottled waters. After the next drink she would cut herself off.

A small cluster of people stood around the bar, but she wedged herself in.
As she reached for a bottle of white, she almost tripped over a woman kneeling
by the ice chest. "Oh, sorry!"

"No problem," the woman said, standing up. It was April. For a second, she
looked at Claire blankly. "Oh, hey! Holy shit. I heard you were back but—wow,
you lost a ton of weight. I didn't even recognize you."

Claire said, flustered, "Yes, well . . . it's been a while."

April looked better than before. Her hair was pulled back in a simple ponytail, and she wore a sleeveless blue shirt with denim cutoffs, clean and not too

short. "Yeah, I guess. Anyway . . . sorry about all that happened." After a pause, she said, "So, how's it going? Dealing okay with the local buzzards?"

Claire was caught off guard by her directness. She was about to change the subject, but something in April's weary, arch expression made her laugh. It was refreshing for a moment to be frank, to not have to pretend. "That's an interesting way to describe them."

"Please," April said, rolling her eyes, "I know all about it. Thing is, you have to not give a fuck. Then they respect you."

"I see," said Claire. Just then, a young girl and boy walked up to April, both carrying towels.

The girl said, "Mom, where can we change to go swimming?"

"I don't know, go look for a bathroom or ask someone." She told Claire, "These are my brats. Two of them, anyway."

The boy was dark and tall and looked nothing like April. The girl was a softer version of her mother, pretty in a checkered sundress, a floral handkerchief tied around her blond ponytail.

Then Claire cried out, pointing to the handkerchief. "Where did you get that? That's—my husband gave that to me." He'd wrapped it around a pair of earrings for her birthday years ago. She noticed it was missing, then forgot about it in the chaos of the last several months. "Where did you get it?" she insisted.

"From my mom," the girl said, frowning.

Claire turned on April. "*How?* I don't understand."

April actually turned red. "I found it somewhere, I can't remember." But the guilt on her face was plain to see, and it shocked Claire to the core.

"You're lying," she said, her voice rising. The implication crashed over her. "Did *he* give it to you?"

She whirled around and ran out of the barn, her head reeling. She hadn't gotten far when someone grabbed her by the arm. It was April, holding out the handkerchief.

"Listen," she said, "he did not give it to me. I found it in one of the houses I clean, in the trash. I don't do that normally, but I thought Cara would like it. It's the truth, I swear."

"Whose house? Why did you lie about it just now, when I asked?"

"I was embarrassed and—oh Christ. Okay. In the house where I found it, their nanny was that girl from the Eternals. Anna. I guess she had it and threw it away."

Claire was dumbfounded by the news that Anna was still in the area.

"Sorry. I didn't want to bring her up and upset you. But you thinking he gave it to me is worse. Here," April said, pressing the handkerchief into Claire's palm.

"Whose house was it, where you found this?"

April hesitated. "I don't work there anymore. It was last winter. I don't even know if she's still there."

Claire wondered why she was being so evasive. Did she think she was going to find the little whore, have a confrontation? Was that in fact what she wanted to do?

"Look, for what it's worth," April said, "she told me nothing ever happened between them. Physically, I mean."

When Claire didn't say anything, she flicked her hands helplessly and walked away. Claire watched her disappear into the barn. She couldn't face more idle chitchat with Jan and her friends. She needed to go home and be by herself, sit in a cool bath and think. It wasn't a long walk, two miles at most, and her phone was in her pocket. She would text Karl later and make up some excuse. She was at the bottom of the slope, sweating profusely, when she remembered she left her hat by her lawn chair. Too late to go back for it now. The sun was directly overhead, with no shade along the road for as far as she could see. As she wiped the sweat off her forehead, a wave of dizziness came over her. She bent forward, clutching her stomach and feeling her gorge rise up. *Oh god, not here. Just let me get home.*

She took in deep breaths, eyes squeezed shut, waiting for the nausea to pass. After a few minutes, it did. She stood up shakily and continued down the road. So much for drinking in the sun. She was probably dehydrated. Walking in the heat with no water was about the dumbest thing she could have set out to do, but now she was committed. Shielding her eyes with her hand, she hastened her pace. Two cars passed her coming from the opposite side. The passengers gave her curious looks. *Fuck off,* she mouthed silently. Had people noticed her talking to April and looking upset? Had April told anyone else about seeing Anna?

"Nothing ever happened with them physically."

So Sebastian hadn't lied about that. Then what could account for his infatuation? What did he see in that plain-faced girl, a cult member no less? Was it simply her youth? Tears welled and mingled with mascara, stinging her eyes. To the friends who still asked, she'd learned to say "He stopped loving me" in a matter-of-fact tone, hoping the act of acceptance would make it come true. But inside, the old pain was still there.

She'd walked for almost a mile when blisters began to form on the tops of her toes where her sandal straps rubbed. Finally, she took them off and stepped away from the road, trudging instead through the tall grass. By the time she approached her house, her feet and ankles were streaked with dirt and mud. Sweat poured down her face, neck, and armpits. To her shock, Frank's truck was parked in her driveway. As she got closer, she saw him at the side of the house on top of a ladder, scraping something off the roof into a trash bag. He was so intent on the work he didn't notice her until she stood right beneath him.

"What are you doing here?" she asked, so parched she could barely speak. "It's Saturday."

He turned slightly and said, "Gonna be a big downpour later. Saw the other day your gutters are clogged. If I don't clean 'em out now water'll leak into the house and cause a big mess."

"Oh," she said, surprised at his proactiveness. She was too tired to ask what this extra service would cost her.

He stopped what he was doing and looked at her—actually really looked at her. "You okay?"

"I'm fine. I was just . . . out for a walk."

He lifted an eyebrow at her standing there holding her sandals, then shrugged. "Anyway, didn't mean to surprise you. I left a message."

"That's fine. I appreciate it." She nodded and went in the house. It was still warm, despite her having left the ceiling fans on and all the windows open. She gulped down two huge glasses of water. Then she went upstairs, took off her sweat-stained dress, and checked her legs for ticks. After running a cool bath, she leaned her head against the tub, closing her eyes, and fell into a light doze.

The sound of something thumping outside the door jerked her awake. She got out of the tub, wrapping a towel around her, and stepped into the hallway. Near the top of the stairs, a huge rat lay thrashing on its side, its head stuck in a trap. The rat had dragged itself from beneath the linen cabinet where Jim set the trap and was trying to shake free. Claire let out a loud, high-pitched scream. It seemed to galvanize the rat. Its long tail whipped up and down, small claws moving furiously, while the trap on its head clattered against the wooden floor. She screamed again and again, nearly sobbing, and cowered against the wall. The rat continued to thrash, scuttling across the floor, desperate and very much alive.

Frank yelled from below, "What's going on? You okay?" In seconds he was at the top of the stairs. He saw the rat and said, "Holy—" Then he noticed her wrapped in her towel and averted his eyes.

"Kill it! Oh god, please, I can't stand it, make it stop!"

He approached the rat and, with the heavy lug heel of his boot, stomped on it several times. She started to look away but was caught by his face, mesmerized, as his usual impassive expression shifted into one of studied viciousness. The transformation was startling. His kicks at first were slow and methodical. Then they became harder, more emphatic. Blood squirted and oozed onto the floor. The tail stopped moving. Frank stepped back, panting, and looked down at his bloodied boot. He lifted his head and met her eyes. He seemed stunned and vaguely embarrassed. When he spoke, the drag in his voice was more pronounced: "I'll . . . clean this up. Let me go . . . get something."

She nodded and watched him go down the stairs. *I should get dressed,* she thought. But she felt unable to move. Before she knew it, he was back, holding a trash bag and some rags. He used one to pick up the rat by its tail and drop it into the bag, then wiped off the blood with the rest of the rags and tossed them in too. Standing up, he said, "You might . . . want to go over that again with a sponge."

She walked over to him, holding her towel in place. "Thank you. Sorry I got hysterical, but I . . . Anyway, thank you." She reached out and placed her hand on his forearm. The skin was rough and warm, the hairs coarse under her palm. He flinched but didn't move away. She slid her hand down to his, feeling the knobby fingers, the thick calluses on his palm. A sense of recklessness came over her. It took so little to turn the impossible into reality; this much she'd learned from the last year. Lifting his hand, she pressed it to her chest, where she had tucked in the towel edge. She dropped her arms, and now only his hand held the towel in place.

The front doorbell rang, startling them both. He pulled his hand away, and in that instant, her towel fell to the floor. He made a small strangled sound and looked away, blushing all the way down to his neck. She bent to retrieve the towel, covering herself hastily as her own face burned.

Her uncle yelled from outside: "Claire? Are you there?"

"Shit," she said, "it's Karl. Tell them about the rat, that I'll be down in a minute. Tell them I'm washing my hands."

He went down the stairs and she ran to the bathroom, throwing her rumpled dress back over her head. As she descended the stairs, she saw them all in the entryway. Her aunt was holding her hat. "Honey, are you okay? Why'd you leave without telling us?"

"I'm sorry. I got so tired all of a sudden. I didn't want to pull you away, so I figured I'd walk."

"In this heat! I'm surprised you didn't faint. We wondered what happened, then the Straubs told us they saw you walking down Route 22."

Karl frowned. "That's not like you. You sure you're okay?"

"I'm fine now." Having Frank overhear this conversation was humiliating. She stole a quick glance his way, but he kept his back turned to her.

"That's one hell of a rat you caught," Karl said. "Frank said it took a while to get dead."

"Yes," she said, shuddering at the memory. Why wouldn't he look at her?

Frank muttered, "I should get rid of this," and slipped quickly out the door.

Karl turned to Claire with a bemused expression. "I see what you mean. He does act kind of strange around you."

———————

Later that evening, the sky cracked open with deafening thunder and heavy rain. It continued all throughout Sunday, but by Monday morning the sun was out again, and the weather balmy. Frank and Jim showed up shortly after eight to resume their work. When Claire saw the truck pull up, she felt both relieved and agitated. She'd spent all weekend indoors, agonizing over what had happened—or not happened—between her and Frank. She replayed the scene over and over in her mind, trying to decide if he'd been excited or terrified. He was caught off guard, but he didn't pull away, not until Karl and Evelyn showed up. What if they hadn't?

She watched the men unload, waiting until she saw Frank by his truck alone before she stepped outside. Her heart pounded as she drew near. "Good morning," she said, trying to sound casual. "You were right. That was some storm we had."

He glanced at her sideways and nodded. "Yep. We were due." He turned away and rummaged for something in the truck bed, clattering tools around noisily. Saying nothing. Refusing to meet her eyes.

Her stomach pitched sharply. She had made a terrible mistake.

He turned around but kept his gaze directed somewhere over her shoulder, just as he did in the beginning. "I'm bringing on an extra guy tomorrow . . . so we should be done by Friday. I won't charge you. I got another job starts next week so . . . best to wrap things up here."

"I see." Her cheeks flamed with indignation. So he'd pay out of his own pocket to be rid of her. *I'll be damned if I let him think I care.* "That's great. The sooner the better. Well, then, I'll let you get to work." She turned and headed toward the house, keeping her shoulders squared, her back straight—even though she knew he wasn't looking.

———————

The lights in the supermarket hurt her eyes, and it was freezing, but Claire figured the cold might sober her up. She'd just had brunch with Jan, where she consumed an arugula salad and two strong Bloody Marys. She hadn't planned on drinking until Jan nonchalantly ordered a mimosa—though *she* stopped at one. "I've got to take Ally to volleyball practice," she said. "You go ahead, though. Enjoy your Sunday." She probably hoped Claire would get drunk and spill gossip, but Claire only got tipsy. Still, the strain of keeping her tongue in check, while the rest of her loosened, gave her a pounding headache. She only bothered to meet Jan for the distraction.

The work on the house was finally complete: the exterior painted, the shutters back up, and Frank and his crew gone. He slipped his final invoice under the front door at the end of the last day. *Good riddance to you too,* Claire thought, still smarting from shame. It was unbearable he should think she was actually interested. She'd been badly unnerved by the rat and overly grateful to him for killing it. Nothing would have happened if she had been in her right mind. She was relieved at least he wasn't a big talker—or much of a thinker either.

She wished it could be like that for her, that she could rid herself of her obstinate memory, her obsessive nature. But of all the ways she tried, the only escape she ever found was through exercise or alcohol. Even sleep eluded her most nights—and earlier that week, she awakened again to find the shadow creeping on her wall. It was definitely a presence, but this time she felt less fearful than mystified. Watching its rhythmic pulsing, she had the distinct sense it was trying to impart a message to her, though she could not decipher what that might be.

"Excuse me," a woman said to her irritably. Claire had paused in the middle of an aisle near the meat section. She moved to let the woman by and caught the savory aroma of roasting chicken. Her stomach rumbled. The salad at brunch was tiny, more like garnish than a meal. She was still hungry. She was always hungry. In her cart so far were salad greens, carrots, brown rice, lemons. Normally she got her vegetables from the farmers market, but she was too tired and buzzed to make multiple stops today. And for what? In the end, a salad was a salad. She was sick to death of them, sick of kale and healthy grains and fiber and fruits, sick of chia seeds and herbal teas and fish oil capsules, sick of never feeling full or satisfied, sick of denying herself, pushing herself, *being* herself—

"And for *what?*" she hissed.

People around her turned to stare. She colored and looked down. Before her, a refrigerated island displayed different cuts of beef, bright red meat with white veins of fat glistening behind plastic wrap. There was a thick, beautifully marbled rib eye—how delectable would that be with a crusty sourdough and butter, some of that good cabernet she splurged on last week? And plain vanilla ice cream for dessert, a whole pint. Her mouth began to water. She tossed the steak into the cart and pushed it forward swiftly through the aisles, searching for the other items. Her heart pumped with something close to joy.

At home, she unpacked her groceries eagerly. She uncorked the cabernet, turned on some music, and began to cook. The meal surpassed her expectations. The steak was perfectly seasoned and seared (how easily it all came back to her), its juices running pink onto the plate, which she soaked up with buttered bread. She savored every bite luxuriously, polishing off the steak, half the ice cream, and the whole bottle of cabernet. It was just turning dark outside when she swallowed the last bite. Leaning back against her chair, she closed her eyes, feeling decadent and satiated. The world teetered pleasantly, as if she were flying through a light turbulence.

It was only when she stood up to clear the dishes that the old despair returned, heavier than ever. Her grand indulgence was over, and now there was nothing more to look forward to. Yet still so many hours lay ahead. And then the days . . .

She stumbled to the kitchen and scraped into the trash what remained on her dirty plate: gristle and bone, chunks of fat and congealed grease. There was grease too in the skillet, with small splatters all over the stove, and a stick of melting butter she forgot to put away. She pictured all that fat and meat in her stomach, already breaking down and digesting. Tomorrow, and the day after, she would have to run extra miles. This was her life: fleeting pleasures and endless retribution. Her mother, toward the end, tried to wax philosophical: "It's not about the life we wanted, it's about the life we were given." But her eyes were full of fear and said something else.

Claire snapped on rubber gloves and soaped a sponge, determined to remove every trace of the meal. It seemed to take forever in her drunken state. She was drying her wineglass when it slipped out of her hands and shattered on the floor. By the time she'd swept up the shards and put everything back in order, she was cranky and spent. Her buzz had faded and her headache was back.

It wasn't even eight o'clock, but she dragged herself upstairs and got into bed fully clothed, falling asleep instantly. An hour later, she bolted awake, her insides churning. The nausea came up suddenly, so fast she could barely react—she was already retching over the bed, the rank smell of it making her even sicker. Cupping her hands over her mouth, she ran to the bathroom, kneeling over the toilet in misery. She expelled everything: the meat, the bread, and the wine—so much of the wine, the toilet bowl turned pink. "Oh god," she moaned, clutching at her stomach. It kept heaving, even when nothing came up but rancid liquid.

At last, the spasms subsided. She flushed the toilet and stood over the sink, filling her rinse glass from the tap. She drank greedily. Then she splashed cold water on her face and neck. Above the sink, her reflection in the mirror showed a drawn face, scrawny arms, pronounced collarbones. From this angle she seemed almost emaciated. But looking down, she could still see the padding of flesh at her midsection, even depleted as she was.

"You're disgusting," she said, squeezing the fat on her belly. "You're so disgusting."

Then she felt it again: the strange, hard lump on her right side. She lifted her shirt and pressed around the area. The last time she checked, she thought the lump had receded. Now it was back, and as she probed, it had a definite shape, like a small . . . it was crazy, but it felt to her just like a tiny fist. Her stomach in fact seemed distended, bigger than she remembered. She turned to look at it in the mirror sideways. The rounded shape moved in and out as she breathed—

She gasped in recognition as the back of her neck prickled. The shadow on her wall. "It's impossible," she whispered. She'd had her ovaries removed thirteen years ago. *But,* said a voice inside her head, *doctors make mistakes all the time.* When she continued to bleed and was told she had cysts . . . what if her procedure was somehow botched? She should be livid, but instead, her heart began to pound with desperate hope.

She thought back to the bouts of nausea and vomiting over the past several weeks, her strange appetites, her growing belly. And before that, the man in Tampa. She couldn't remember if he used a condom or not, it all happened so fast. He looked like Sebastian—how fateful that now seemed. The irony was that Sebastian might have been the infertile one all along. But if she were to claim him as the father, who could dispute her? Only Sebastian, and he probably wouldn't even care. Her pulse was racing. She forced herself to take deep breaths. Something was unfolding—something too extraordinary for her to quite believe.

She wondered if the mini-mart down the road at Pete's Pump carried pregnancy tests. But even if it did, the chance of running into someone who knew her, and the ensuing gossip, was too risky. The CVS in Greenville was safer and only four miles away. If she left now, she'd get there before it closed.

She was wide-awake as she drove there, made her purchase, and drove back—yet all the while she felt outside her body, as if her actions were propelled by an external force. When she got home, she settled herself in the small downstairs bathroom, trying to ignore the sharp smell of rust. Her hands shook as she read over the instructions. She'd never taken a pregnancy test before, never allowed a life to grow inside her. Once, the very idea made her panic. Even after marrying Sebastian, she chose to wait. She went straight from birth control to barrenness. Or so she thought.

Carefully, she removed the tester swab and sat on the toilet seat. She urinated onto the swab and held it in front of her, staring at the indicator. She waited for what seemed an eternity, listening to her own shallow breathing. When the test turned positive, she burst into tears. Feelings she could scarcely contain overwhelmed her: shock, wonder, humility, and gratitude. Her life had seemed a series of disappointments. And then, somehow, this unthinkable grace—this miracle. She had never believed in miracles or in the existence of a god. But now she fell to her knees and, looking upward with streaming eyes, said fervently, "Thank you, thank you, *thank you.*"

4
REUNION

June 3, 2010

Dear Luke,

I know I shouldn't be writing, but I heard from Adina back home in Milton that you've been sick with Lyme. I asked if she wouldn't mind inquiring with your parents on my behalf, and their response was more than generous. I hope they weren't wrong in encouraging me to write to you directly.

We are no longer husband and wife, and I've wronged you in ways I can never amend. You have every right to hate me. But we've known each other since we were children. You were my most trusted friend. I don't want to upset you, but I just want to know you're okay. It sounds like you were very sick. I'm so distressed to hear it.

Luke, if you don't answer this, I'll never bother you again. But if you want to reply, please send a letter through your parents, and they'll make sure it reaches me. If you could find it in your heart to set my mind at ease, it would mean so much. You're forever in my heart and in my prayers.

Anna

———————

June 12, 2010

Dear Anna,

I wasn't upset by your letter, only surprised—by you and by my parents agreeing to help, going against the elders' wishes. I suppose I'm going against them too. But somehow I feel it would be even more wrong not to reply. I can't explain it, why doing what's wrong feels right, or at least correct. Maybe God is testing me. I've been in a strange state of mind lately, so forgive me if I don't make sense. It's the illness, mostly, but I suppose you could also call it a spiritual crisis. I'm praying very hard to be lifted from it.

As for my health: I am getting better, thank you. I started feeling sick around the end of April, but I thought it was just the flu, so I pushed myself, probably too much. Then I felt worse and got a bad rash on my leg, so Esther knew it was Lyme, and I saw a doctor. I've been on antibiotics, but my recovery has been slow. It's frustrating, because you know I'm never sick. Now Gabriel has to tend to the goats on his own. Well, I'm sure this will pass.

You don't mention anything about your life. I thought you would stay in Milton, but I heard you left after only a short time. So then I thought you must have gone somewhere far away. I've often wondered to where. There's so much on my mind, but I can't seem to turn these thoughts into words. I do know this: I could never hate you. Before, when you couldn't explain yourself, I didn't understand. I assumed the worst. But now I'm struggling to explain myself too, and failing. So I'll end this letter by saying I'm grateful you've kept me in your prayers and in your heart. You've remained in mine as well.
Luke

———————————

June 25, 2010

Dear Luke,

I was so happy to see your letter, though I'm very sorry to hear you're still not fully recovered. And that you're suffering from a spiritual crisis. You've had to bear so much sorrow. I know I'm a part of that.

When I left Caliban, I was also in a spiritual crisis. I thought I was unworthy of God and questioned if I still had the right to pray to Him. I've come to see even those doubts were a form of vanity, the same vanity that led to my disgrace. Worthy or not, I kept seeking His guidance and forgiveness. He has shown me both. I know if you keep praying, He'll show you His mercy too.

You wanted to know about my life now. I live with a family not far from Caliban, taking care of two little boys. You remember how I used to watch Rebekah's girls? I couldn't think what else to do, and if I stayed in Milton, I'd only bring more shame to my parents. So I came back to the only other area I've lived in, though of course not the same town. It was frightening at first, living with strangers. And their youngest was a newborn when I arrived. That was hard.

My employers don't know about my past as an Eternal, though I don't really think of it as my past. It's still my faith, still who I am. Even though, as you say, I'm going against the elders by writing to you. But when I heard you were sick, I felt the same way you did, that somehow it was worse not to reach out.

I'm so grateful you don't hate me. You can't know the weight it lifts from my heart. I so wish I could do something to help. I so wish I didn't forfeit that right. Please forgive me if this brings you pain. I've tried to bear my punishment and be strong. It's just that I don't know how to live in this world. The ways of this family are so strange. Aside from the children, their concerns are mostly about work and money. Holy days are occasions to entertain the children. They sit down to eat with their phones. They insist I carry a phone too, in case of emergency. I know this goes against our rules, but now that I live in their world, I must abide by it.

I know God means to show me the spiritual vacancy of those who live without His grace. And that, even in isolation, my life has more purpose. But I miss sharing that purpose, feeling lifted by others who also believe. Forgive my rambling. Writing to you perhaps gives me too much comfort. But I'm so grateful you've allowed me to. Please just get better, Luke. I'll continue to pray for you.

Your Anna

She signed the letter the way she used to in the early days of their betrothal, when they passed secret notes to each other during evening prayers—a habit carried over from childhood throughout study hour. It was an unconscious slip, but she decided to leave it. She hoped he wouldn't find it presumptuous, that instead it might please him.

"My Anna," he used to whisper to her in moments of intimacy. The Eternals did not use the word *love* to express their feelings for each other; love was a pledge sacred to God. Still, when Luke used his private endearment, she felt him declare his heart. It moved her and at times bewildered her. Was she his? Did she belong to him? Though she understood this was the nature of marriage, some part of her resisted. Yet, when he released his claim, she did not return to herself. If anything, there seemed less of her than before. And then she understood what she had lost, what her curiosity and hubris had cost her.

She had told April she left Milton to protect her parents from the fallout of her shame, and it was the truth. It seemed right that she did her penance among other sinners, in the outside world. But she was also intrigued by the possibility of what she could see and learn. The elders in Milton agreed it would be best for her to leave and helped her find employment as a nanny, teaching her the basics of using a computer, allowing her access to the phone, and providing good references. She asked for only a modest wage, so several families were interested. After the Burnetts hired her, the elders gave her money to buy some modern clothes and a train ticket to the Rensselaer station.

Her first few days with the Burnetts were a difficult time of adjustment. She felt awkward in her new clothes, sleeping in her new room, living with these strangers in their huge, wasteful house. Michael had to teach her how to turn on their house alarm, TV, DVD, and other various gadgets. For the children's sake, they got her a phone and insisted she learn to drive (she omitted this last point in her letters to Luke).

It got better once she grew comfortable with the boys and had April to talk to. As Laurie grew to trust her, she became more friendly and confiding. But Anna could never truly relax in her company. There was a barrier, unspoken but clear. While Laurie and Michael were kind, it was more than obvious that they saw her and April as peripheral, there to serve a domestic function and nothing more. Yet that absence of attention could at times be liberating. Anna alternated between enjoying her hours of solitude and feeling crippled by loneliness.

Memories of Luke and her parents, her friends from Milton, her daily exchanges at the Horizon Café—all these fragments from her old life would flood through her at unexpected moments. Sometimes Sebastian would intrude into her thoughts as well, leaving a ripple of shame and remorse at how she could have been so reckless. Even before she left Caliban, she'd heard he and his wife were already gone. She wondered if they ever returned, if he at least was able to save his marriage. But this was something she could never ask Luke.

Sometimes, on her days off, Laurie let her take one of their cars for a few hours, and she would often drive to Cornwallville Creek. It reminded her of the farmhouse in Caliban. How strange that she should miss it, when she had felt so out of place before. So constricted.

Now, she was able to read and look at whatever she pleased; she could do anything in her free time. But she found the novelty of these distractions small comfort in the face of her profound isolation. There was no one who truly understood her. She missed the Eternals' rituals and spiritual communing. And she missed Luke. Most of all, she felt heartsick at her betrayal of his trust.

In the hospital, the morning after their baby's death, she could hardly look at him or answer his questions without breaking down. Finally, he said something that stunned her: "Anna, please, at least tell me . . . what did our baby look like?"

"What do you mean? Didn't you see him?"

He shook his head. "Hiram insisted I shouldn't. I had to let them take him. You know there can be no funeral or gravestone, since he didn't live. But they'll bless him and lay him to rest with the Eternals."

"When?"

"I don't know. It doesn't matter, we're forbidden to be there."

She was dumb with fear and disbelief. She knew that parents of stillborn babies were discouraged from displays of mourning, as it impeded their chances of being blessed with a new child. But the elders forbidding them to witness the burial meant they considered her baby's birth to be shameful.

"What did he look like?" Luke asked again.

She could see the small blue head, the tiny lifeless limbs. "He looked peaceful," she said softly. "He looked like he was asleep."

After she was released from the hospital, the Eternals allowed her to recuperate in their convalescent room, with the understanding she was to leave them as soon as she was well enough.

On the eve of her departure, they held the denouncement ceremony in the back parlor. Everyone wore dark clothing and stood in a large circle. In the middle of it, Anna knelt on the hard floor with her head bowed. Hiram gave Luke a large sharpened cleaver, and he lifted the heavy black plait of her hair. As he moved the blade just under the base of her head, Anna had a sudden, vivid memory of the first time he saw her hair unplaited, how he ran his hands through its silken weight. Later, he covered his face with the long strands, murmuring into her neck, "I could die here, like this. That would be glory."

His hands shook as he ran the blade back and forth, pausing several times in his effort. She flinched, trying to stifle her sharp inhalations. It seemed to take forever. When it was finally done, he dropped the plait to the floor and said in a trembling voice, "I disown you." All the Eternals said in unison, "You are disowned," and the deed was done. The men left the room, and the women stayed, using small scissors to cut the rest of her hair to the scalp.

Before she left the next morning, she approached him outside their room. He opened the door as soon as she knocked, holding a small bag in his hand. "Oh. I was going to bring this to you." He stared at her newly shorn head, and she flushed.

"Thank you," she said, reaching for the bag.

"I can take it down."

"No. I'll have to carry it anyway." She looked at him directly for the first time. His eyes were red, but his face was composed. "I wanted to say goodbye. And that I'm so sorry for everything." Her voice quavered with her next words: "Luke, he asked me to sit for a portrait. That's all. But I know it was wrong. I deserve to be punished, but you—I can never make it up to you, never."

She stood still, waiting for him to speak. Nothing in the moment seemed real. She felt as if she were suspended from above, watching them. When he remained silent, she turned to leave. As she approached the stairs, she finally heard him say, "Goodbye, Anna." She looked back and nodded, pressing her lips closed to stop their trembling. Then she went down the stairs and left through the front door, walking away from the world she knew and into the outside world, where only God could protect her.

July 6, 2010

Dear Anna,

I don't mind your rambling. I miss it. Writing to you gives me comfort too. I've cherished your letters—they are the best medicine. Rest assured that I am getting better. It comforts me that you're so close, though it also pains me, knowing all this time you've had to stay hidden. It's funny . . . I was feeling down and full of self-pity, being bedridden this long—yet my illness was the reason you finally revealed yourself. God's ways are truly wondrous.

You talked about purpose, and I've been thinking a lot about what His purpose might be in reconnecting us. I believe you are truly remorseful. I believe your sin was due more to poor judgment than poor character. I can tell by your letters that you remain devout, maybe even more so now. Some of us knew the outside world before we became Eternals, but you were sheltered from it most of your life. You didn't know the ways of outsiders, or how easily you could be led to fall.

I don't bring this up to hurt you. Anna, I have forgiven you. I never wanted to send you away. I've often regretted allowing the elders to decide our fate. Everything happened so fast. My mind wasn't clear, I couldn't think how to stop it. But if you trust me, I'll try to defend you now. Will you allow me to petition for your return? If I succeed, would you come back to me?
Luke

The waiting area inside the Hudson train station was nearly empty; only a handful of commuters paced around the small, air-conditioned space. Their footsteps echoing against the hard floor made a cold, unwelcome sound, making Anna feel more anxious. The last time she passed through, on the day she was sent away, the station was crowded, and the weather chilly. The ghost of that bleak day still lingered. It seemed a lifetime ago—and yet, it could just as well have been the day before. She sat on the same bench as she did then, wearing the same long dress.

She'd put the dress away while she lived with the Burnetts. The night before she left them, she took it out to launder and iron. It was handsewn and made of brown-checked homespun, with a high plain collar and long sleeves. At first, it felt strange to put it on again. It disturbed her to realize she'd grown accustomed to the ease of modern clothes. But as she studied her reflection in a full-length mirror, slowing her gestures to be more modest, she began to recognize herself again, and the person she had been the past several months fell away. It was like waking up from a long, puzzling dream. When she came out of her room wearing the dress, Laurie gaped at her in offended silence. She was upset about Anna's abrupt departure, refusing to say goodbye before Michael took her to the Rensselaer train station.

Now, people in the Hudson station also stared. Anna was discomfited but took it as affirmation that she looked like an Eternal again, even if her hair was still too short to plait. She lowered her head to avoid their glances but kept her eyes on the entrance doors, nervously anticipating Luke's arrival. His last letter relayed the miraculous news of Hiram's consent to absolve her. He wrote that the elder relented because of her youth, her obedient nature before her sin, and because Luke had been so sick and despondent. There would be a tribunal by the elders upon her return. They needed to feel assured that in the future she would be more temperate. The prospect of their judgment frightened her, but she was determined to earn back their trust.

A train pulled up to the platform. Everyone rushed outside except her. Minutes later, a crush of passengers spilled out of the train, heading toward the parking lot and waiting area. Suddenly, the room was crowded. It thinned out as, one by one, people met their respective parties and left. Then she was alone again. Even the ticket taker behind the counter was gone. The big clock on the opposite wall showed it was a quarter to one; Luke said he would arrive around noon. She had been waiting for almost an hour.

She was beginning to fear something had gone wrong when one of the doors opened. It was Luke, though at first she hardly recognized him. He was greatly altered, so gaunt his clothes hung on his tall frame. His cheeks were sunken, his complexion sallow. But when he saw her, his eyes came alive.

Behind him stood Ezra, an elder, one of the few Eternals permitted to drive. She felt a pang of disappointment. Of course, she knew someone would accompany Luke, but she'd hoped they might have a private moment. Her frustration and pent-up nerves, with the shock of his condition, were all too much. She felt the start of tears, and only Ezra's presence forced her to stay composed. When she looked back at Luke, his face too quivered with suppressed emotion. Their eyes met, and his seemed to telegraph to her, *Be careful.*

The elder stepped forward and asked coldly, "Are you ready?"

She stood and inclined her head in deference. "Yes."

5
THE CREEK

A nna was in the confinement room sorting through the mending basket when Tamar entered without knocking. There was no lock on the door, but footsteps coming up the creaky stairs always gave her some notice. "Esther needs you in the kitchen," Tamar said, leaving without waiting for a response. Anna had grown used to these abrupt comings and goings, the interruption of one chore for another. Much harder to accept was the aloof, even hostile manner most of the Eternals adopted toward her; to reconcile familiar, formerly kind faces turning away in judgment. The women were especially harsh. Even the children were told to keep their distance.

The confinement room was a small attic space with high, angled ceilings, where in certain lights she could look up to see a vast network of lacy cobwebs stretching from beam to beam. It had poor ventilation and, to Anna's horror, the occasional rodent. A lone window overlooked the sprawling backyard, with its rows of clotheslines, chicken coop, vegetable garden, and greenhouse, and the wide ribbon of the creek weaving along the rear of the property.

For the past month, she'd spent her daylight hours in this room, assigned to pray for her sins and attend to her chores, even taking all her meals there. Hiram blessed their marriage reunion, but she was allowed to join Luke in their room only after evening prayers. She still had another month left to fulfill this part of her correction. Then she would be allowed to integrate with the rest of the

Eternals under strict supervision, forbidden to leave the property or engage with outsiders for an indefinite period.

In the kitchen, Tamar and Sarah bustled about preparing supper while Esther stood at the center island in her apron, sharpening knives on a brick of whetstone. "There you are!" Esther cried. "I need you to go slaughter a hen. Bring it here after."

Anna's heart sank. Of all the farmhouse chores, this was the one she hated most. Even as a girl, she was squeamish about slaughtering, and she realized that, in the time she worked for the Burnetts, she'd grown used to not having to. Esther would probably make her gut and defeather the hen too. She wondered if the woman sensed her aversion, then immediately squashed the churlish thought. "Yes, I'll do that now."

"Take this," said Esther, wiping off one of the knives. "It should be very sharp."

Anna put on an apron and took the knife outside. It was early evening and still warm, though the turning leaves signaled fall's approach. She and Luke used to walk along the rolling stretch of highway at exactly this time of day, when the houses were quiet and the sun was starting to fade. It was their way of getting to know the town when they first arrived. She looked toward the highway now, hoping to see Luke and Gabriel returning from the dairy farm. Luke was still not fully back to health, but he had grown stronger and, in the last week, had resumed light duties.

She set the knife by the killing cones and went into the coop, grabbing a hen by its legs. When it was calm, she placed it upside down into a cone and, steeling herself, swiftly sliced the head off. She winced as it hit the bucket below. While the hen bled out, she put the knife down and stepped away. She was dismayed to find a large splash of blood near the hem of her skirt—she'd forgotten to tuck it between her legs. Seeing the blood brought back the night she lost her baby, and she winced. Before the stain could set, she cut across to the creek to wash it off.

The Catskill Creek stretched for more than forty miles, all the way from Schoharie County to the Hudson River, gushing in some areas and barely trickling in others. There were several spots to wade along the creek, but one of the best swimming holes was right in the Eternals' backyard. The water there was nearly thirty feet across at its widest point and eight at its deepest. Technically, half the creek belonged to Greene County; the other half, facing the farmhouse, was private property, but as far back as the 1930s, every owner of the farmhouse, including the Eternals, allowed locals full access to the swimming hole.

Earlier in the day, the creek was crowded with families, but now it was empty and serene. Anna removed her shoes and sat on a rock at the edge of the bank, scrubbing at the stain furiously. When it was gone, she felt better, though Esther would likely see her wet skirt and chide her for it, unless she could go back upstairs unnoticed. She allowed herself a moment to sit and dip her feet in the clear, cold water. The quietude and sensation of the flowing current lifted her spirits and gave her solace. She closed her eyes and prayed, asking God to give her the strength to bear her sentence with grace, to be patient and worthy of forgiveness, and to quell her misgivings toward the elders and matrons. She fretted over her inconstancy. When she lived in Caliban before, she was lured by the outside world; once there, she longed for her old life. And now . . . what did she want now? As she prayed, these words came to mind: *Be patient. When your correction is over, everything will be much better.*

After several minutes, she stood on the rock and looked back toward the coop, steeling herself to clean out the bucket. A colorful object caught her eye, several yards away on the lawn. Curious, she stepped out of the water, retrieving her shoes, and walked toward it. As she got closer, she saw it was a red-and-yellow-striped T-shirt—a child's—with a scuffed pair of black sneakers beside it. She examined the items and looked around. "Hello?" she called out, though she'd seen no one. Usually, swimmers entered from the other side and didn't wander onto the Eternals' lawn. She went back to the creek and walked along the water's edge, peering in all directions.

When she saw the child moving a few feet below the surface, she exhaled with relief. Then she realized it wasn't the child moving but the rippling water. She gasped and jumped in. The child lay in a shallow section, facedown in the silty bottom. Long sandy hair fanned above a bare back, dark shorts, thin, pale limbs. She tried but couldn't lift the small body, shocked by its inert weight. She ran out of the water toward the house, screaming hysterically, *"Help! Somebody, help!"*

From a distance, she saw Gabriel sprinting across the lawn, with Luke behind him, struggling to keep up. "Help me!" she screamed. "There's a child in the creek!" Whirling around, she raced back to the spot. The men followed and plunged into the water. They heaved the child onto the rocky bank, the left arm dangling at an impossible angle, like the snapped wings of birds that sometimes flew into the farmhouse windows. Luke turned the child over, and now Anna could see it was a boy, dead, the flesh already bluing, the eyes brown and wide open, as if surprised to see the sky once more.

————————————

The farmhouse was in chaos. Outside, several Eternal women stood watch over the child's body, weeping. In the kitchen, Hiram and the elders debated what to do while they waited for the police to arrive. Luke pleaded with them not to involve Anna. She only saw the boy and ran to get help, he said. It could just as well have been him and Gabriel who found him. There was no need for her to break her confinement and be subjected to interrogation.

"But, Luke," she said, "we can't lie to the police."

"Hush," said Hiram sternly, his dark, hooded eyes flashing impatience. "It's not for you to decide. Now tell me again what happened." After listening to their accounts, he was silent for a moment. Then he said, "It would be better if she wasn't connected to this. Her baby died last year. With all the superstitious talk that went around, it might cast a motive on her, and on us."

Anna blinked in horror at his implication.

Jonah, another elder, nodded. "Our reputation with children is already tarnished. Let's not make it worse, if we can avoid it." He was referring to several lawsuits in the last decade filed against certain Eternal communities for violating child labor laws. The Caliban branch had never been accused, and eventually all the cases were settled, but some hostile locals continued to hold those and other accusations against them.

Hiram told Anna, "Go retire to your quarters. And change out of those wet clothes." Then he turned to Esther. "Bring in that slaughtered hen and the knife. Hurry."

Anna went up to the small, tidy room she shared with Luke, furnished simply with a bed and dresser. Her mind was spinning, unable to accept what had happened. Peering out the window at the group gathered below, she saw that someone had placed a blanket over the body. She turned, averting her eyes, and gasped. There, twenty feet to her right, a large owl was perched on the branch of a hemlock tree. It hadn't been there before, not on all the other nights. The round yellow eyes seemed to bore into hers. Then its head swiveled abruptly away, turning an impossible, near-complete rotation before swiveling around again. Satan's fowl. She reared back from the window. "Dear God," she whispered. "Why? What have I done?" Had she incurred His displeasure for her thoughts alone? Why punish her, and the boy, when she'd prayed so fervently for His guidance?

She was starting to strip off her dress when Zebiah walked in. "Give me those wet things. Come on, what's wrong with you?" Anna's hands were shaking, and she could barely undo the buttons on her bodice. Zebiah batted her hands away and unfastened them for her, yanking the dress down. As she gathered the wet clothes, she sighed. "You do end up at the center of things. I don't know why Hiram keeps showing you such leniency. Know that it's a testament to his affection for your husband, and be grateful."

Anna felt stung by her words, amplifying her fear that she was somehow at fault for the boy's drowning. Before she could think how to respond, they both started at the sound of approaching sirens.

It was almost nine by the time the police finished questioning Luke and Gabriel. The EMT had taken the boy away hours ago, but some neighbors still lingered at the edge of the property as policemen roamed over the yard and creek with their flashlights. Finally, when they left, the last of the spectators did too. The Eternal women assembled a late, cold dinner, but Luke had no appetite and went upstairs to join Anna.

She ran to him as soon as he entered the room. "I've been so worried. Did you talk to the police? Did they believe you?"

He nodded. "They seemed to. Though they asked a lot of questions—especially about the boy's broken arm. But I told them the truth, that it's how we found him. I honestly don't know how it happened."

She shivered, remembering the horrific sight. "That poor little boy. Do they know who he is?"

"Zebiah said he's a local, that his family lives down the road. His father identified him. He was only missing for an hour or so." He shook his head sadly.

"Oh, how terrible. If only I'd seen him earlier, I might have . . . Luke, I know you wanted to protect me, but it doesn't seem right that we didn't tell the truth about me being there."

"It's our sacred duty to protect our women, especially against outsiders. You know that, and so do the elders. Besides, we saw what you saw, just a few minutes after. There's going to be an inquest next week. Gabriel and I have to give our statements. I can't imagine you going through that."

She sat on the edge of the bed, still uneasy. "Zebiah doesn't seem to agree. She thinks Hiram favors you, and that's why he's been so lenient with me. She made it seem like . . ."

"What?" he asked, sitting next to her.

"I don't know. It's not so much what she said, really. It's more my own feeling. Like maybe this happened because I came back."

"Anna," he said gently, "you know that makes no sense. You're in shock. It's normal to feel guilty. He was just a child, and taken far too soon. Yet we're alive."

She nodded, unconvinced but wanting to acknowledge his comforting. "You look exhausted. I don't want this to set you back. We should try to get some rest."

But Anna's sleep that night was fitful, filled with intense images so brief they could hardly count as dreams. She kept seeing the cold blue face of her baby and the lifeless eyes of the drowned boy, one sometimes changing into the other. As she lay in bed, unable to shut off her mind, she was aware of Luke twitching and sighing beside her, wrestling with his own subconscious troubles. She assumed the source of their disturbance was the same. But the guilt it provoked from her past was her own.

———

Anna's adoptive parents once belonged to the Unification Church, led by Reverend Sun Myung Moon. The reverend, who encouraged interracial families, matched Cathy, a white girl from Indianapolis, to John, a Korean American from San Jose, in a mass wedding ceremony at Madison Square Garden in 1982. The young couple weren't able to conceive, so in 1985, they adopted a four-month-old baby from an orphanage in Busan, naming her Pearl. They lived a peripatetic life, recruiting and fundraising, but eventually left the church, disillusioned by the reverend's ongoing accusations of fraud, his engagement with politics, and what they considered the church's corruptive overpopularity.

They yearned for a simpler, spiritual engagement with the world and found it when they met members of the Eternals at a green market in Boston selling produce grown on their farms in Milton. These were good people full of compassion and integrity, and despite how they stood out in their old-world attire, they seemed more at ease and assured than their contemporary peers. Their adherence to the Old Testament, with God as the single divine being, resonated as pure and truthful. They rejected the modern world's fixation with the idea of progress, which led to avarice and, ultimately, destruction. It wasn't a sacrifice to leave the ills of that world for a virtuous, purposeful existence among this peaceful community. John was allowed to keep his name, but Cathy changed hers to Deborah, and Pearl became Anna.

In Milton, Anna and her parents lived on a rural communal compound of six houses. All Eternal children slept in a room with their parents, but from age four onward, when the parents had private time, they stayed in different rooms with other children, supervised by a rotation of women. These overnight separations happened twice a week. Anna remembered them as fun evenings spent giggling with her friends, being gently chastised to go to sleep by the women watching over them. Boys and girls were put in separate rooms when they turned twelve, but until then, everyone tumbled onto large mats pushed together on the floor to make one.

Luke's family joined their community when Anna was eight and he was ten. His entire family was tall with white-blond hair, which Anna found fascinating. He was a quiet boy, awkward around everything except nature. He knew how to mimic birdcalls, raise butterflies, and train baby goats to sit up. She considered him and the other Eternal children her siblings. They all called each other "brother" and "sister," prayed together, studied together, played together, ate, slept, and did chores together.

Once, when Anna was nine, two friends woke her during the night to spy outside their parents' rooms while their guardian dozed. They heard loud snoring from one room, nothing in the next, and, in the two after that, beds squeaking in tandem with strange, muffled groans. Her friends suppressed their giggles, but Anna was disturbed. As they approached her parents' door, she was full of dread. To her relief, all that came through was her father's deep voice in prayer, followed by her mother's low murmur, both of them reciting Isaiah. She felt a rush of pride. Everyone knew, and here was proof, that her parents were among the most devout. Then one of her friends said her parents prayed during private time because they couldn't make babies anyway. She wasn't exactly sure what it meant, only that somehow they were deficient.

The following year, their community hosted an Eternal couple passing through on their way to visit their son's family, who lived in another community in Maine. They stayed in Milton for six days while they waited for the next driver to transport them, along with a delivery of soap, yarn, and other homemade goods. The man, Aaron, whittled funny creatures from branches and gave them to Anna and her friends. They liked the toys but not the sour way he smelled.

One afternoon, he came up to Anna from behind while she was pinning sheets to the laundry lines, sticking his hand down her bodice. She turned and saw his face, then felt the shock of his fingers on her bare chest. His breath was hot against her ear as he hissed, "Shh!" Hidden by the laundry lines, he continued to grope as he pressed and worked something furiously against her. The rankness of his breath, his sweat, made her gag. Finally, he groaned and went still. Something wet seeped through the back of her dress. Then he let her go, walking away quickly.

She washed her dress. She told no one. For days, she lived in terror of seeing him. The terror lingered long after he left. Later, when she understood better the relations between men and women, she wondered if she had been the only one—or if he picked her because she looked different. She asked her father once why there were so few Eternals who looked like them. He told her it was a matter of time; that while their beliefs were ancient, their religion was still new to most people. "It doesn't matter," he said. "God doesn't see us as different." *Then why did He make us this way?* she wanted to ask, but was ashamed to.

When Anna turned twelve, she had her bat mitzvah celebration, marking her entry to womanhood. Her friends Adina and Rebekah had their celebrations the year before. Rebekah was the prettiest and, at sixteen, was chosen by Ephraim, a widower eighteen years her senior. They married, and she gave birth to twin girls a year later. Anna watched the changes in her friend's face, body, and demeanor with wonder and abhorrence. Rebekah told her what they did to make babies was "not so bad." Ephraim was a good husband, and her babies were beautiful. But she looked bewildered, exhausted, much older than seventeen.

Anna knew she was plain and strange looking; her eyes were too small, her nose too flat, her face too round. For the first time, she felt glad about it. None of the boys or young men ever paid attention to her except Luke, who was like a brother. No one would choose her, she felt certain. And then, when she was eighteen, someone did. Caleb was a heavy, shy twenty-eight-year-old who worked in the lumber mill. A Gulf War veteran, he had been an Eternal for only three years, but the elders considered him a good, righteous man. Her parents agreed.

"But he's old," Anna protested, "and he's ugly. Please don't make me."

"Shame on you, Anna!" her mother cried. "He's neither of those things, but even if he were, would that make him less worthy in God's eyes? Is your judgment above His?"

Her father said, "You disappoint me. Where's your compassion? He's a repentant, true believer."

She was stunned by their rebuke. Privately, her mother lectured her further: "You know your father and I were matched. One of God's greatest tests is whether two people unknown to each other can grow to love and accept the other. Our only regret is that we couldn't bring children into this world. But you were entrusted to us—and when you marry and have children, our duties as your parents will be fulfilled. You're eighteen, Anna. These are the crucial years."

She agreed to let Caleb begin to court her. Their conversations were strained. His discomfort never eased, and she wondered why he chose her. On one of their walks, she asked him directly. He took a moment to reply, as if the question was too personal. "I knew a Malaysian girl once," he said finally. "You remind me of her."

Something about his eyes frightened her. He had second-degree burns on his right forearm, and two of his fingers were missing their nail beds. She couldn't imagine ever loving him. When she told Luke, in tears, about her betrothal, he became distressed too. "Oh no, Anna. I would have chosen you myself," he said, coloring, "if I thought you wouldn't mind."

"I wish it were you."

As the wedding drew near, she prayed fervently to God: *Please, I'll do anything, I'll be so good, but please, God, don't let this happen. Don't let it be him.*

Four days before the wedding, Caleb had an accident at the lumber mill. He was cleaning out a chipper with a cable while the machine was running. Somehow the cable got caught in the chipper and struck his neck, throwing him off the four-foot platform. He suffered cervical fractures and couldn't move his hands, torso, or legs. Since he could no longer father children, the betrothal was annulled. When Anna heard the news, she felt shock, then guilt at her relief, awe that God had heard her prayer, and fear for the repercussions.

She became careful with her prayers, unsure how God might interpret them. But during her pregnancy, she allowed all her terrors of motherhood to take hold. And then she indulged in Sebastian's attentions, the heady novelty of his admiration—this handsome stranger who smiled for no one but her. When her baby died, she knew she was culpable. With this boy who drowned . . . of course

Luke was right. She'd done nothing to cause it. Still, there seemed something fatalistic about her proximity to these deaths, some kind of lesson or message she couldn't interpret. *"You do end up at the center of things."* Was she the harbinger of misfortune? It struck her as horrific that the whole time she was praying at the edge of the creek, the poor child lay only yards away, lifeless, at the bottom.

———

In the days to come, they learned more about the drowning from the inquest and through gossip from the neighbors. The boy's name was Patrick Clay, and he was nine years old. He was the youngest son of Brian and Jody Clay, who lived down the road from the Eternals. The autopsy indicated he drowned sometime between four-thirty and five-fifteen. The boy's clothes and shoes yielded no suspicious clues, and the cause of his broken arm was undetermined; it was possible he slipped on the rocks before falling into the water.

Hours before he went missing, Jody took her boys and their friends to the creek. Shortly before four, they all headed back to the house. When Patrick didn't come downstairs after she told him to wash up, Jody told his brother to go find him.

At first, they thought he must be hiding. The house was a large bungalow with several rooms, closets, an attic, and a basement. He wasn't in any of those places, nor in the garage or back shed. Brian came home around five thirty and tried to make sense of their panicked accounts. They looked up and down the highway, but it was empty. They knocked on the doors of their neighbors, who saw nothing but offered to help search. While Brian and the neighbors went canvassing, Jody stayed at the house and called the local police. Soon after, her phone rang. It was Brian, calling from the Eternals' backyard.

———

The following month, Hiram received a notification in the mail from attorneys representing the Clays. They'd filed a wrongful death suit against the town of Caliban and the Eternals, seeking $5 million in damages. The list of claims included negligence, inadequate supervision, and attractive nuisance, citing the failure of both parties to barricade the swimming hole when so many children lived nearby.

It was an unexpected blow. Hiram talked to the Eternals' attorneys and Ralph Edmonton, the town supervisor, and then called everyone into the dining room to discuss the lawsuit. Even Anna was told to join. She noticed Zebiah's disapproving glare, but she wasn't sure if she was angered by Hiram granting another exception or if she actually blamed Anna for the lawsuit too. The week before, Zebiah had brought up the owl that had begun to roost in their yard and how it always seemed to be looking toward Luke and Anna's window. They tried to shoo it away by throwing rocks in its direction, but though it would take flight in the moment, it always came back.

Hiram sat at the head of the table with the other elders: Jonah, Matthew, and Ezra. They were elders not so much for their age (Ezra was only fifty-four) but because they founded the Caliban branch of the Eternals in the late eighties. In the beginning, there were only four families and eleven members. Now there were almost fifty members, their numbers steadily growing. They worked hard over the years to gain the trust of locals, offering their carpentry and farming skills for low wages, and volunteering help for town events and fundraisers.

"Our standing in this town is at stake," Hiram warned. "This lawsuit could affect our businesses, our livelihood. When we first came here, people would have nothing to do with us. You don't know how easy it is to destroy the good relations we've formed."

"What does it mean, 'attractive nuisance'?" Matthew asked. "Are they saying we're baiting these children to harm them? Don't they realize we also have children on this property we want to protect?"

"We kept the swimming hole accessible for their sake," said Jonah. "I feel terrible for that family, but to put the blame on innocent citizens? On a whole town? It's unreasonable. They have no grounds."

"Regardless, we must be careful not to provoke our neighbors," said Hiram. "Most of them know the Clays and will be sympathetic. Whether we win or lose this case, it's going to be unpleasant. And costly."

The following week, the town council held a meeting to declare the swimming hole off-limits indefinitely, requesting people steer clear while investigators continued to gather evidence. The police had already blocked the area around the creek with garish yellow tape that ran along the length of the Eternals' property, as well as the grassy field opposite. The visual was jarring and indicting, suggesting the scene of a crime.

Soon after, on the advice of their attorneys, the Eternals put up PRIVATE PROPERTY: NO TRESPASSING signs in their yard. Within days, both signs were defaced.

6
SETBACK

The dream was always the same: It was dusk and she was cutting across Buckhorn Meadow, cradling a pillow in her arms. The meadow stretched endlessly beyond the horizon. The pillow grew cumbersome and heavy; she could barely hold on to it and keep walking. The only sound was her shoes crunching through the tall, dry grass. It grew dark. Just as she began to feel anxious, the highway appeared before her with its welcome lights. Then she was back in her house in Caliban, the rooms upstairs quiet and dark. Down the hallway, she could see Justin's bedroom dimly glowing. She set the pillow down and walked toward it. Justin was sleeping on the far side of his bed, the sheet covering his face. "Justin?" she whispered, leaning over to pull the sheet away. But it wasn't Justin. It was Patrick, his flesh pale and ice cold, his lifeless eyes staring up at nothing.

Sometimes April screamed herself awake, or imagined she did but only whimpered, because Justin almost never woke up. She sat up now and looked at his silhouette across their tiny room, listening for the sound of his breathing. *It's Justin,* she told herself, her heart still racing. Even worse than the dream was its aftermath—how it made her feel afraid, for the first few moments, to approach her son.

Patrick's death haunted her waking hours too. Seeing his body was a shock she would never recover from. She could go for hours without thinking about him, and then something small—a boy on TV with dark blond hair; a box of Rice Krispies, his favorite snack; or coming across his name, so common, in print—would punch the air from her chest. Then the surreal, leaden sorrow would wash over her again.

The morning of the drowning, she'd dropped Justin off at Jody's so he could go to the creek with her boys. When she went to pick him up at the end of the day, she walked into a frantic household. Patrick was missing, and Jody was beside herself. They'd looked everywhere, she said, and called their neighbors, but no one had seen him. She was waiting on the police while Brian canvassed the area.

Justin and Patrick's brother, Ethan, sat in the living room, watchful and quiet. April said to Justin, "I want to go help Brian search. Can you stay here with Ethan? Will you be okay?" He nodded, and she crushed him against her, kissing his head. "Don't worry, we'll find him." She truly believed it. Theirs was a safe, close-knit community; people kept their doors unlocked. Patrick was prone to mischief, and when he was younger, he used to hide in obscure corners and fall asleep.

April caught up with Brian and three other neighbors farther along the highway. As they neared the Eternals' farmhouse, she noticed several members of the group on the back lawn, huddled together in a large circle. Some of the women were weeping. When she was a few yards away, she realized within the circle something lay on the ground, covered by a dark blanket. One of the Eternals looked up and stretched out his hands. "Don't come near!"

Most of the search party stopped and stood still. But Brian stepped forward. "Please," he said, his voice breaking, "we're looking for my boy."

April watched as they moved aside for him. A moment later, she heard his anguished cry. Her whole body went numb with refusal. She had to see for herself and pushed her way into the circle. At first, she saw only Brian hunched over the shape on the ground. She called his name and reached down to touch his shoulder. He turned, and then she saw Patrick: his wet tangled hair and blue-white skin, the blank staring eyes.

"Oh god," she whispered.

"Do you know him?" one of the Eternal women asked. April nodded mutely, too stunned for tears. It was impossible. Just that morning he was as alive as her own boy. As Brian sobbed over his son's body, she thought of Jody, how her heart was about to be ripped out, and felt her own breaking. But beneath that grief flared a burst of gratitude it wasn't Justin.

Later, when the nightmares came, she took them as punishment for that moment of selfish relief. In the light of day, she dismissed the idea; she wasn't a superstitious person by nature. But each time she woke in terror it always came back to her and felt truer than logic. Part of it was that Jody had distanced herself. The funeral was the last time April saw her, though she left texts and messages after. When she heard about the lawsuit, she was surprised; it didn't seem like something they'd do. Secretly, she couldn't see much basis for it, though she didn't say so. The town was divided over the issue. Some people worried litigation would raise their taxes and permanently close the swimming hole, while others firmly sided with the bereaved family. She thought Jody might be upset because she hadn't expressed support for her lawsuit and called her one more time, leaving a rambling, halting message when she didn't pick up. A few days later, Jody sent her a text: *Thanks for your message. I know you mean well, but seeing you and Justin right now is too hard. It's not your fault, but I need time.*

April knew grief sometimes caused unexpected rifts. If the situation were reversed, how could she know what she would feel? Still, it hurt. They'd been friends since high school. When Jody asked her to be Patrick's godmother, she said, "Don't worry, if anything happens to us, the boys will go to my folks or Brian's. You'll be more like a fairy godmother." But they never discussed the possibility of something happening to the boys. And now that they had to live through the unspeakable, no words or gestures could ever be adequate.

It was hard to tell how Patrick's death affected Justin. In the early days, he cried and let her comfort him. Lately, he preferred not to talk about it. He was always a stoic child, and it was hard to know if he was really okay or just pretending to be.

She could hear his sweet, even breathing. Her eyes adjusted to the darkness and she slid out of bed to walk over to him. He lay on his back, his face clearly visible. Of all her children, he claimed a special tenderness that frightened her. Was it because he was her baby or the only boy, or because she'd loved his father the most? After a moment, she went back to her bed. In another year, Justin would need his own room. By then Maddy would be out of the house, and April could sleep in the room she shared with Cara or take the sofa.

Where would Maddy go? She was smart enough for college, and motivated. But she'd still have to work. All her kids would, as soon as they were old enough. Her failure to do better for them was a constant source of shame. April's mother had been a Tremaine, one of the first families to settle in the area in the 1830s. Her great-grandfather James built their house in Caliban and a few others in Pine Hollow and Medusa. Now April cleaned one of those houses. The work had aged her. Her hands were lined and chapped, her knees were always bruised, and her lower back twinged when she stood up too quickly. She could physically handle it for another ten, fifteen years, and then what?

Some days, when she was down to canned soups and condiments, she'd remember her mother's Sunday dinners, her father's prized Trans Am, family vacations, and wonder how all their luck had turned. Her father was a civil engineer and volunteer fireman who, thirty years ago, saved a man's life at the cost of his own. Her mother died of an aneurism just before she turned sixty. Her brother, Mark, did well as an electrician but was now entangled with ex-wives and alimonies. As for herself, she'd blown all her looks and sass just to end up back in the same town she grew up in, with barely a home, no man, and no real skills to make a decent living. She'd wanted her life to be bigger, but never had the patience to wait for something she couldn't see.

"What a mess," she once heard someone say about her, thinking she couldn't hear. People were always full of opinions. She'd lived in the area so long she knew almost everyone except for some of the newcomers—and the Eternals, who mystified her, had difficult names she couldn't remember, and dressed so alike it was hard to distinguish between them. In any case, aside from Anna, she never had much to do with them. Since Patrick's drowning, it seemed others had stopped engaging with them too.

The town in general had gone quiet. It was early January and bitterly cold; with the holidays now over, people mostly stayed indoors. Each new blizzard provoked tired complaints about plowing, heating bills, boilers breaking down.

April hated winter. She hated trudging through slush, digging out her truck, wearing fat padded coats and cumbersome layers, her extremities numb with frostbite. Most of all, she hated the constant dreary darkness that lifted for only a few short hours each day.

She could see a cold gray light seeping in through the blinds now. At the same time, she felt her lids grow heavy and let out a huge yawn. Checking her phone, she hissed softly, "Fuck." Her alarm would go off in forty minutes. She'd have to wake up Justin, get him on the school bus at eight fifteen, and get herself to Hudson by nine. A long drive just to clean one house. Then her CVS shift in Cairo, thirteen miles away, from eleven to five. Some kind of dinner after. There was always work, school, meals, endless errands. If only she could nap in the truck between jobs. But turning the heat on while the car idled was dangerous, Eli told her—people died of carbon monoxide poisoning. "That's all I need," she mumbled drowsily. As her mind finally shuttered, she thought how strange it was that she should wake up and fall back to sleep thinking of death.

—————————

It was just past six and already pitch-dark outside by the time Claire came home from the office. The holidays were over, and her bosses had scheduled an all-staff meeting to kick off the new year. She hadn't been back in almost a month, and the long day had taken its toll. She looked and felt wretched; twice during the day, she'd squelched a wave of nausea and managed not to vomit. But on the drive home, she had to pull over and expel the protein shake she'd had in lieu of lunch, leaving a large purple puddle in the snow.

As soon as she walked into her house, she felt sick again and raced to the bathroom. The rusty smell made her more nauseated, but this time, nothing came out except a thin trickle of saliva. She left the bathroom, closing the door behind her, but the odor still lingered. She found a scented candle in the front closet, lit it, and set it on a small bench in the entryway. Then she went to the living room to lie down on the couch, pulling the throw blanket up to her chin. It was too damn cold in the house; even with the space heater inches away she shivered, unable to get warm. Though hours later, she'd probably wake up bathed in sweat, racked by another hot flash—a by-product, like the nausea and fatigue, of her latest treatment.

The last four and a half months felt like a blur, and she still hadn't processed all that had happened. Certain facts were indelible: she was not pregnant; her home test was a false positive. An appointment with her gynecologist prompted more tests and an ultrasound, which showed a mass in her uterus, eighteen centimeters long and six wide, with smaller clusters around her cervix. A visit to her oncologist and more tests produced a grim diagnosis: stage three uterine cancer.

She had surgery in late September to remove the tumors, undergoing a full hysterectomy, followed by three doses of radiation the month after. It made her pubic hair fall out. She pondered the irony of her newly smooth pubis, with its suggestion of undefiled innocence, when everything inside was used up and scraped out. November brought a reprieve and the hope she could stop treatment. But in early December, her CA-125 was still elevated, so Dr. Sominian, her oncologist, recommended a three-month course of Taxol—one week on, two weeks off—as an extra precaution. Claire had tolerated the radiation fairly well, but the chemo knocked her flat. It made her feverish, weak, and nauseated, especially on the second and third days of her "on" weeks.

Worst of all, her hair was starting to fall out, and she'd done only two courses. She could wear knits caps for now, but if it continued, she'd have to invest in a wig. She didn't want people in town to know; being the subject of more gossip, or worse, their pity, was unbearable. The only ones she told were Karl and Evelyn and, because she had to, her bosses, who promised to be discreet. She was grateful for their understanding, but worried constantly that they might question her ability to still do her job. Which was why she made herself go in today, despite having a chemo infusion three days ago.

Finally getting warm, she grew drowsy and succumbed to the sweet pull of sleep. Twenty minutes later, she startled awake to the sound of an owl hooting. In her half-conscious state, its reverberating cries filled her with a melancholy both aching and nostalgic. Since childhood, it signified life in the country, and here she was, living it—but not in a way she ever imagined. She lay in the darkened room, lit only by the orange glow of the space heater and, beyond the arched doorway, the flickering glow of the candle in the entryway. As the flame's shadow played against the wall above the staircase, its shifting forms began to resemble strange figures, not quite human or animal, and she turned away before they solidified into something disturbing. *No. Not again.* She'd become fearful of shadows and the various forms they suggested, of the way her imagination played tricks with her mind. For the sake of her sanity, she *had* to stop indulging it.

She forced herself to get up and go to the kitchen. She had no appetite but knew it was important to eat. Evelyn kept bringing over leftovers, homemade soups, and roasted vegetables, and though this coddling annoyed her at first, now she was grateful. It saved her from having to cook or get groceries and run into people. The only times she ventured out now were to her chemo appointments in Albany or to work. After heating up some minestrone, she smelled the broth and was relieved it didn't disgust her. She was losing weight even without exercise, which she had no energy for. Running had been the only thing that helped her anxiety, besides drinking. Now that was off the table, except in limitation. But her numbers were dropping, so the chemo was working, which meant she had to continue. Two more months, she told herself. And then, hopefully, remission.

———————

Promptly at six on Wednesday night, Eli swung by to pick up Justin and April for their weekly dinner out, his treat. The dinners were part of a routine they established, along with the "boys only" outings Eli and Justin had together every other Sunday. Those Sundays were a hard-won privilege April allowed only in the last few months, in part to make up for Patrick's absence.

After a year of careful observation, April felt pretty certain Eli wouldn't endanger her son. He held on to his job at the body shop and checked in with his parole office every month. He went to AA meetings twice a week and, as far as she knew, hadn't fallen off the wagon. She was on familiar terms with his sponsor and caseworker. She'd even developed a civil relationship with Aiyana, who doted on Justin (to April's satisfaction, the feeling wasn't quite mutual). They all forged a cautious alliance toward one goal: keeping Eli from fucking up.

He stepped through the door and leaned down to kiss April's cheek, a neutral embrace she permitted. Once in a while, when no one was looking, he'd give her ass a little pinch for old times' sake. Her usual response was to calmly give him the finger. Now, as always, she was struck by the way he dwarfed the room, his head only inches below the low ceiling.

"Where is he?"

"Getting his coat." She turned and yelled, "Justin! Eli's here!"

"The girls coming?"

"Nope. Maddy's working, Cara's at a friend's."

Justin came out and Eli grabbed him, lifting him a foot off the ground. "Hey! So, what do you feel like tonight?"

"Pizza?"

Eli looked at April, who shrugged. "I don't care."

"You never care. That's why we split," he told Justin. "She never cooked."

She rolled her eyes, and Justin smiled. They all knew the real reason. It was a good thing, she supposed, that they could laugh about it now.

"Come on, let's go," she said, shoving Eli lightly. As they walked out, he gave her a quick backward glance full of mirth. He looked happy and handsome again, she thought with some resentment. Clean living had done him good, and she was sure he took full advantage of it. She never asked nor did he volunteer any details about his private life. She figured there was nobody serious, or Justin would have mentioned it. But she knew what a horndog Eli was. After all that time in prison, she could only imagine what a fuck palace his place must be. Whereas she hadn't gotten laid or even tried for almost two years. Part of it was that she wanted to set an example to Eli. But the other part was she no longer felt able to compete.

Years ago, she flaunted other lovers to make him jealous. Now she was as pointed in displaying her abstinence: *This is what I sacrifice—so don't you complain.* The casually flirtatious manner he sometimes slipped into with her was annoying. She had no interest in reviving their past, but the way he teased, it was as if the very idea were now a joke to him. That stung. Sometimes she couldn't help feeling bitter, watching him reap the benefits of all her hard work raising Justin. She knew it was petty to begrudge him his role as a father, since she was the one who allowed it. But Justin accepted Eli so completely, and as he grew older, he'd need his father more and her less.

At D'Amico's Italian Kitchen, she watched how they sat together, Justin laughing at the way Eli folded his slice and shoved it in his mouth, eyes bulging. An older couple in the next booth looked over and smiled. April imagined them thinking, *What a nice family*, and snorted inwardly. She craved a cold Stella but never indulged in front of Eli. Justin mimicked Eli and took a big bite of his pizza. A second later he spat it onto his plate. "Ow, it's hot!" Some of the sauce landed on his T-shirt.

"Goddamn it, I just washed that."

"Sorry, Mom." But he was still laughing.

She scowled at Eli. "Nice, teach him how to be a pig."

"I'll get him a new shirt."

She snickered. "Right."

Justin said, "I have to pee."

"Take your napkin with you and clean that spot," April said. When he was gone, she told Eli, "Don't act like you're all flush in front of him and then not come through."

"What are you talking about?"

"You know! You want to be in his life, great. That means more than picking up dinners here and there and going to the movies. I need you to help with his expenses. I'm tapped out and I'm fucking exhausted. It's not fair."

He looked alarmed. "Well, shit, April. You know I don't make much. After rent and food and parole fees—"

"I know what you make and what you can spare. We've been talking about a budget for months now, but it never happens and I'm sick of it. I'm doing the hard work, and meanwhile, you just come and go as you please."

"Wait a minute," he said, his eyes flashing. "I see him as much as you let me, which isn't much. You want me to split his expenses, I should be able to spend equal time with him."

"Please, as if you could handle it. As if any court would let you. And I'm not talking about splitting things down the line, I'm talking about a fair, regular, monthly payment I can count on, you cheap bastard." Before he could answer she said, "He's coming back."

Justin knew as soon as he sat down that something was up. The rest of the dinner was quiet, and April was relieved when the waitress brought the check. On their way out, they passed the bar, where two young women sat perched on stools. One of them swiveled around and cried out, "Eli! What's up? Hey, that was fun the other night." She had a hard pretty face with a halo of frizzy hair.

"Hey, Jess. Yeah, good times. Well . . . I'm heading out."

"I can *see* that." She took in April and Justin, pursing her bright mouth. "Catch you later."

Fun doing what? April wondered. She had every right to ask—it concerned Justin. But since he was there, she refrained, and Eli acted like nothing had happened.

She was still cool to him when he picked up Justin on Sunday, barely exchanging words beyond asking what they planned to do and when they would be back.

"We're playing ice hockey," said Justin.

"Again?"

"He's getting really good. Then we'll go see the new *Tron* movie, maybe swing by and say hi to Aiyana after."

"Just be back by five thirty."

Eli nodded and let out a huge yawn.

"Late night?" she asked pointedly.

He shrugged. "Long week."

She kissed Justin and let them leave, planning to revisit her argument with Eli when they were alone. She spent the rest of the morning nagging Maddy and Cara to help her clean. No matter how often she yelled, they failed to pick up after themselves. Justin alone was tidy. During the week she'd leave luxurious dwellings, made spotless by her hard work, and come home to chaos and squalor. But she'd be damned if she was going to be the help in her own house.

By noon, the place was more or less in order. Maddy left for her job at a local deli, driving the used car Eli got her and fixed up for cheap. Cara stayed at home while April ran errands, ending up at Price Chopper in Greenville, where she loaded up on a week's worth of groceries. Later that afternoon she planned to cook up a vat of chili, some corn bread, and a pan of baked ziti to freeze. Then dinners during the week would be done.

On her way home it began to sleet, melting the snow and turning the roads icy. She flicked her headlights on and drove carefully. Nearing Caliban, the highway narrowed into two winding lanes with hardly any traffic. The only businesses were Gilly's, an Irish pub, and Pete's Pump, the gas station and mini-mart. She noticed the slight figure of a girl about twenty yards ahead on the overpass above the creek, looking as if to cross. It was a startling sight. People rarely walked the highway, much less in this kind of weather. As her pickup approached, the girl paused and turned, raising a hand to shield her face against the headlights. Now April could see by her long dress and cloth satchel that she was an Eternal. She wore a short coat and boots, but no gloves or hat. April braked to let her cross. As the girl walked past, she turned and nodded, lifting her hand in thanks.

"My god," April said. She rolled her window down and called out, "Anna!"

The girl stopped and looked back. Then her face lit up. "Oh! It's you!"

"Get in. I'll give you a lift."

"No, no," Anna said, "I'm fine walking, thank you."

April beckoned at her impatiently. "Oh, for chrissakes, come on. I'm pulling over." She steered off the road and parked a few yards beyond the overpass. Sticking her head out the window, she yelled back at Anna, "What're you, nuts? Dressed like that! It's freezing out here!"

Anna glanced around quickly, then walked to the truck and reached up to clasp April's hands. It was an odd, touching gesture, formal yet strangely intimate. "I've wondered about you. You're doing well, I hope? And your children?"

"Yeah, yeah, we're okay. Get in and warm up."

Anna shook her head. "I really can't. I have to get back to the café. I was just at Pete's. We ran out of vegetable oil, of all things."

"Wait—you've gone back to the Eternals? To your husband?"

"Yes." Anna's cheeks flushed. "He petitioned for me."

"Wow. When did all this happen?"

"Last summer. By God's grace. I'm so grateful." As Anna smiled, her teeth began to chatter.

"You're freezing! Get in, for crying out loud. I'll drop you off."

Anna laughed lightly. "Well, it wasn't so bad when I set out. But I'll be fine. Thank you." She stepped back and waved. "It was so good to see you again."

April said, confounded, "But—but *why* are you so set on walking? It's another mile, and I could get you there in two minutes."

"I can't. I have to be more careful now with outsiders. I mean, those outside our faith. After what happened before . . . I hope you understand." Seeing April frown, she said, "Oh, I don't want to offend you, of all people! I'll never forget how much you helped me. But I can't disobey—not after all Luke did for me. Usually I don't even go outside, but everyone's been sick, so we're short-staffed."

Jesus Christ, April thought. *This was what she chose to go back to?* "Well, I could still drive you a little ways and—okay, never mind. I get it. I guess." She stared at Anna, curious. "So, this is what you wanted, right? And you're happy? Now that you're back and not repenting anymore?"

Anna's smile turned gentle, indulgent. "There's no end to repenting. But yes, I'm grateful to be back. It's more than I expected or deserve."

A life of constant rules and judgment—and she was grateful. April could not wrap her mind around it. "Well, then, that's good," she said. "Guess I'll see you around." But it seemed unlikely, and anyway, what was the point if they had to pretend not to know each other? She waved and rolled up her window. Driving off, she watched Anna's figure in the rearview mirror retreating, growing tiny, until it disappeared into the swirling sleet. She could have imagined the whole encounter, it was so brief and bizarre. She had the distinct feeling if she turned back, Anna might not even be on the road.

———————————

On Monday morning, as April helped Justin hoist his school backpack on, he winced when it touched his left arm. "What's wrong? Are you hurt?"

"It's just heavy."

"Well, what do you have in there? Take some stuff out."

"Later," he said. "I'm gonna miss the bus."

She thought nothing more of it until the next morning, when she was standing in the bathroom doorway, making sure he brushed his teeth. As he reached for the toothpaste, she noticed something on his inner left forearm. "Hey, what's that?"

"What?" he said, twisting away.

"Justin." She put an edge to her voice that meant business, and he let her take hold of his arm. Under the bright light, she could see a mottled bruise, about two inches in diameter. "What happened here?"

He just shrugged.

"Justin, this is a huge bruise! Did you bang it against something, maybe when you were playing hockey?"

"I don't know, I just noticed it now."

"You must have hit something, or something hit you. Was your dad around? Did he—"

"Leave me alone!" he said, shaking her off. She reared back in surprise. He'd never spoken to her like that before. An instant later, he was contrite. "It's just a bruise, Mom. Can I rinse now?"

She decided not to press him. But as soon as he got on the bus, she called Eli. He picked up after four rings. "Hey, what's up?" She could hear clanking and loud machinery.

"Did something happen to Justin on Sunday? He's got a huge bruise on his left arm. He can't remember how he got it."

"A bruise? No."

"It's the size of a fucking baseball. He's being really weird about it. Did he fall or something, or were you guys roughhousing? If something happened just tell me, I won't get mad."

After a beat he said, "Really? 'Cause you sound pretty pissy now, and I didn't even do anything."

"I'm just asking if you saw anything."

"No, you're not. Jesus," he said bitterly. "Look, I don't know how he got that bruise, but he's a boy, you know? They get banged up. Don't overreact."

She snorted. "Right. Go back to work."

That night, she insisted on examining Justin's arm again. The bruise had spread and turned slightly yellow. As she peered closer, her breath caught. Were those dark, mottled spots finger marks? For a moment, her mind went blank with disbelief. It couldn't be Eli. He loved Justin. And he was never physically violent. Still, she remembered in their early months together how he lost patience with the girls, how careless he could get when he was tired. When he first got out of prison, friends warned her about letting him get close to Justin. "Be careful," they said. "Watch him."

"Justin," she said, trying to keep her voice steady, "I need to ask: Did Eli do this? Did he hurt you, even by accident? Maybe he didn't know his own strength."

"No, it wasn't him."

"Then who was it?"

He looked down, pressing his lips together as if to keep the words inside.

She said as gently as possible, "What is it? Why won't you tell me?"

"I tripped on my way to the bathroom 'cause I had my skates on. I must've hit something when I fell."

He was lying. She knew it instinctively. "Your dad didn't see you fall? He doesn't know anything about this?"

"No, Mom, I swear. He didn't *do* anything!" His eyes met hers and didn't waver. Now she felt confused. It seemed incredible he could have forgotten or failed to notice hitting his arm as he fell. On the other hand, if he was lying, he'd learned very quickly, like his father, to be convincing.

On Wednesday morning, Eli called to ask if they were on for dinner.

"I think we should meet tonight without Justin. We have some things we need to talk about."

"Okay, if this is about the money, I'm working on it. I'm making a budget so I can pay you on a schedule, like you said. We can talk before dinner or after. But I want to see him. We agreed it's good to do these things."

"Yeah, well, I'm not so sure about that now."

"What do you mean?"

"I'm saying this isn't good for him in the long run if you can't be responsible. I don't just mean about money, though that's part of it. The other part is I have to trust you to take care of him. He got hurt the other day, Eli. There are finger marks on his arm! If you say you don't know anything about it, you're either lying or totally clueless. And if you're hanging out with skanks like we saw the other night, that's not the kind of company I want around my kid."

"What?!" he sputtered. "You're saying *I* hurt him? I told you I didn't see anything happen, and if something did, then I'm sorry, but shit, April . . . he never got hurt around you? Or the girls either? And that girl the other night—I barely know her. Is that what this is all about? You're punishing me 'cause you're jealous?"

"Jealous?" she said icily. "*Please.* Don't compare me to that trash heap—or you! Things happened with the kids, sure. The difference is I never acted like they didn't. Get your shit together. Till then, fuck off."

"Hey, calm down. Look, let's just you and me have dinner and we'll talk, okay?"

"Fuck your dinners too. We've had our talk, far as I'm concerned. You don't like the way it went, blame yourself," she said, and hung up.

———

Claire was sorting through the mail that had just arrived when her heart skipped, seeing Sebastian's handwriting on a small gray envelope. She tore it open to find a brief note:

Hi Claire,

Hope you're well. Lars forwarded your Xmas card—thank you for that. I meant to send one back but missed the window, so . . . here's to another year bygone, and all good wishes for the next one. I'm in Albuquerque now, teaching at UNM, and will be here through at least the summer. After that, we'll see. It's been an

adjustment, but it's nice to have some stability and make a little income. Anyway, just wanted to let you know you can reach me at this address if you need to.
All my best,
~S

The return address was a P.O. box number. *Well,* she thought, *it beats a postcard.* The note was written on plain but expensive paper, the envelope handmade with his signature deep flap. Receiving it felt bittersweet. His notes to her in the past, though rare, were treasured: beautiful cards for special occasions he made from thick matte vellum.

She wondered why he decided to communicate with her this way instead of through an email or text. Was it that he preferred the distance, the impossibility of an immediate reply? Or was there something more sentimental about his choice? Though the tone of his note was anything but. She'd sent him a Christmas card out of impulse and curiosity, as she hadn't heard from him since the summer, when she'd complained about his postcard. Her message was brief, an olive branch, with no mention of past discord or current troubles. That he responded at all, she supposed, was validating. Except that it put her back into a spiral of confusion, overanalyzing every sentence he wrote for possible clues about his intentions.

What did he mean by *after that, we'll see* and *you can reach me at this address if you need to*? With all her health issues, work challenges, and constant negotiations with her insurance provider, there were days when she never even thought of him. But in other moments—when she felt physically exhausted or sat in the chemo ward getting her infusion, or when the house was dark and too quiet—sometimes she ached for him. Those moments of weakness filled her with shame. *You ought to be able to move on.* She resented his ambivalence, the power it wielded. Why couldn't he just ask for a divorce and be done with it? Why couldn't she?

That night, she had trouble sleeping, even after taking a Xanax. She'd be on the verge, then float back up to consciousness, too tired to read but unable to turn off her mind. It had begun to sleet outside, and she lay with her eyes closed, listening to the wind and drizzle tapping her window. It was a soothing sound, but after twenty minutes, she still couldn't sleep. Taking another Xanax would just up her tolerance. "Fuck," she said out loud, pushing her duvet aside. She reached for her robe, as her feet felt around the floor for her slippers. She still had half a case of red in the pantry; what harm would one glass do her?

Snow reflecting the full moon gave enough illumination so she didn't have to turn on any lights, which would have jarred her out of drowsiness. But the house was chilly, and she padded down the stairs quickly. As she crossed the kitchen to the pantry, she heard a swishing sound from the backyard and, turning, saw something glide past the French doors. Frowning, she walked up to the paned glass to peer out. The sleet was now turning to snow, sheets of it drifting sideways across her yard as the wind gained force. Then her breath caught.

There, by the maple tree, stood two figures in long gowns, their backs turned toward her. Something about them was familiar but also a little off; they seemed not quite solid, almost phosphorescent, and their gowns didn't move, despite the wind. Her heart beat faster. She was wide-awake now, sleep a foregone loss. "Is this real?" she whispered. Either answer, yes or no, would be troubling. But she would prefer not to be losing her mind. *It's the chemo,* she told herself. She'd read it sometimes caused delusions. In that moment, another gust blew up drifts of snow, and when it settled, both the women were gone.

Finally, the snow started thawing and the sun lingered later each day. As the weeks went by, the temperature rose to the fifties, palpably lifting everyone's moods. Warmer weather also meant spring cleaning, which always brought April more business. Clients who cut back during the winter now called her to set up schedules. She was vacuuming a new client's house one afternoon when she felt her phone vibrate in her back pocket. It was Eli's caseworker. "Hey, Alan," she said, frowning, "what's up?"

"Listen, I don't want to alarm you, but a couple weeks ago Eli canceled an appointment, said he had some stomach thing—fine. Then last Friday he shows up looking real raggedy. I ask him what's going on, and he says he's been putting in a lot of hours at work. I call Charlie, and he says nope, actually he's missed three days this month and was late twice. Now that's bad. But what's worse is him telling me such a stupid lie. Now he's not calling me back. Can you talk to him, find out what's going on?"

She sighed. "The thing is, Alan, he's not talking much to me either these days."

"Why's that?"

She hesitated saying too much. "We're having some arguments about Justin. He thinks I'm being too strict."

"Oh. Well, aside from that, you haven't noticed anything?"

"No. But I'll find out what I can and let you know. Really appreciate this." She hung up and cursed softly. "Damn you, Eli, what are you up to now?" Over the last couple of months, he'd gone from pouting and insulting to remorseful. Then he started giving her $200 on the first of each month, to get back into her good graces. But not a week went by that he didn't pester her to reinstate his Sundays with Justin, which she had revoked after their fight. She told him they'd talk about it again once school let out. Until then, he could see Justin twice a week in her presence.

Justin didn't like her chaperoning any more than Eli did. She tried to reason with him: "We'll still go to the rink, if you want. Eli can come—"

"I don't like hockey anymore."

"Come on, Justin. I know you're not happy, and I'm sorry. But your dad's got to be more on the ball—about you and about some other things between him and me."

It gave her no satisfaction now to know her caution appeared to be justified. Eli told her the same story he gave Alan about working more hours. If that was all bullshit, how was he making the extra cash? She remembered how he lied to her when he got busted years ago. Instinct told her not to call but instead confront him in person. His face would tell the truth.

She finished cleaning shortly before four thirty and sped from her last house in Freehold to Charlie's Auto Repair in Medusa, hoping to catch Eli before he left at five. Traffic was light, and she got there in fifteen minutes. Eli was in the driver's seat of a low white sedan, one long leg sticking out the open door. She called his name, and he peered out, looking astonished to see her.

"What's going on?"

"You tell me. Alan called and he's worried. He says you missed an appointment a couple weeks ago, then you lied about why, and now you're not calling him back. What the fuck, Eli?"

He stepped out of the car. "Lied? What do you mean?"

"You told him you were working overtime—same as you told me. But he checked with Charlie, okay, and he said you were out a few days and you're coming in late. So, be straight with me: What kind of bullshit are you up to?"

His expression went dark. "Charlie told him that?"

"Jesus, what do you think? He's your boss, Eli, not your friend. You think 'cause he's nice he's gonna cover your ass?" When he said nothing, she asked again, "What is going on with you?"

He looked over his shoulder toward the rear office, where they could see Charlie through the window, talking on the phone at his desk. "Okay," Eli said, avoiding her eyes. "I had a little stumble a few weeks back. I missed work one day, and I canceled on Alan 'cause I knew I wouldn't pass the marker. Then I called Donna."

Donna was his sponsor, a straight-shooting DMV clerk in her late fifties who'd been sober almost thirty years. Eli liked her a lot, and so did April.

"Anyway," he said, "she kicked my ass back onto the wagon, but I had to miss work another few days. It was a setback. I've been dry now eleven days. Call her if you don't believe me."

She gaped at him. "You fell off the wagon a few weeks ago, while you were begging me to see Justin alone. And you wonder why I can't trust you! How're you giving me money if you're not working overtime?"

His face flushed and now he looked at her. "I *did* work overtime, four shifts! Go in there and ask. I've been saving money too. Maybe if you trusted me in the first place, none of this would've happened. I didn't do anything to Justin, I swear to god I didn't. And I never took a drink, ever, until you put all that on me."

"Oh, so it's my fault. You take no responsibility."

"Of course I do," he said angrily. "I know I fucked up. But it didn't help, you taking away my biggest incentive."

She rolled her eyes. Typical of him to own his guilt one minute and blame her the next.

"Are you going to let me see him again?" he asked, suddenly fearful.

She thought about Justin's reaction if she were to ban Eli outright. "Yes," she said finally. "If you promise not to fuck up again. Don't let your kid down. I will kill you if you break his heart."

"I won't. I mean it. Thank you." He tried to touch her arm, but she jerked away and walked back to her truck. Halfway there, she stopped and turned around.

"Call Alan right away. Don't tell him you fell off the wagon, for chrissake. Just convince him you're okay. Make up some story. You're good at that."

7

EVIDENCE

The line of customers at April's counter had grown to six, her dinner break was eight minutes overdue, and there was still no sign of Brenda, who failed to come back from her break on time. Brenda was an affable woman whose laziness was overlooked because her nephew, Clark, was the manager at their CVS. She finally rushed in as April rang up the last customer. "Sorry," she panted, "couldn't get off the phone with my sister. She's a yapper."

I'll bet, April thought, then said out loud, "Going on my break now." She grabbed her parka and bag and clocked out in the back office. As she walked through the feminine hygiene aisle, out of camera range, she pocketed a box of tampons as a "fuck you" to Clark and his nepotism. She had to admit it felt good. Maybe she'd have to get off on shoplifting now instead of sex. *Probably cause me less trouble.*

Out in the parking lot, she fished in her pocket for her cigarettes, lit one, and inhaled deeply. She closed her eyes, lifting her face to the sun's last rays, and took another drag. The week before, Justin got into a fight with another boy who called him a "fat tomahonky." He'd been subjected to such slurs before, told he was a bastard and his dad a crook, and though it happened less as he got bigger, there was always one or two kids who persisted in taunting. This was the first time he'd lashed out. The other kid ended up needing stitches on his right cheek, and Justin spent a week after school in detention. He was angry, resentful, and so withdrawn she couldn't reach him.

At the sound of footsteps approaching, April opened her eyes. A woman was walking toward her—with a shock she realized it was Claire Pedersen. Her face was hollowed out, her hair hidden beneath a dark knit cap. She saw April and stopped. "Hey," April said. "Long time no see." The last time was in the summer, when they had that awful confrontation at the Erikssons' barbecue. Claire had already lost a lot of weight then. Now she was even thinner, to the point where she looked downright unhealthy. April recalled hearing rumors about her being anorexic.

"Yes. I've been kind of occupied." Claire's thin cheeks flushed, as if she too remembered their last encounter. "Well, I better go in. Have to get my prescription filled before the pharmacy closes."

"You got a couple hours. They're open till eight."

"Oh." Claire took in April's custodial blue shirt and name tag, visible beneath her open parka. "You work here?"

April scanned Claire's face for judgment. Detecting only curiosity, she nodded. "Four years. On a break right now." She dropped her cigarette and put it out with the toe of her shoe. "Never seen you come in before."

"I usually go to the one in Greenville, but they were out of my prescription, so they sent me here. Anyway, enjoy your break." Claire waved and went inside.

Well, April thought, at least she was polite. She pulled her sandwich from her bag and ate quickly. Then she had one more cigarette and walked back to the office. On the way, she passed the pharmacy and saw Claire waiting with three other customers on the bank of hard plastic chairs. She gave April a wan smile and shrugged. She really didn't look well. April hesitated, then went up to the counter and whispered to the pharmacist, "Hey, Max."

He leaned toward her. "Yeah?"

"Can you fast-track the Pedersen scrip?"

"Okay. Friend of yours?"

"Neighbor. Thanks."

She clocked back in, hung up her parka, and went to the bathroom. A few minutes later, walking past the pharmacy again, Max called out to her. "Hey, your neighbor just left and forgot her credit card. You want to call her? Maybe she can come back or you can drop it off."

"Uh . . . sure. Give me her number."

She called from the store to seem more official. To her surprise, Claire answered on the first ring. "Yes?"

"Hi. It's April, here at CVS. You left your credit card at the pharmacy. We'll hold it for you if you want to come back."

Claire groaned. "I can't believe I did that. Shit! I just got onto the highway and there's all this traffic going the other way. How long can you hold on to it?"

"I guess till whenever." April knew they weren't exactly careful about their lost and found. "Look, why don't I just drop it off to you later?"

"I couldn't ask you to do that."

"It's okay. You're like five minutes away from where I live. I can swing by after eight thirty."

"Well . . . if you're sure you don't mind. That would be really helpful. Thank you."

"If you're not home, I'll just leave it on the porch."

But when she drove up to her old house almost three hours later, the porch and front windows were lit. April rapped on the door three times. There was no answer. She scrawled a note on the envelope containing the credit card and was about to wedge it under the door when it abruptly opened. Claire stood before her in a thick sweater and sweatpants, their bulk only emphasizing her thin neck and small head. April noticed her hair looked shorter and stringy. She held a glass of red wine. "I thought I heard knocking. Why didn't you use the buzzer?"

"Does it work now?" April pressed it and heard four chime-y notes echo through the entrance. "Huh. Nice. Anyway," she said, pulling the card out of the envelope, "here you go."

"Thank you so much. Won't you come in? I've just opened a fairly decent cab."

"Thanks, but I don't really drink wine."

"Right, you drink beer. Shoot. I don't have any of that, but there's some scotch I keep around for Karl. It's Macallan, good stuff. Please, at least let me offer you a nightcap." Her eyes glittered with insistence. April thought she might already be tipsy. She knew how it was, not wanting to drink alone. But while she was curious to see the house, she was also apprehensive. Back in the fall, she noticed new paint on the exterior and shutters and felt the old stab of loss.

"Of course," Claire said, "if it seems too weird . . ."

Her perception made April feel exposed. "No, it's okay, I can come in for a bit."

Stepping inside, she could see right away it was clean and more modern, though sparsely furnished. A large candle burned on a table in the entryway, emitting a woodsy scent. The stairway banister was repaired, the walls were a smooth off-white, the wooden floors gleamed. Gone were the finger smudges, food smears, and ink scribbles that, at one time or another, marked those surfaces as far back as her childhood—all replaced by this pristine, adult, tasteful rebuttal. For a moment, she wondered if Claire meant to show off.

"You sure did a lot," she said politely. "It looks good." Suddenly, she dreaded the obligatory house tour, but to her relief, Claire didn't offer it. If anything, she looked slightly embarrassed.

"Oh, well . . . thanks. Please, sit down." She pointed to a beige leather sofa next to a glass coffee table stacked with large books and magazines, an open bottle of wine at one end. Setting her glass next to it, she said, "I'll go get you that drink. Neat or on the rocks?"

"Ice is good."

Claire walked to the kitchen, and April sat at one end of the sofa, checking her phone for the time. The room was cold and she kept her parka on. She was surprised Claire would skimp on heating. She assumed the woman had plenty of money. Looking around, she saw other signs of scarcity: the near absence of rugs and wall decorations and even pictures, the naked windows, the fact that the house was dark except for the room they occupied. The light bulbs in the candelabra were different, she noticed—and in that instant, all eight of them flickered off and back on.

Claire came back, holding a tumbler filled with ice and the bottle of scotch. She poured to the top and, handing the glass to April, noticed her holding her phone. "Everything okay?"

"Yeah, Maddy's home. Though I can't stay long."

Claire sat on a matching square ottoman next to April. "Maddy's your oldest, right?"

"Yep, seventeen. Ready to leave the nest soon." She took a sip of her drink, savoring the smooth welcome burn in her throat. The stuff tasted expensive.

"Is she going to college or . . . ?"

April shrugged uncomfortably. "She'll probably work first, save some money. It'd be good if she could go one day and, you know, make something of her life."

"Though these days, a degree doesn't guarantee much. I mean, I've got two and I still lost my job. I make less now than I did ten years ago—and I'm lucky! Some of my friends are still looking."

But you used to make money, April thought. *It let you buy this house.* "You're a lawyer, right?"

Claire made a soft, self-deprecating sound. "I was. Right now I just do paralegal work. Actually, my firm is representing the Clays in their civil suit." Seeing April flinch, she asked, "What's wrong?"

"Just . . . Patrick was my godson. His mom and I were close. And he was friends with my boy."

Claire looked stricken. "Oh god, I'm so sorry."

"It's okay, you didn't know."

Claire nodded but seemed disturbed. After a moment, she said, "We probably shouldn't discuss it. I don't want to be insensitive, but . . . I just don't want any conflict of interest with my job."

"Don't worry," April said. "I'm not involved in all that anyway. She's been keeping to herself." In fact, Brian and Jody were selling their house, and the family left weeks ago to stay with his parents in Connecticut. When April heard, she couldn't believe Jody would leave without saying goodbye. But when she saw the realtor sign at their house, she knew the rumor was true.

For a moment, they sat in awkward silence, sipping their drinks. Then Claire said, "I sometimes pass by that place in Hudson . . . Mackey's. Do you still go there?"

April snorted. "No. Too busy. And it's not like I ever met any winners there."

"What about around here?"

"Please, you've seen how it is. Here they're married or old or drunk or stupid. Sometimes all the above." April couldn't believe she was talking about men with Claire, of all people. But what else was there to talk about? "Doubt I'll meet anyone if I stick around here."

"Then why do you?"

The question caught April off guard. "I don't know. I mean, where else would I go? This is where I grew up . . . this town, this road—" She stopped herself from saying *this house*, but the words hung unspoken in the air. "What about you? No one since . . . ?"

"No. Not really." Claire looked away, and April shifted in her seat, taking another large sip of her drink. She wanted to finish it and get out of there. Something about Claire and being in the house, the way it was now . . . it gave her a cold, constricted, *sad* feeling, one she never experienced in all the years she lived there. For all its upgrades, the place creeped her out now, almost as if it were haunted; only rather than some unseen presence, what she felt was a palpable absence. Her place was small and messy and ugly. But there was life in it.

"There's something I wanted to ask," Claire said hesitantly, "if you don't mind. When you mentioned Sebastian and that girl, Anna: Did she ever say anything about him wanting to become more religious? What did they talk about, if they weren't having a real affair?"

April shook her head. "Honestly, the only time she mentioned him was to set me straight about, you know . . . that they didn't. Otherwise, all she ever talked about was God and suffering—oh, and the afterlife."

Claire leaned in curiously. "What did she say about it?"

"Well, not sure I remember this right, but something about how suffering makes you more open to God. How He reminds you of your mistakes, so you can get them right in this life and go on to heaven or wherever."

"Isn't that big of Him," Claire said dryly. "I consider myself an agnostic, but years ago, I explored different religions. I read somewhere that once we learn our lessons in this life, we're ready to move on to the next. That always kind of made sense to me."

"So, you think there's a life after this one too? I don't."

"No?" Claire asked with a puzzled smile. "You believe we're just . . . extinguished? Body, mind, and soul, all just dust? That seems so final and sad. You don't think our spirits can somehow find a way to linger?"

April thought of Patrick and wondered if recurrent nightmares could count as a kind of lingering. "I don't know. That's what's weird when someone dies . . . it's like, where do they go? Both my parents are gone, and I'd like to think they're still around somewhere. But I've never seen any proof to make me believe it. Sorry."

"Don't be. You're entitled to your opinion. Sebastian felt the same way. He found my spiritual quests rather naive, I think." Claire looked down at her wineglass for a moment, then said quietly, "I was with him for a really long time, but when I think about it now, it all seems like it happened to a different person. It's funny to think about that person. The things I accommodated. You know, one time when he wanted to be hurtful, he told me, 'No one really likes you.'"

"Whoa, that's harsh."

"But, in fact, he was right. People don't like me. I've never been able to figure out why." She gave April a sudden, piercing look. "Do you know?"

"Me? Why?"

"Well, you didn't like me. Even before I bought this house. You didn't like me back when we were girls. You don't really like me now."

April couldn't think how to respond. "I don't know you," she said finally. It was an evasive answer but not untrue.

"You probably want to keep it that way," Claire said with a short laugh. "Sorry, I didn't mean to put you on the spot. Anyway, that was my ex. A real keeper. But everyone in this town already knows that."

April wasn't going to go there. Instead, she said neutrally, "There's gotta be someone somewhere who's decent. Think you'll ever want to try again?"

Claire drained her glass and set it down on the table. "I don't know." She shrugged and let out a long sigh. "Maybe all that's done for me."

April nodded slowly. "Yeah. Maybe for me too."

They were quiet again for a few moments. This time, the silence felt communal. Then Claire spoke. "I had cancer, you know." She said it so softly April wasn't sure she heard right.

"What?"

"Uterine cancer. Stage three. But I got treated and they're pretty sure they got everything."

April absorbed the news with mild shock. All that talk about the afterlife—no wonder. "Wow. When was this?"

"Back in the summer and fall . . . Well, until last month, actually."

It made sense to April now why she hadn't seen her around much. "How'd you find out?"

"I went to see my gyn. My belly was swelling and . . ." Claire laughed bitterly. "You know, I actually thought I might be pregnant?"

"Oh!" *So there was some action,* April thought.

"I even took one of those home pregnancy tests. But turns out it was a false positive. Not a baby but a tumor. Isn't that classic? You ever feel like the universe is playing tricks on you? Like you just keep misreading the signs?"

April was uncomfortable with these vague, hocus-pocus concepts and found it odd that Claire and Anna, otherwise so different, were both so interested. "I guess I don't really think about all that stuff. But I'm sorry about your cancer. You're okay now?"

"So they say." Claire lifted the wine bottle. "Think I'll just have another drop. And you?"

She pointed to the bottle of scotch, but April said, "No, I'm good. Actually, I should—" She stopped at the sound of something creaking from above. Then they heard a crash outside.

"What the hell?" Claire ran to the door.

From the porch, they could see the weathervane lying on the front lawn, snapped off at the base. April gasped. The weathervane had crowned the peak of the roof since her childhood. She remembered the day her father installed it as she and her brother watched from below.

"Goddamn it," Claire said. "I don't believe this."

"How weird," said April. "It's not even windy outside." She walked over to examine the oxidized axis of arrows and letters. "It's still in pretty good shape. Maybe just needs a new base."

"Forget it," Claire said heatedly. "Every time I fix it something else goes wrong. I'm sick of this thing! Honestly, there's enough here to freak me out, without—" She caught herself and stopped short.

"What?"

Claire started to make a dismissive gesture, then looked at April intently. "Look, did you ever notice anything odd when you lived here? Weird smells, or scratching noises? Strange shadows in the rooms at night—or in the yard?"

"Like a ghost?" said April, clearly incredulous.

Claire colored. "I know it sounds crazy. Never mind. Probably just the house settling. I can spook myself sometimes. I guess I'm still not used to living alone." She shook her head. "Anyway, that weathervane's been nothing but trouble since the beginning. It's just not meant to be."

"If you don't want it, I can take it off your hands. I mean," April said awkwardly, "if you'd sell it to me."

"Oh!" Claire seemed startled by the request. "Why don't you just take it?" she said, and walked over to pick it up.

As she held it out, April asked, "Are you sure?"

"Yes. It obviously means more to you than me."

"Well. Thanks." April took the weathervane and said, "I should probably get home. My kids . . ."

"Sure," Claire said quickly. "Thanks again for dropping my card off. That was more than nice."

"No worries. And, well, take care of yourself. If you ever need anything . . ."

"That's kind." Claire gave her a brief, wistful smile. "See you around, I hope. Good night."

As soon as she got in her truck, April checked the time. She'd been in the house for thirty-five minutes. It felt twice as long. Something about the place *was* different now, and disturbing. She felt relieved to be out but also guilty, especially since Claire had been nice about the weathervane. She couldn't say why she wanted it so badly. It would look ridiculous on top of her mobile home. But since Claire had no use for it . . . and if her gift was an act of charity, at least she didn't make her feel it. She pictured Claire alone now, pouring herself another glass, maybe even killing the bottle. Probably not the best thing to do after having cancer. But with her run of bad luck, who could blame her?

It might have been her conversation with Claire that unsettled her or being back in her old house, but that night, April had another nightmare. This one was different in a way that shook her. It started out the same: crossing the darkening meadow, holding the clumsy weight of the pillow in her arms. For a long time, she walked in the pitch-black night. Then, slowly, the rising sun illuminated her path. She was on the Eternals' back lawn, with the farmhouse behind her and the creek shimmering ahead. All around her it was still and quiet. Just at the creek's edge, she saw a dark, familiar shape on the ground, covered by a woolen blanket. Her heart began to pound with dread. *Don't look, you know what it is.* Still, she drew closer, her fear overpowered by the need to see. She set the pillow down and stood above the small, hidden body. When she pulled back the blanket, it was Justin.

On a Thursday night two weeks later, April drove up to one of the filling stations at Pete's Pump. The gas was overpriced, but it was past ten o'clock, and she'd just gotten off work and didn't feel like driving out of her way to find a cheaper place. The air felt balmy when she got out of her truck. It was early spring, but she could already anticipate summer's arrival—and how quickly it would all go by. Every year she got a little older, and nothing else really changed. She swiped her debit card and fed the nozzle into her tank, looking around the lot idly. Then she frowned and leaned forward.

Across from the filling station, about twenty yards away, was the mini-mart, with two cars parked out front. One of them looked like Eli's blue Nissan. The pump clicked off, startling her. She set it back, capped her tank, and walked over to the car, checking out the license plate. It was his. She peered at the mini-mart but didn't see him through the brightly lit windows. Whirling around, she ran back to her truck and started the engine. She reversed toward the edge of the station lot, away from the lights. Then she turned off her headlights and waited.

After a few minutes, Eli came out of the store, eating chips from a large bag. He walked steadily and appeared sober. He clamped the bag of chips with his teeth while he unlocked his car and got in. A moment later, she saw the girl from D'Amico's saunter out in her tight jeans, taking a swig from a paper bag before getting in the car too.

April felt as if someone had punched her in the stomach. It wasn't jealousy, exactly; it was disappointment and, behind that, vindication. She followed his car as he drove east along the highway, staying back as far as she could without losing them. She'd never tailed anyone before. It was to her advantage that the highway was only two lanes, normal for one car to be behind another for several miles.

They drove past her old house and April glanced over briefly, noticing one lit window upstairs. In less than a mile, she passed the turnoff to Pine Hollow. All her kids were home. Justin and Cara were hopefully sleeping, but she'd have to let Maddy know if she was going to be much later. She figured Eli was heading to West Durham, to his apartment complex close to Aiyana's and his ex Naomi's. If she was still an ex. Who could keep track of all the women he'd fucked or was fucking? Fucking wasn't a crime, but partying could be—for him. And April could tell that girl he was with was looking to party.

To her surprise, instead of staying on the highway to West Durham, Eli veered north onto the road leading to Medusa. This road was isolated, narrow, and dark. April hung back until she could just see his taillights in the distance. She turned the radio off, the silence somehow making her feel less visible. After a few minutes, she saw ahead to her left a low building dotted with dim, evenly spaced lights. His car turned in that direction. As she got closer, she recognized the building: the Nitey-Nite Lodge, a budget motel from the sixties. Back in the Catskills' heyday, it attracted tourists and families on vacation. Now its reputation was sleazier, its occupants mostly campers and truckers, the occasional short-term renter.

Each dim light illuminated a doorway. Most of the windows were dark. She pulled over across the road and, with her engine still running, watched as Eli drove slowly through the sparsely filled lot. He disappeared behind the back of the building. She waited a moment, turned off her headlights, and followed him. The lot in the back was crowded, with several rooms on that side lit up behind the curtains. Eli's car pulled in front of one of the rooms. April steered several yards away toward a spot in the rear of the lot, keeping him in sight. He stepped out of the car, carrying a dark messenger bag, and the girl got out too. He knocked on the nearest door. It opened a crack, then wider. Some kind of music thumped in the background, and a thickset, muscular man quickly ushered them in. April had the impression of other people in the room before the door closed.

She killed the engine and pondered what to do. Something about the whole scene felt off. . .the way that man had rushed them through the door without a greeting. "Eli, you piece of shit," she muttered. She was sure he was dealing again. But how could she prove it? Her phone showed it was now ten thirty-five. She sent a text to Maddy: *Have to do some restock so home late. Everything ok?*

She could practically hear Maddy's sigh in her response: *I guess.*

Good. Not sure when done so don't wait up.

Nothing for a minute. Then: *Are you drunk?*

Christ, she thought, *everyone's a narc.* She texted back: *No!*

After a few minutes, the muscled man came out of the room, followed by another man, balding and older, holding the arm of a scantily clad girl. Her head was lowered, and she tottered in her heels. April was struck by her slumped, defeated posture. They walked over to the next door. The muscled man let the other man and girl inside, then closed the door and went back to the first room. April released a long, shaky breath she hadn't realized she was holding in. A bad, ugly feeling settled over her. The girl was obviously a sex worker, but unlike those April had seen in the past, this one seemed reluctant and fearful.

April had two strong opposing impulses: to flee as far and fast as she could, and to stay and call 911. Except if the police came it would cause trouble for

Eli. He was a lying, manipulative loser, involved in something worse than she could have imagined—but he was still Justin's father. She wished there were someone she *could* call, someone she could trust. Donna came to mind. But it was late. Did this count as an emergency? Or would it be better to wait until tomorrow, when they could confront Eli together? She sat holding her phone, debating.

Then Eli walked out of the motel room. He was alone, with the messenger bag slung over his shoulder. Before she could decide what to do, he was already in his car starting the engine. She started her truck too, determined to confront him. She caught up to him in the front lot, flashing her high beams and honking her horn to get his attention. He looked back through the rearview mirror, eyes wide with alarm, then narrowing in recognition. He stopped, got out of his car, and stomped over to her.

"What the hell—what're you doing, following me?" he yelled. "Are you crazy?"

She stepped out of her truck too. "Yeah, I followed you! I saw you at Pete's with that girl and I knew you were up to something. You're dealing, aren't you, you fucking liar!" His face twitched, trying to settle on an expression—outrage, denial, shame. She would have laughed if it wasn't so pathetic. "What else, are you pimping too? The girl who came out with that fat, creepy guy? Jesus, Eli!"

"I've got nothing to do with any of that. I didn't know that was going to be the scene, that's why I got out of there."

"What about your girl? Why'd you leave her behind?"

He snorted. "They're her friends. I was just giving her a lift."

"You are so full of shit! I saw the bag you took in and brought out, okay? You really think I'm that stupid?!"

His lips compressed tightly. Then he opened his mouth, but before he could speak, a loud boom and flash came from behind them. They turned around and saw smoke billowing from what looked like a blown-out hole at one end of the motel. Seconds later, lights in the other rooms flicked on and people came running out, some only in T-shirts and underwear.

"What's going on?" a woman screamed. "What's happening?"

"Fire!" a man yelled, pointing to the smoke, which now bloomed higher, with flames shooting out through the gaping hole. An acrid chemical stench filled the air.

"Shit!" the woman said, dashing back to her room.

"Oh, *fuck me*," said Eli. "Don't tell me some asshole was trying to freebase. I can't fucking believe this night!"

More people began to run out to the lot, several coming from the rear of the motel. Everyone was frantic and screaming: "Holy shit, did you *see* that?" "The window blew out!" "Someone call 911!"

"Wait here," Eli said, running toward the back of the building. April nodded mutely, staring as the flames reached the roof, the short, hot sparks licking at the sky. Sounds crashed around her in jumbled chaos, but it seemed as if everyone moved in slow motion. Some people drove off in their cars, but most, like her, stood at the scene gaping. She had always been in awe of fire, ever since she could remember. After her father's death, that awe turned to terror.

The woman who rushed back to her room came out with a heap of clothes piled in her arms. She looked over her shoulder and screamed, "Brianna, get *out* here, come on!" before running ahead to her car.

A little girl with tangled blond hair stepped through the doorway, eyes wide and panicked. April ran to her, horrified she was left alone. "Go on, honey," she said, nudging her gently. "Go to your momma."

The girl stared up at her, then tottered forward. Clutched to her chest was a pillowcase overflowing with clothes, the head of a baby doll sticking out from the middle. She struggled to catch up to the woman, trying to balance the pillowcase in her arms. As April watched, she felt a cold, familiar horror. Her nightmare—here, in real life.

Suddenly Eli was back again, grabbing her arm. "We have to go *right now*. Get in your truck and follow me."

"Did you find her?"

He shook his head frantically. "Too crazy, everyone's running in all directions. We gotta get out of here too."

"What was going on back there?"

"Sweet holy Christ," he said, nearly sobbing, "the cops are gonna come any minute, and when they do, *I can't be here*, do you understand? I'm fucking dead if that happens." He coughed, turning away for a moment, then looked into her eyes. "Listen. I'm asking you to help me, for the last time, I swear. Not just for me but for us. For Justin."

"Oh, don't you dare." But she knew he was right. She made the mistake of allowing him into their lives, and now she'd have to make sure he came through okay. Far off in the distance, they heard the sound of sirens approaching.

"Come on!" he cried.

"Where are we going?"

"Just tail me."

As she pulled out of the lot, she looked back once more at the fire, which now seemed to engulf nearly half the building. Then she sped forward to catch up to Eli. This time she followed him closely, and though he drove fast, he made sure she didn't lose him.

They backtracked to the highway toward West Durham, staying on it for the next five miles. She had a feeling they weren't going to his apartment, and she was right. Just as they entered the town, he detoured south at the junction leading to Ashland. About a mile farther on, they approached a mini strip mall. Eli turned into the parking lot, and she did too. The lot was empty, lit only by neon signs for three businesses: a nail salon, dry cleaner, and hardware store. When April got out, she noticed two vacant storefronts with FOR LEASE signs taped to the windows, something she'd grown used to seeing in almost every town over the last two years.

Eli stood beside his car holding the messenger bag, waiting for her. Something tense about his posture, and her awareness of how isolated they were, made her suddenly fearful. Did he mean to harm her? What if the bag contained not drugs but weapons? For a moment, she could barely breathe. Slowly, she backed away from him. "What are we doing here? Why do you have that bag?"

"Jesus, relax." He took two steps toward her, then stopped. Now she could see his expression, the genuine bewilderment. "You're scared of me? Shit," he said softly. "You actually think I could hurt you? You're the mother of my kid. What the hell's wrong with you?"

As he spoke, her fear abated. But she was still unnerved. "Look, I need to know what's going on. What were you doing there tonight?"

He sighed heavily. "I was doing what you thought, okay? Jess said she knew of a party, people looking for some blow. She's hooked me up before. So, we go there and do the deal. I've got the cash right here," he said, tapping the bag. "Anyway, it was a weird scene. Not the usual party, you know . . . all those hookers. I wanted to cut out, but Jess didn't. So I left."

He was so dismissive about the girl, April had to believe there was nothing more between them. "Shouldn't you call her, see if she's okay?"

He shook his head. "No way. Not till I know how this'll play out. But first I have to show you something. It's important." He led them to the far end of the long building, where a darkened PUBLIC STORAGE sign hung above a metal door and large, gated window. Two American flags swayed from the low roof. He pulled out his keys and opened the door to a small entryway that lit up as soon as they stepped inside. There was another door about fifteen feet ahead. He opened it, and they walked through a narrow, harshly lit corridor lined on both sides with several locked storage units.

He stopped in front of a small cube, inserted a key, and swung the door open, revealing a large metal box secured with a padlock. Holding it out to her, he said, "Open it. The combination is Justin's birthday." It took her a moment to think of the date as numbers. When she lifted the lid, she let out a small gasp—not at the money, which she'd expected, but at the amount. The surreal sight of it. There were several stacks of hundred- and twenty-dollar bills, along with some tens and fives, all separated by rubber bands.

"Holy shit. How much is in here?"

"About forty-two thousand." He unzipped the messenger bag and produced another thick wad of bills, which he added to the box. "Plus eight hundred."

"But . . . how can there be so much? I thought all your money went to your lawyers."

"Some of it did. Not all. And then I made some more."

A slow rage began to burn in her. "And all this time you cried poor! You lying piece of *shit*."

His face reddened. "Aiyana thought I shouldn't tell you. She said to save it all for Justin. And I didn't want you to get suspicious. Hell, if I knew you'd stop our outings—"

"That bitch! I was asking for Justin! You thought I was going to spend it on myself? Take a five-star cruise around the world?"

"I'm sorry. But listen: I'm giving it all to you now. Do you understand?"

"Why?" she asked, suspicious.

"In case they connect me to what happened tonight."

"But you didn't have anything to do with that explosion."

"Doesn't matter. They'll do a full sweep of the building, and there were a lot of drugs at that party. I don't know if those guys had time to clean out before they ran. And all those witnesses. Let's just say I'm a lot more paranoid now than I was ten years ago." He closed the box, locked it, and put it back in the storage cube. Then he pulled off three keys from his chain and gave them to her. "The smaller one's for this locker. Write down the number. These two are for the doors outside—don't lose those keys. There's only one other set, and no one but me knows where it is, not even Aiyana."

"Does she know what you've been up to lately?"

"No. And if this blows over, I'd prefer she never does."

April shook her head in amazement. "How do you even keep track of what you tell to who? And why this big confession now? What if nothing happens? You gonna take the keys back and switch lockers?"

"No. I'm telling you now 'cause I have no choice. You busted me. If they come after me, you keep the money for Justin. Consider it a show of trust. All I'm asking is that you do the same."

"Eli, are you—how can I trust you?" she sputtered. "You've been lying to me for months, just like you lied to me ten years ago. All I can trust is that you'll lie to me again. Your money's not going to change that."

"I'm trying to make things right. Jesus—fine, okay, don't trust me. Just keep an open mind, is all I'm asking."

"About *what*?"

"About me. I know that's asking a lot right now. But I was in a good place for a while. You know it. I was doing really well until you started doubting me."

"Please, let's not go there again."

He started to object, then stopped. "All right," he said finally. "Hold on to those anyway. We should get going, it's late."

She hesitated. Accepting the keys felt like a bribe. But it made sense for her to safeguard the money. Who knew how long he could stay out of trouble?

"Come on," he said, turning to walk down the hallway. "Show me how you lock up."

She stared at the locker for a moment. Then she pulled out her phone, took a picture of the number, and caught up to him.

———

The motel explosion was big news in the area, reported on all the local stations and in several papers over the next few days. Firefighters discovered the charred body of a man later identified as a white thirty-four-year-old former FedEx employee with a history of drug abuse. As Eli guessed, he was using his room as a makeshift freebase lab. There was no mention of other casualties or suspicious activities.

To be safe, Eli tossed his phone and got a new one, replacing the SIM card. Almost two weeks went by and nothing happened. Then, just as he began to relax, two officers arrested him at work one afternoon, taking him in for questioning. He called his former attorney's office from the police station but was told she was out of the country. He agreed to a court-appointed attorney and learned the police had found some small baggies of cocaine in the motel room. It turned out one of the hookers that night was a trafficked woman who escaped in the chaos. When she described her captors and other people she saw, she mentioned "a really tall guy, maybe Mexican or Indian," which led them to Eli. Later, she picked his face from a series of mug shots. They saved the worst news for last: his prints were lifted from one of the baggies.

———

The next month for April was a blur. Eli was in the Columbia County Jail waiting for his next hearing, and his future was uncertain. The prosecutors offered a plea bargain if he gave up his customers and helped identify the sex traffickers. If he cooperated, they could reduce his sentence to a year, possibly even avoid imprisonment altogether. He considered taking the plea but worried snitching might cause him trouble later. On the other hand, going to trial would be costly. Hiring someone good like his old attorney would wipe out the money he'd saved for Justin, with no guarantee of acquittal.

When Justin asked why his dad was back in jail, April was blunt: "Because he made a stupid mistake. He sold drugs to some bad people. And he was in the wrong place at the wrong time." She figured by now he was old enough to know the truth and, hopefully, take a cautionary lesson from it. The reality was Eli could be incarcerated for years. It killed her, the first time she took Justin to visit him in jail, seeing how upset it made him. And seeing Eli's acute shame. It was exactly what she had feared might happen.

She tried to keep Justin occupied by getting him back into a sport. Since he'd lost interest in hockey, she signed him up for soccer. The weekend before the first practice, April took him to the Walmart in Catskill to buy cleats and shin guards. They were heading toward the checkout lines when they ran straight into her long-ago ex Harlan with his trust-fund loser sidekick, Duncan.

"Well, if it isn't Tweedledee and Tweedledum," she said. "What trouble are you all up to?"

"Ha ha," said Harlan. "Always gotta be funny." He was about to say something else when he noticed Justin holding all his gear. "Hey, sport. You play soccer? Gonna be a World Cup champ someday?"

Justin had gone shy, practically hiding behind April. She shrugged and said, "We'll see. He starts practice next week."

Duncan told Harlan, "Hey, man, let's go." He seemed antsy.

"You okay?" she said. "Gotta go barf somewhere?"

Duncan didn't even look at her. Harlan snickered, shook his head, and said, "Okay, be good now. See ya around." They walked away.

She snorted and muttered, "Losers. Sorry, let's go."

"Why'd you tell him about practice?" Justin said, visibly upset.

"What's wrong?"

"You told him about practice! Now he's gonna go, and I don't like him!"

"Harlan? I don't like him either, but—"

"Not him!"

"You mean Duncan? What's the problem?"

He shook his head and stalked toward one of the lines. She caught up to him and asked again, "What is the problem with Duncan?"

He wouldn't look at her. He seemed on the verge of tears.

A cold, ugly fear began to snake through her. She lifted his face, her hands shaking. "We are going to find him in this store and I will make you ask him yourself, I swear to god, if you don't tell me what he did *right now.*"

His voice was so low she had to lean in to hear: "He's the one who grabbed me that time at the rink. He's the one who twisted my arm."

"Duncan?" She couldn't believe it. He was just a drunken moron, more a threat to himself than anyone else. Then her shock turned to rage. She forced herself to ask calmly, "Tell me what happened."

He kept his head down and mumbled, "I went to the bathroom, and he came in right after. He asked if I remembered him, and I said yeah. He had a pack of gum and asked if I wanted one. I said no, but he kept saying 'Come on,' so I took one and said thanks. Then he said, 'That's all? Come here, give me a hug,' and just grabbed me. It was weird . . . I didn't like it, but I couldn't get away." He paused, and she noticed his chin was trembling.

She placed her hands on his shoulders and said gently, "Go on, I'm listening."

"I said, 'Let me go,' but he wouldn't. My face was like smashed into his chest, and I couldn't breathe. No one was around, and I got scared . . . I kept pushing at him, and he said, 'Stop it, stop fighting!' and he got mad and started twisting my arm real hard. Then this older kid came in, and he let me go. But while that kid was peeing, he said real quiet if I told anyone what happened, I'd be sorry. He said he knew all these bad things about Dad, and if I told on him, he'd make sure he got in trouble." He looked up at her and said, "Now Dad's in jail—but I swear I never told anyone before."

She pulled him into a tight embrace. "I know you didn't. I'm so glad you told me now. Your dad's not in jail because of Duncan. And it's sure as hell not because of you, okay? Duncan said that to scare you. He's a liar. He doesn't have that kind of power."

But as she held her boy, her heart pounding with fury, she realized Duncan had had enough power to hurt him, and wondered what it would take to avenge him.

8
BLAME

Anna was shifting in bed, trying to find a comfortable position, when she felt the weight of Luke's arm around her shoulders, his breath warm against the back of her neck. She sighed in sleepy protest, but he only threw his leg over hers and drew her closer. She felt his erection pressing against her bottom and his hand lifting up her nightgown to caress her belly.

"Anna," he whispered, "are you awake? Can we . . . ?"

His asking for what he meant to take provoked a flash of irritation. She remembered Sebastian, how purposefully he'd led her, and felt an inchoate longing followed by intense shame. Murmuring assent, she placed her hand over his. "Be careful, the baby—"

"I know."

She was six months along now and could lie comfortably only on her side, which was the way he entered her. Miriam, the elder midwife, told them it would be safe to have relations up until Anna delivered, provided he was gentle. And Luke was always gentle—up until the moment just before it was over, when he became changed, frightening, almost a stranger.

"What is it?" he asked her once, stopping abruptly in his exertions.

"Nothing," she whispered, pressing him closer so he would finish.

Now she grasped his hand, concentrating on that pressure and not the other thing he was doing. Whatever he wanted, she was determined to give him. And what he wanted above all else was a healthy child. A boy.

When the morning sickness came on, she was stunned. The fact she conceived and was due to have this baby close to the same time as her first one filled her with superstitious dread. But Luke was thrilled and took her pregnancy as a sign of God's forgiveness. Like before, her nausea was ever-present. She was weak and miserable, unable to keep food down. Her alarming weight loss prompted Miriam to make her a special porridge high in nutrition, so that this baby would be stronger. The dish was a dark green color that made her think of algae. It had a strange, gristly texture and odor, killing any appetite she had. They made her eat it anyway, twice a day, even if she was sick only moments before.

"You have to think of the baby," Miriam insisted, when Anna tried to refuse. "Come now. This is one of the smaller sacrifices you'll make for your child."

Anna much preferred Rachel, Miriam's apprentice, who had guided her with her firstborn. Miriam was more experienced, but her constant scrutiny made her uncomfortable. As much as for the baby's health, she ate so she could get better and no longer require monitoring. She forced herself to swallow the food, holding her breath so she wouldn't have to smell it.

"Chew slowly," Miriam said, pushing another spoonful in her mouth. "It will help you keep it down." But the slower she chewed, the more she could taste it and want to gag. It seemed to her a perverse form of torture, enforcing the method designed to do exactly what they forbade.

She could taste the foul gruel even now, as Luke gripped her tighter, the crook of his arm pressing against her throat. She began to gag and panic—she couldn't breathe or swallow, she was choking, he was choking her!—and then he finally groaned and his arm relaxed, trembling against her. After his body quieted, he crawled over to her other side to look at her. In the faint moonlight, his face, damp and flushed, was back to the way she knew it: sweet, loving, and concerned.

"Are you okay?"

"Of course," she said, wiping the sweat from his cheek. She liked these moments after, when they could lie next to each other calmly.

"Your hair is getting long again," he whispered, wrapping some strands around his fingers.

"And you've regained your strength," she said, smiling.

"It's hard to believe, isn't it, that it's almost been a year. To think how miserable I was before, and now . . . I'm so happy, Anna. We are so blessed."

"It's true," she said.

The elders had relaxed their rules, allowing her more autonomy outside the farmhouse and even in the café. When they first sent her back to work there, she was confined to the kitchen, away from customers. Now that there were less customers, she also worked the cash register. Since the boy's drowning and the lawsuit, the Eternals noticed an unmistakable distancing from their neighbors. Exchanges were civil but no longer extended. No one attended their Shabbat on Friday evenings, and two carpentry jobs were canceled. Business in the café was almost nonexistent during the winter. As the weather grew warmer, it picked up again, but locals were no longer their mainstay, replaced instead by random tourists.

Zebiah still kept a watchful eye on her in the café, as did Esther at the farmhouse, and Miriam at mealtimes. Even before her disgrace, they were always reserved. She assumed that as matrons, they were meant to set an example for the younger women. She was thankful at least some of the latter, like Rachel and Sarah, were friendly again. Rachel was especially considerate of her condition, offering to take on her chores when she looked tired. Anna was touched but never accepted, mindful of criticism. What she wanted was simply to blend back into the community, neither shunned nor the object of special treatment. *Once the baby comes,* she told herself, *their attention will no longer be on me.*

Miriam felt certain she was carrying a boy, and she was right the first time. Though no one predicted he would die. Anna knew her doubts and fears had poisoned her womb before. With this baby, she was determined to be courageous. *Please, God,* she prayed now, *don't let it happen again.* She hoped that Luke was right, that the child she carried was proof of His benevolence. For her, relief could only come once she delivered safely. At that moment, as if on cue, the baby began to kick. "Feel," she said, placing Luke's hand on her belly. "He's stirring."

The following week, Anna was sorting bills with Zebiah at the cash register when Luke walked into the café, carrying several packages. "What are you doing here?" she said, startled but pleased to see him.

"I was going to the house for lunch and ran into Matthew on his way to the post office. He said there was a big shipment, so I offered to help. These are your supplies."

The Eternals always had their mail delivered to the post office rather than to the farmhouse or café. It was a precaution that all their communities established years ago, to prevent former relatives and hostile strangers from too easily seeking or harassing members in their communal homes.

"Thank you," said Zebiah. "And how long did Sandy detain you today?"

Sandy was the postmaster and frequent epicenter of town gossip. She was also one of the few locals who remained friendly to the Eternals.

"For quite a while, actually," Luke said, frowning. "Some woman accused that drunk, Duncan McAuley, of molesting her son. Says he harmed and threatened him."

"What? When was this?"

"Last winter, at the Albany Y. He cornered the boy in the bathroom and, I guess, touched him inappropriately. When he tried to get away, Duncan grabbed him and injured his arm. Said if he told anyone, he'd get his father in trouble—or more trouble, I should say. Apparently, he's a convicted criminal."

"Who's this woman?"

"Someone named April Ives, a local."

Anna stifled a gasp. She'd never told anyone, even Luke, about working with April at the Burnetts'.

Zebiah said, "This happened in the winter and she's accusing him now?"

"Apparently, she only found out recently. Sandy said April pressed charges, but she doesn't have a chance because Duncan's family has influence. People are saying she's just out to get money."

Zebiah shook her head. "Another lawsuit in this town, imagine."

Luke sighed unhappily. Anna knew he dreaded the upcoming deposition, when he and Gabriel would have to answer questions under oath. Alvin Baumann, the Eternals' attorney, said it would happen by the end of summer. He warned them the Clays might be present.

"It will be a relief when ours is over," he said, "with a good outcome, I hope."

Zebiah nodded, then said, "Luke, I almost forgot. A coyote got into the coop last night—it dug under the mesh. We lost two chickens and a quail."

"A coyote—are you sure? Not a fox?" They'd had problems with the latter before, but coyotes rarely ventured onto their property.

"I know the difference between predators," she said with a note of impatience. "It was a coyote. I saw tracks this morning from the henhouse going across the creek to the woods. We need you to fix the mesh before nightfall."

"All right. I'll do that straightaway, once I leave here. And set up some noose traps too."

Anna grimaced. "I hate those things."

Zebiah said, frowning, "You would hate to see what that coyote did to our fowl."

"I'll take care of it," Luke said again, to end the subject.

"Thank you. Anna, bring him some chili from the kitchen and set it there on that table. You can eat now too if you like."

It was an unexpected kindness, which Anna assumed was for Luke's benefit. Then she chastised herself. *Why do I have such ungrateful thoughts? Why do I constantly question my own people?* She went to the kitchen to prepare their lunch, still unnerved by what she'd learned about April.

When she set their bowls down, Luke leaned over to smell Anna's porridge. "It does have a strange odor," he said, wrinkling his nose. "What's in it?"

"Bone marrow, they said, and medicinal herbs. It makes me want to be sick every time." She bolted it quickly, then ate some corn bread to mask the taste.

Luke chewed his chili slowly, with a slight frown on his face.

"Does it not taste good?" she asked.

"No, it's fine," he said. "I've just been thinking about something odd Sandy mentioned: she said that woman, April, was Patrick Clay's godmother, that he was good friends with her son."

Anna gaped in silence. Hearing the drowned boy was April's godson made the hairs on the back of her neck rise.

"Strange those two boys knew each other," Luke went on. "I was trying to think why it bothered me, hearing that Duncan grabbed this boy's arm . . . It reminds me of how Patrick's arm was broken."

"Are you suggesting there's a connection? That Duncan might be involved with the drowning?"

"I don't know." He shook his head. "It's just a feeling . . . I can't prove it. At the very least, he's a dangerous man, if what that woman says is true, and living just up the road."

She looked around to make sure no one was listening. "Luke, I should have said something earlier, but that woman, April—I know her. She used to work at the Burnetts' when I was there. She cleaned their house. I never told you because I thought it would bring up bad memories."

"You knew her? What do you mean, 'bad memories'? Did she mistreat you?"

"No. She was very kind. I meant bad memories because it was such a hard time for me, being sent away. And the house where I lost the baby"—she looked down for a moment—"she used to own it, before the Pedersens. I didn't know Patrick was her godson until today. And to think I was the one to find him. I can't tell you how horrified it makes me feel."

He sat still, looking distraught too. "It is all very strange," he said finally. "Have you been in contact with her since?"

"Only once, back in the winter. I was walking back from Pete's, and she pulled over to offer a ride. I told her I couldn't, that I had to be more careful now with outsiders." Her cheeks turned pink at this reference to Sebastian. "I haven't seen her since. But she's a good, honest person. I feel awful about what happened to her son, especially knowing she must be grieving Patrick too."

He measured his next words carefully: "If you say she's honest, then her account must be true. Is there anything else you've kept from me I should know?"

"No, I don't think so," she said, taken aback by his tone. She had disappointed him, she could tell. "I'm sorry, Luke."

"All right. I'm glad you told me now. Compose yourself, Zebiah is looking."

The busiest days at the Horizon Café were always Sundays, even though they closed by three o'clock. Their extensive brunch was still popular with locals, and even tourists who heard about it flocked to the café. Anna had started to clear the dishes from a large group when she was overcome by a sharp wave of nausea. She set the dishes down abruptly, bolted to one of the bathrooms, and began to vomit. Someone rapped on the door.

"Anna?" Zebiah called out. "Are you sick? Let me in, child. Let me see."

She lifted her head and gasped, "I'm okay, I just need a minute."

"Let me in. Don't flush!"

She was still retching when Zebiah rushed in with the master key. Anna was so outraged by her intrusion she almost forgot her misery. Zebiah began to beat her upper back lightly with both fists, murmuring, "That's good, let it out . . . let it all out." When she was finally done, Anna raised herself slowly to the sink to rinse her mouth and face. Zebiah peered intently over the toilet bowl. It was filled with brackish green liquid, darker than anything Anna had ever expelled. Zebiah closed the lid and looked at Anna with a strange expression. It seemed like satisfaction, possibly even approval.

"You can go home now," she said. "There's not much left to do."

"I can't eat that porridge anymore. I won't." After a moment, Anna added, "Please."

"You don't have to. All the toxins are expelled. Now go home and rest."

Anna nodded, relieved but still furious. What did they feed her to make her so sick? How could it be good for her or the baby? She had the sudden fear that they meant to harm her. She pushed the blasphemous thought away, telling herself she was just exhausted.

On her way home, she felt a wave of fatigue and had to pause to catch her breath. She stood outside the secondhand store, looking at the window display. There was a vintage wheelbarrow, several planters, and a red-and-white rocking horse, the latter so small that only a toddler could ride it. She remembered Mikey J. had a wooden rocking horse he'd outgrown, pushed to the corner of the boys' room until the baby, Sam, could one day use it. Anna hadn't permitted herself to think about them much, but now she missed them. She regretted the abrupt way she had to leave, without being allowed to even say goodbye.

Feeling a presence nearby, she turned and saw a woman across the road, staring at her. The woman was panting and sweaty, wearing workout clothes that revealed her lank, nearly emaciated body. She had dark hair pulled back in a short ponytail and a small face with familiar, piercing eyes. She crossed over to Anna, stopping only a few inches away. "You're back," she said in a flat, strangled voice.

"Excuse me?"

"When did you get back?" the woman said, her voice rising. "Whose baby are you carrying now, you little *whore*?!"

Anna covered her mouth in horror. It was Claire Pedersen. She'd feared this confrontation ever since she first came back and heard the woman had as well. But as the months went by and nothing happened, even once she was allowed to venture out, she relaxed. Claire never came to the café now, and they'd had only one brief encounter when she did before, with Sebastian. She was much curvier then, cool and standoffish, with a streak of gray in her hair. Everything about her today was different—everything except her eyes. Those were the same, and they took in every detail about Anna, raking over her body from head to toe, finally settling on her belly.

"I can't believe it," she whispered, as if to herself.

"I'm sorry," Anna said, "please—"

"You're *sorry*? About what?!"

Anna flinched at the pure hatred in the woman's face. "I never meant . . . Please believe me, nothing ever happened—"

"Oh, I'd say a lot happened," Claire said, her voice shaking. "A lot fucking happened *to me*. But you—you get to come back and just pick up your life again?" She looked upward, fists clenched. "Goddamn it, it isn't fair!"

"Please, you have to believe me. There was nothing ever between me and your husband." But Anna knew, even as she spoke, that this wasn't entirely true.

"Little Miss Innocent, oh no, you didn't do anything!" Claire hissed, leaning in closer. "How'd you get knocked up this time, immaculate conception?"

Seeing Anna blush, she became even more enraged. "Oh, please! *This* is what he slobbered over? You're no virgin saint. You let someone stick it in, okay, just like the rest of us—"

"Stop!" Anna cried, pressing her hand over Claire's mouth. Claire lunged forward and clamped her teeth down hard, whipping her head like a rabid dog. Anna screamed and wrested her hand free. There were four small puncture wounds on her index and middle fingers. She watched in horror as blood began to well and trickle down her hand.

Claire, seeing the blood, seemed shocked too. She wiped her mouth and spat. "You'd better take care of that," she said shakily, backing away.

Anna turned and continued up the highway in a daze. Her fingers were throbbing. She would have to clean the wounds thoroughly to avoid infection, and hide them too. There was no way she could tell anyone, even Luke, about what happened without reminding them all of her disgrace. She reached into her pocket with her good hand and pulled out her handkerchief, wrapping it tightly around her bleeding fingers.

As she neared the farmhouse, she was still shaking. She took several deep breaths to collect herself and walked into the house, relieved not to encounter anyone. In the large washroom just past the entryway, she found bandages and antiseptic. After she cleaned and dressed her hand, she stepped into the front parlor. From there she could see the large dining room table, already set for supper. The room was empty, but she heard singing coming from the kitchen, at the rear of the house. It sounded like Esther and Tamar, and after a moment, she recognized the hymn, "Adonai Ori" from Psalm 27. Usually it soothed her, but today, she found their perfect harmonizing eerie. Then the singing abruptly stopped. After a moment, she heard their voices joined in humming, softly at first, then building in volume until they sounded like a loud tuning fork. Curious, she walked toward the kitchen, stopping just before the wide doorway.

Both women stood by the sink beneath the large window, facing each other with their eyes closed. They were gripping something pink and slimy over the sink, each of their fists interchanged over the other's. It was some kind of animal intestine. She knew Esther sometimes made sausages and other dishes from goat intestines, but why were they holding it and chanting like that? She retreated before they could see her and went back to the front of the house, puzzled and disturbed.

As she ascended the stairs, she heard muffled thuds and footsteps. When she reached the landing, no one was in the long corridor. Then she noticed the door to her and Luke's room was ajar. Just as she approached, he stepped into the corridor, followed by Gabriel.

Luke seemed startled to see her. "Anna! You're home early. Are you okay?"

"I'm fine. Zebiah said I should come back and rest. Did you slaughter a goat today?"

"What? No, you know it's not harvest season. Why?"

"I—never mind."

"Well . . . we have a surprise for you. Come see." He walked toward her, smiling, and reached for her hand. "You're hurt! What happened?"

"It's nothing," she said, tucking her hand in her pocket. "I broke a glass at the café."

"Oh, you have to be more careful." He took her elbow and led her into their room. She nodded at Gabriel, who stepped aside shyly to let her pass through the doorway. At the far end of the room, where their dresser had been, stood a wooden baby crib. It was the same one given to them two years ago, when she was expecting their first child. The crib was made of pale birchwood, hewn by one of the Eternals' most skilled cabinetmakers. She remembered how touched she and Luke were when the elders presented it to them as a special honor, welcoming them as a family to their new community.

The last time she saw the crib was hours before the death of her baby. When she came back from the hospital, it was no longer in their room. Seeing it again made her blanch with horror. The past hour had seemed like a prolonged nightmare—and now this. She struggled to control her face. Of course they would need a crib. But why *this* one? What could Luke be thinking? She could not understand why he continued to pay homage to their dead child when it was strictly forbidden and, to her, unbearably painful.

"Gabriel and Sarah thought we should have it," he said. "Their Ada has grown so much, she's ready for a bigger bed. And it's still practically good as new."

So, the crib had been given to them. If they had no superstitious qualms about inheriting it, why should she feel so averse to taking it back? She turned to Gabriel and willed herself to smile. "Thank you." Her voice came out small, breathless. "Please extend our thanks to Sarah—and to little Ada too."

"She slept very happily in it," he said. "We wish the same for your baby."

She wondered if his words were meant to dispel any lingering bad luck, but as she searched his face, it was clear he was only being polite. He was simple, Gabriel, well-meaning but simple—and then, turning to Luke, she saw him beaming at his friend with happy gratitude, oblivious to her distress, and realized he was the same.

The following Sunday, Anna and Luke were delivering logs of cheese to the Milk Pail, one of the market stands that opened at the mini-mart lot on weekends. It was early, but a small crowd had already gathered, and as they stood waiting for Janet, the vendor, to settle their invoice, they heard a couple nearby gossiping about April.

"She's broke," the man said, "and now she's accusing Duncan McAuley of child molesting? Timing's awfully suspect." He was tall with white hair pulled back in a short ponytail.

The woman next to him said, "But he's got nothing. Sure, his family does, but if they cared, why let him live the way he does?"

"I know Angus McAuley, and it's one thing, his son being a drunk, but a pedophile? No way he's gonna let their name get dragged through the mud like that. She oughta be ashamed, trying to squeeze them. Just trash, always has been. Her and her half-breed bastard." Then he noticed Luke and Anna, possibly sensing their eavesdropping. He glared at them, pale eyes blazing, and muttered, "Look at them, popping out more babies, just so they can put 'em to work."

"Hank," the woman chided.

The man ignored her and raised his voice: "Child labor, child drownings, pedophiles—we didn't have none of that, not a whiff, before they all came here."

People turned to stare. Anna felt Luke tense up and placed a cautious hand on his arm. "Walk away," the elders always instructed. "Don't incite."

Now Janet spoke up: "That's not fair, Hank, for shame."

"You're taking up for them?" he said in disbelief.

As the two of them began to argue, Anna whispered to Luke, "Please, let's go," and convinced him to walk away.

"What a horrible man," Luke said, once they walked back to the highway. "He was deliberately trying to provoke us! And what he said about April—obviously, he's not as fond of her as you are."

"I don't understand how anyone could take sides with Duncan over her. But I don't think people in this town are as kind as back home, to us and even to each other."

"Are you not happy here?" he asked, looking troubled. "I thought all you wanted was to come back."

"I did," she said quickly. "I do." But she had begun to realize that what she meant by coming back was returning to him and her life as an Eternal—not so much Caliban nor, if truth be told, the elders and matrons who seemed bent on judging her.

===

In early June, a grand jury dismissed April's charges against Duncan McAuley for lack of evidence. It was a swift decision, and news of it spread through town even faster. Anna found out by overhearing three women eating at the café:

"Really, what was she thinking? The McAuleys have money, sure, but they also have a lot of clout."

"I'm surprised they dropped it so quickly, though, since it involved a child."

"But it's all hearsay. I mean, don't you think it's suspicious, she suddenly finds this out when her baby daddy needs bail money?"

Anna was outraged by the jury's decision and the casual, vicious gossip. She wondered if April was aware of the nasty things people said about her. If so, that on top of this latest outcome, and the harm done to her boy, must be terrible to bear. It upset her too, knowing Duncan would not be punished. She thought back to herself as a child, how no one was able to protect her. And now a man who hurt children practically lived next door.

Luke tried to console her. "Everyone now will be more on guard. And at least he's gone." No one had seen him since his preliminary hearing. It was rumored he was at his family's estate, Blackbriar, about ten miles north, supposedly getting sober.

Anna sighed. "That doesn't give me much comfort—nor April, I'm sure."

The following week, Esther sent Anna to the nursery to buy seeds for lettuces and root vegetables. It was a balmy afternoon, and she was happy to be given such a rare, pleasant task, though she was careful not to show it. Other than her fear of running into Claire again, any opportunity to leave the oppressive confines of the farmhouse was welcome. She was almost never alone, and the sense of freedom was exhilarating as she walked along the highway, breathing in the scent of sweetgrass and pine.

In another few months, summer would be over. And then, God willing, she would be a mother, and her life would change forever. She didn't know what would come after; only that this was her destiny and purpose, and that whatever fears she had must be overcome by her faith.

She crested the hill and reached the town cemetery, pausing to catch her breath in front of the arched iron entrance. From where she stood, she could see the entire expanse of wild meadow with its scattered gravestones, many of them several centuries old. Somewhere within the small acreage reserved for the Eternals, her son lay in an unmarked grave. The other day, Luke told her when she was sent away, he was so lonely, he often knelt at a vacant plot to pray in secret for their baby's soul.

Hearing this broke her heart and softened her misgivings about the crib. If only he had been able to see his son's face, even once; he might have something tangible to mourn and not a phantom idea of a child. She closed her eyes now and prayed silently to God to grant them a healthy son this time, to help them heal from their loss. Then she continued up the road to the nursery.

There were only a few other customers roaming among the plant beds. Two women who were shopping together gave her cold looks. Anna felt her face grow warm. She had never grown immune to the rudeness of nonbelievers. Lately, it was hard to know why people stared—whether it was due to her condition, her different face, or the fact she was obviously an Eternal.

She made her purchases quickly, filling her cloth satchel, and then asked the cashier what time it was. "Two twenty-five," the woman said.

"Is Hempstead Road nearby?"

The cashier nodded. "Just the next two signs up that way."

Anna thanked her and walked back toward the highway. Would she have time? The idea had formed on her way up from the cemetery. She remembered April saying she lived up the road from the nursery, on Gibson Lane just off Hempstead Road. There was no guarantee she would even be home. And if Anna was caught in this infraction, what would she say? Her heart began to race, remembering the last time she was with child and disobeyed. But since she learned about April's connection to Patrick, her plight weighed heavily on her mind. She felt indebted in a way she couldn't articulate and guilty about having to avoid her—especially now, when other people were renouncing her.

She turned decisively, making her way up the road as fast as she could. When she got to Hempstead, she walked north for another few minutes until she saw Gibson Lane to her left. The dirt road opened onto a wide lot with three homes raised on stilts. Farther off to her left was a slight ditch with a worn-down picnic table and corroded grill. There were patches of dried grass around the table and bench, and a dusty soccer ball nearby. Three vehicles were parked to her right: a metallic beige sedan, a yellow two-door compact, and April's large green pickup.

She stared up at the houses, unsure which one might be April's. Then she noticed a small bicycle lying in the crawl space beneath the house set farther back. She thought the bicycle might belong to April's son. As she approached the house, she heard strident female voices from inside. She walked up the planked steps and knocked on the door. The voices stopped and footsteps thumped toward her. The door swung open and a tall, skinny girl stood before her, wearing frayed shorts and a cropped T-shirt. She had pale freckled skin, spiky red hair, and several small tattoos on her arms and exposed belly. Her light green eyes opened wide when she saw Anna. "Who're *you*?"

Anna blushed at her boldness and skimpy attire. "Excuse me. My name is Anna Marten. I was looking for April Ives. Does she live here?"

The girl's right eyebrow lifted. She turned her head and yelled, "Mom! Someone's here for you!" Then she whirled around and left her standing at the doorway.

"Who is it?" she heard April ask. A moment later, she came to the door. She gaped at Anna, taking in her protruding belly. Her face looked tired and drawn. She wore shorts too and a denim shirt that hung on her wiry frame. "Anna," she said in a low, scratchy voice, "what're you doing here?"

"I—I was wondering if I could talk to you. If this isn't a bad time."

"Are you all right?"

"Yes, yes. I was just at the nursery, and I remembered you said you lived close by."

April looked skeptical and took a moment to answer. "Okay. But you mind if we talk over there by that table? The house is a mess, sorry. I'll be out in a sec." She closed the door.

Anna made her way to the picnic table and sat on the bench facing the house. After a few minutes, April came out in a pair of flip-flops, clutching a lighter and cigarette pack. She stood several feet away and lit a fresh cigarette, cupping her hands around the flame. After a deep drag, she turned her head to the side and exhaled, blowing the smoke away from Anna. "Sorry. I'll stay here so you don't get any." She gestured toward Anna's belly and said, "Congratulations—I hope? How far along are you?"

"Thank you," Anna said, blushing. "I'm due the end of September. We feel blessed."

April nodded. "That's good. So, what are you doing here? I thought you weren't allowed to, you know, socialize."

"No, I'm not. But . . . I just wanted to tell you I'm so sorry about what happened to your little boy. I felt awful when I heard."

"Thanks." April sighed and gave her a flat, tired look. "I guess you know the jury tossed the case too. So that's that."

"Yes. It's so distressing and unfair. I don't care what the jury says. I believe you. I know other people do too." When April didn't respond, she asked, "How is your son?"

April shrugged. "He's a tough little guy, but it's been a rotten year. Between this, his dad, and Patrick . . ." She sighed and took another long drag.

Anna nodded, her heartbeat quickening. "I only found out recently he was your godson. I'm so sorry."

April tossed the butt and ground it out before sitting on the bench opposite. Now she looked at Anna directly. "How'd you find out Patrick was my godson?"

Anna said haltingly, "Well, because . . . my husband heard it from someone at the post office."

April let out a short laugh. "Right. I'll bet that's not all he heard. This town sure loves to talk."

Anna was upset with herself for letting the conversation go in the direction she'd wanted to avoid. "I told Luke how I knew you from before, when I was working for the Burnetts. He feels terrible for you too. And we know about town gossip. Some people have been hostile to us since the lawsuit with the Clays." She stopped short, struck by a sudden thought. "I hope—I mean, do *you* blame us for what happened?"

April shook her head. "No. I know it was an accident." Then she said, "Your husband's the one who found Patrick, isn't he? The one who pulled him out of the creek?"

"Yes," Anna said. "Him and Gabriel." Lying about Patrick to April made her feel especially wretched. "I was there too, right after."

"You were? I didn't see you there when I—when we found him." She stared past Anna, lost in remembrance. "I saw him, though. When he was dead, I mean. I really wish I hadn't." A shudder flitted across her face. "I have dreams about him, a lot. Bad ones."

Anna nodded. "I still . . . I keep seeing his eyes. The way they were open but . . . not there."

"Yes," said April, suddenly looking directly at her. "I only saw him for a second—but I'll never forget it."

For an instant, Anna could feel the boy's cold skin, the surprising weight of his body. She wanted badly to tell April the truth about what happened. But there was no way to do so without maligning the Eternals. And she suspected it would only cause April more pain, when what she hoped to do was give solace. "I am so sorry for your loss," she said quietly. "So sorry for everything." It felt inadequate.

April nodded but said nothing. After a moment, Anna thought it might be best to change the subject. "Was that your daughter who answered the door? She's so pretty."

April gave her a brief, rueful smile. "Doesn't she know it. Yeah, that's Maddy. My other kids aren't here right now."

"Oh, I was hoping to meet your son. But maybe the less people who know I'm here, the better. I should probably head back soon."

"I'll tell Maddy to keep it quiet." A shadow of amusement crinkled April's eyes. "Guess I shouldn't bother offering a ride."

Anna smiled. "The walk is good exercise. Our midwife encourages it."

April looked dubious, but all she said was "Well, thanks for coming all this way. You really didn't have to."

"I wanted to. I'm glad you were home. It was important to me to tell you in person how sorry I am. And that you're always in my prayers. I've never forgotten your kindness."

"I didn't do anything," she said with a shrug.

"That's not true. You were good to me, and I—I reciprocated by ignoring you. I'm so sorry for that."

April shook her head. "You didn't do anything either. As for Duncan, his family's got money and they call the shots. I don't know . . . maybe if the case went ahead, it would have been worse for Justin. Kids are already hassling him. Adults too. It's sick. I don't care what people say about me, but my kids . . ." She clenched her jaw, still shaking her head. "I don't know . . . I feel like I opened up this big can of worms, and all I did was make a mess of things. He swears

Duncan only grabbed him, and I hope he's telling the truth. His dad's about ready to lose his mind. I think he'd kill Duncan if he wasn't locked up. That's probably my fault too."

"Please don't torment yourself. You did what you felt was best."

"It doesn't matter," she said, and to Anna's dismay, her eyes suddenly welled. She stood and flicked away a tear impatiently, as if it were an insect. "It wasn't enough."

9

FORECAST

The psychic lived in a narrow brownstone on a quiet, tree-lined street in Hudson. Just before Claire approached the stoop, she flipped nervously through her small notebook, where she'd jotted down her questions, then checked the recording function on her phone. When she called to make the appointment, the psychic, Tamara, suggested she might want to tape the session. "That way you can be fully present during your reading, instead of trying to write everything down."

Claire had seen her discreet business cards at the yoga studio, only a few blocks away on the main strip of Warren Street. The yoga classes were part of a wellness package from Karl and Evelyn, after her doctor determined in March she was in remission. One of the yoga regulars, Shannon, saw Claire pick up a card and said, "She's *really* good. I went to her a year ago, and she blew my mind."

"What's the difference between a spiritual reader"—that was what the card read—"and a psychic?" Claire asked.

"Semantics?" Shannon laughed. "Try her, you won't be sorry."

Claire pressed the buzzer, and a voice said through the intercom, "Claire? Just take the stairs up to the second floor." When she reached the landing, she saw a woman at the end of the hall waving from her doorway.

"Nice to meet you," Tamara said with a smile, pressing both of Claire's hands between hers. She was a middle-aged woman with small blue eyes and graying brown hair, dressed casually in a short-sleeved top and capris. She could have been a suburban mom.

Claire noticed her feet were bare and asked, "Should I remove my shoes?"

"Only if you want to. I'm always barefoot indoors, especially in the summer. Speaking of which, is the AC okay or too cold?"

"Maybe a little cold?" Claire said apologetically. She kept her shoes on.

Tamara went to adjust the thermostat across the room. The apartment was small and clean, the furnishings modest but comfortable looking. Late-afternoon sunlight poured in through the south-facing windows. There was a round wooden table in the living room with a stack of cards placed facedown in the middle. Tamara beckoned her over. "We'll sit here."

Claire sat and took her phone out. "Should I start recording now?"

"In a minute. Let me explain what I'll be doing, since this is new for you. We'll start with a palm reading, then consult the tarot for an overview, and after, you can ask me specific questions. Does that sound good?" When Claire nodded, she said, "Okay. Are you right- or left-handed?"

"Right."

"Give me your left then. And now you can start to record."

Tamara pressed and peered at her hand, squinting in concentration. The contact felt both intimate and impersonal, almost like a medical exam. She made a series of matter-of-fact comments: "You've had a lot of separations in your life—some of them quite abrupt. You carry a lot of fear, and your compensation method is control, though you're trying to be more open. Your early life was difficult, lonely . . ." She went on to describe more past struggles and personality traits that Claire felt could apply to many others.

Then she asked, "Were your parents divorced?"

"Yes."

"And were you divorced recently?"

"Well, not exactly. We're—we've been separated for a while. We haven't spoken in months."

"I see. You're estranged from your father too, and your mother . . . has passed?"

"Yes."

"She was relatively young, no? Some cancer of the reproductive organs . . . ovarian?"

"Yes," Claire said again, the back of her neck prickling.

Tamara asked her gently, "Were you ill recently too?"

Claire nodded mutely, all her skepticism gone. Tamara was slightly off in pinpointing her type of cancer, guessing ovarian too, but accurate about the timeframe. She knew that Claire was a lawyer and liked photography, and had benevolent parental figures in her life; that her marriage involved a betrayal, and that she'd had some bad luck related to a house purchase. As she continued to talk, the sun began to drop, and the room turned golden. The magic hour, Claire's favorite time of day. She tried to take comfort in it.

Tamara finally released her hand. She instructed her to shuffle the tarot cards, divide them into three stacks, and combine the stacks into one again. She spread them out on the table facedown and asked Claire to pick out ten, placing them in a cross pattern. Then she turned them over. Claire leaned in and saw some of their titles: the Tower, the Fool, the Hanged Man. Other cards had no titles, only images.

"Some of these look ominous," she said.

Tamara shook her head. "None of them alone are bad, per se. It depends on the whole. For instance, the Fool in this case is a good card, if you stay open-minded. It means you're at a crossroads, which your next actions can determine. This one," she said, tapping the Hanged Man, "means to pause, take stock of your surroundings. Or surrender. He's upside down, but see his face? It's peaceful." Claire saw she was right, but the dichotomy disturbed her even more.

As she continued with the reading, Claire grew increasingly depressed. Everything seemed to suggest hardships to either overcome or accept. She'd hoped for answers, but the cards only confirmed her present state of irresolution. Tamara, seeing her face, said, "You're discouraged. Don't be. The cards are only a snapshot of your current influences, not a prediction. There's a lot of growth and strength here—this is all positive."

Claire's smile was bitter. "It doesn't feel very positive."

"But it can be. The answers are in you. The thing is, Claire, nothing is set in stone. You have agency. Some people find that unpredictability terrifying. But it can also be liberating." When Claire didn't respond, she asked, "Do you have questions for me?"

Claire looked over her notes. Most of them had been addressed, if not satisfactorily, except for the two foremost on her mind. "About my marriage . . . Sebastian. Is he okay? Will there be a future for us?"

Tamara had her select more cards and spread them in a different pattern. She turned them over and sat back for a moment. "There's a lot of murkiness emotionally. It prevents him from being available to you or anyone else. He has to learn on his own how to manage his depression. You're used to doing that—but his issues aren't yours to correct right now." She looked up and said softly, "I think you need to move on."

Claire digested her words in pained silence. Her voice tremored as she asked her next question: "My cancer. Is it going to come back? Am I going to be okay?"

She picked more cards that Tamara set in yet another, different pattern. Claire waited, her heart pounding, as she turned them over. Finally, she spoke. "You'll have some more challenges to face. You need to be emotionally prepared. But you're on the right path . . . you're listening to your instincts more. They brought you here. Keep those channels open. Nothing is definitive."

Claire sat very still in her chair, a small knot of dread forming in her stomach. She stopped the recording and reached numbly into her bag for her wallet. After she paid, Tamara looked up at her wall clock. "You're my last appointment for the day. I don't normally do this, but if you have a few minutes, I could run a bit of energy on you. No charge. If you're interested."

"What does that entail?"

"I place my hands on your shoulders while you relax and close your eyes. Ideally you should be lying down on the sofa. If you're familiar with Reiki, some people find it similar, though I think they're quite different. Would you like to try?"

Claire moved over to a large brown sofa and lay down at one end with her head propped on some cushions. Tamara pulled up a chair behind her and rested her hands on her lightly. "Now just breathe evenly and easily, and allow your mind to drift. Feel whatever you feel."

Claire closed her eyes. For several moments she fidgeted, tried to get comfortable, heard the clock ticking. Tamara above her was silent except for her even exhalations. Claire began to match her breathing to hers. Minutes passed. At last, her body relaxed. She felt herself begin to dip and float, in and out, in a tidal rhythm. Something lovely and warm trickled through her, like the gentlest vibration, barely discernible but there. The feeling slowly grew until the vibration became distinct, stronger; the warmth more intense and pleasurable. A heaviness inside her heart loosened, spilled open. The warmth blossomed into an exquisite sorrow. Tears coursed down her cheeks. She felt her body convulse, but there was no alarm or pain—just a rush of relief thrumming through her body, absorbed by the larger vibration. She continued to weep quietly. After a long while, the tears finally stopped. The vibration did too. She became aware of sounds outside: a car honking and, from a distance, the off-tune jingle of an ice-cream truck.

"You can sit up now," Tamara said.

Claire opened her eyes. She sat up in a daze, wiping at her wet cheeks. Dust motes shimmered in the waning light from the window. She felt she had traveled somewhere light-years away and back, as if her cells had played a trick with time. When she could finally speak, she said, "That was—wow. I'm not sure what happened."

"Something shifted for you. That's excellent. You were very responsive."

On her way out, Claire still felt light-headed. She turned to Tamara, flush with gratitude. "I was almost feeling sorry that I came to see you. I'm not now. Thank you."

"I'm so glad." Tamara clasped both her hands again. "Be well, Claire."

———

Anna's belly was now so huge that bending over was difficult and she tired easily, but she was careful to never complain or appear lazy. In addition to working at the café, the Eternals gave her other chores such as mending, sewing, and any miscellaneous errands they needed. By the end of the day, she was so exhausted that in the brief moments she had between washing up and supper, she often fell asleep, and Luke would have to wake her to go downstairs.

"Won't they give you a little reprieve?" he finally asked, concerned for her and the baby. "Do you want me to speak to Hiram?"

"No." She shook her head emphatically. "That will make it worse with Zebiah. It's only for a little while longer. Miriam says next month I can stop going to the café. And once the baby comes, I'll have a month to rest." She hesitated, then said, "Do you think they'll ever accept me? I thought once I was expecting, they might relent, but it seems like it's only made it worse. Like my being this way reminds them of before. Or maybe they think I don't deserve to have a child."

He sighed as he rubbed her swollen feet. "I know it hasn't been easy for you with the matrons. But after you have the baby, I'm sure things will get better. Especially if you have a boy."

"And if I don't?"

"Then we'll have a beautiful girl. And she'll win them over too. You'll see."

That night, after supper, he searched his Bible for an appropriate passage to read to her, reciting from Psalm 128: "Blessed is everyone who fears the Lord, who walks in his ways! You shall eat the fruit of the labor of your hands; you shall be blessed, and it shall be well with you. . ." She fell into a hard sleep and didn't hear the rest.

She could not recall being worked so hard when she was expecting the first time or seeing other pregnant Eternals do as much either. Bearing her husband's child was a woman's most sacred duty, and giving him a boy, her greatest triumph. The Eternals were suspicious about identifying a baby's gender before birth, so she wouldn't know if her child was a boy until she delivered him. Sometimes she felt the matrons wanted to punish her for her past disgrace—because she had carried a boy and, through her own folly, caused his death.

In her darkest moments, she questioned whether they wanted her to have this baby at all. She feared that in their eyes she was still tainted, and any child of hers, boy or girl, would be too. She kept these profane thoughts to herself, expressing her frustration to Luke only at unguarded times, when her body and spirit felt depleted. But though he tried to console her, she sensed his discomfort at her suggesting the matrons' instructions were meant to be punitive rather than helpful.

Now that she was in her seventh month, she had weekly checkups in Miriam's room. Anna hated having to lie on her examination plank, unclothed from the waist down, with her dress bunched up to her neck. Miriam's probing around her genitals was invasive and often painful. Once, when Anna flinched, the midwife said impatiently, "Goodness, stop being so sensitive! You've delivered a baby before, haven't you? You were not so modest then, I'll wager."

At the next appointment, when Miriam finished her examination, she rubbed a pungent oil briskly all over Anna's belly. It would help with stretch marks, she said, and the aromatics would absorb and be beneficial to the baby. At first it felt pleasant, tingly. But after several minutes, a burning sensation spread throughout her abdomen. The baby became more active—it seemed to her agitated—and she felt acute discomfort.

When she told Miriam, the woman frowned and placed her palm on her belly. "It could be indigestion. There's no redness or heat coming off your skin. See . . . is there?"

No, she had to concede there was not. "But I feel it inside. And the baby feels it too."

Miriam sighed. "If there's something wrong, I can help you. But I can't indulge your imagination." She gave her a hard squinting look and said, "It's not uncommon toward the end of one's term to have moments of hysteria, even delusion."

The burning sensation lasted several hours, into the night. The baby continued to kick and turn, and Anna had trouble sleeping. She shifted from one side to the other while Luke, now used to her constant movements, slept on undisturbed.

Sometime in the deepest hour of night, she finally fell asleep. She dreamed that her water broke while she served lunch in the café. The wetness gushed out and she slipped, dropping the plates she held. A rat scuttled over to eat from the plates, and she screamed. The customers stopped what they were doing to stare. Blushing, she looked down and saw a large pool of water at her feet. The shattered plates started to float away. The water spread and rose, but from where she could not tell. Soon she was knee-deep in it, the hem of her long dress twisting around her. The tables and chairs began to float too, and then the baby started to crown, pushing out forcefully between her legs. Her mind cried out, *No, not here!* and she reached down, trying to hold him back. But with one more push he slipped past her hands and was gone, lost in the water.

———————

The last time Claire heard from Sebastian was back in February, when he sent that card letting her know he was in Albuquerque. After some internal debate, she sent him a brief, friendly letter back. She didn't mention the cancer, thinking it would be better for another time. But five months had gone by with no further response. She berated herself for believing there might be.

Two weeks after her reading with Tamara, Claire texted Sebastian asking if they could set a time to talk by phone. *It shouldn't take long,* she wrote, *but it's important.* To her surprise, he responded within the hour and said he could be available that night. It threw her, but she decided it was best to be done with it. Half an hour before the scheduled call, she calmed herself by doing some deep breathing exercises. Then she went to the kitchen and poured herself a glass of wine. She drank most of it before calling.

He picked up after the second ring. "Claire. Hi."

"Hi." She felt sick with nerves. "It's weird to hear your voice."

"I know. Same here." There was a long pause. "So . . . have you been well?"

Oh, Sebastian. For a moment she wanted desperately just to tell him everything, but it would sound pathetic, a blatant plea for sympathy. "Yes, fine. What about you? Are you still teaching?"

"I've been off for the summer, but it starts up again next month."

"And is it . . . Do you like it?"

He let out a soft, ironic laugh. "Does anyone like adjunct teaching?"

Adjunct, she thought with some shock. She'd assumed he was at least a visiting associate. Twelve years ago, he'd turned down tenure-track positions. It saddened her to realize he'd become just another casualty of ageism and the recession. To some degree, she felt responsible. She could pinpoint when his ambition and hope began to bleed out: six years ago, on the day he started working at the Guggenheim. It was a job he was lucky to get, through one of her contacts. He'd never had a regular job, and she was worried he might behave horribly. But to her surprise, he was responsible and meticulous. He didn't talk about his job much or complain, which she took as a good sign. In retrospect, she realized from that time on he produced very little of his own work. How demoralizing it must have been for him to install shows for other artists who were his contemporaries and, in many cases, far less talented. But then, she once had ambitions too. Why were his dreams any more important than hers?

"Claire," he said, "tell me what you wanted to talk about."

"Okay." She took a deep breath. "The thing is, Sebastian, we've been separated for almost two years. It doesn't sound like you have any plans to change that soon . . . do you?" When he didn't answer, she said, "I can't stay in this holding pattern. I need to move on, and I need to start taking care of myself. Do you understand what I'm saying?"

"Yes. You want to legalize our separation. You're saying you want a divorce."

She was relieved he said it first. "There seems no point not to, don't you agree?" Silence again. She felt a flash of irritation. *Every single time, I have to make the decision.* "I've spoken to an attorney, and if we can come to an agreement on our assets, it'll make the whole—"

"Whatever you want, Claire, I'll sign it. And I won't take anything either. The house, the car, whatever's in the joint account—it's yours."

For a moment she was speechless. "Are you sure? You don't sound exactly flush, and I want to be fair."

"It's fair. We both know you floated me for years. If you can cover the attorney fees, I don't need anything else."

"Well . . . thank you. But what about your paintings? Should I ship them to you?"

He was silent for a moment. "I don't really have the space here, and I'm not sure how long-term this will be. Could I think on it and let you know? I know you want to move on, but—"

"Of course. They're just in the basement." She realized how that could sound demeaning. "They're stored away safely—and they'll be worth something someday. I know you don't believe me. . .but I still believe in you. Please don't give up."

"We'll see," he said quietly. "I appreciate what you're trying to say."

They were both silent for a few moments. "All right," she said at last. "I'll give my attorney your contact information. Thanks again for making this as easy as possible." She searched for something more to say, but there was nothing. Still, she felt reluctant to hang up. "Well, so . . . I guess this is it for now."

"Yes. Maybe for a little while. Thanks for handling all this."

They disconnected. She let out a long, slow breath. She had expected to feel more sadness, and it was there, but mostly she just felt hollow. It was better than pain. And it was a decision, at least. A step forward. She didn't feel celebratory, but she wished there was some way to mark the occasion. In that instant she pictured April making a toast, saying in her blunt way, *Huh, so much for that.* It brought a smile to her lips. She went to the refrigerator and poured herself another glass. "Well," she said out loud. "Here's to me."

When Hiram heard from Alvin Baumann again, he expected to get an update on the deposition schedule. Instead, the lawyer had good news—far beyond what anyone expected. "Hiram," he said, "I think I might convert to your faith. They've dismissed your wrongful death suit, if you can believe it. I just spoke to the presiding judge."

"The Clays dropped their lawsuit?"

"*They* didn't. The judge did! The Clays' counsel was late paying a cost bond I filed for months ago, and this new judge is less lenient than the one before, so . . . that's it. I have to say, in over thirty years, I've seen this happen only twice. But it's dismissed. There'll be no deposition, no court or trial—it's over."

The Eternals reacted to this incredible event with stunned elation. Everyone exclaimed it was a miracle. Some of the women even hugged each other impulsively, shedding tears of joy and relief. "Praise be to God!" cried Zebiah. "It's a sign of His blessing." That a problem so large and looming could disappear so swiftly was surely proof of God's immense power.

When the jubilation subsided, Hiram led them in a long, fervent prayer of gratitude: "Thank You, Lord, for this unforeseen blessing You've bestowed upon us today by lifting this terrible burden. We, Your servants, thank You for protecting us from those who would harm us and for guiding us through difficult times. We thank You for surrounding us with plenitude and the love of our brothers and sisters. May we forever remain deserving of Your benevolence, and never forget to show our gratitude in prayer. Thank You, Lord, thank You. In Your name. Amen." Then, in a sober tone, he warned them all to be circumspect in expressing their happiness around the townspeople. "Let us be humble and not provoke unnecessary anger. We mustn't forget that at the heart of this matter lies the tragic loss of an innocent child."

In their room later that night, Luke and Anna marveled over the improbable turn of events.

"Can it really be over?" she said, still incredulous.

"It seems so hard to believe," he agreed. "It's funny how suddenly things can change. I was really dreading that deposition. I was having nightmares again. But now we can put this behind us and look ahead to happier days. And our baby will be here soon. It's all so strange and wonderful."

"It is," she said softly. "God's work is truly mysterious."

She was just as relieved as Luke that there would be no deposition, no further need to lie. Now, aside from her constant fatigue and concern about the baby, all that troubled her was April's misfortune and the harm inflicted on her son. Her only consolation was that even if Duncan escaped punishment from mankind, he would have to face God's judgment. And that, at least for now, the town was rid of him.

Claire didn't see the email until she was about to head upstairs for bed. It was from Scott, one of the partners, and it was curt: *We need you to come in tomorrow.*

My office at 8:30. Bring your laptop. The subject line was "Meeting." Sent after hours, at 6:38 P.M.

She read the words with a knot of dread in her gut. Scott was always economical in his communications, but this felt wrong. She wasn't scheduled to go in the next day. As for the "we"—it was probably Richard, the DA she did most of her work for. Or someone from HR.

Another layoff. Goddamn it.

She thought they liked her. When she was sick last year, they expressed support and sent flowers to the hospital after her surgery. She took two weeks off unpaid but got right back to work after. She wondered if the whole episode put them off, and they waited just long enough to let her go so it didn't appear that way. It wasn't even a job she really wanted or liked. It was tedious and beneath her skill set. She stayed only because of the health insurance and the feeling she owed them some loyalty for standing behind her. It appeared she'd miscalculated.

All she could do now was reply: *I'll be there.*

She hardly slept that night. In the morning, she dressed professionally, in a jacket and skirt, and took care with her makeup. At least this time she would go in prepared.

When an assistant ushered her into Scott's office, he looked up from his desk with a hateful glare that froze her. Mallory from HR sat facing him from the opposite side. There was an empty chair beside her, where Mallory indicated she should sit.

As soon as she did, Scott lit into her: "Do you know what happened yesterday? The judge dismissed the Clays' lawsuit. Do you know why? Because we failed to pay the cost bond on time. I should say *you* failed to pay the cost bond on time. Can you explain how the hell you missed that deadline?" His voice was clipped, furious.

"I don't understand," Claire said. "I submitted payment as soon as I got the quote."

"I don't care when you got the quote! It was due on October twentieth, and you paid on the twenty-fifth. So, it's outside jurisdiction and we have no case. Do you know what you've just cost us? Months of work and billable hours, and now we might be liable for legal malpractice. Richard should have caught it, and we'll deal with him. But you're terminated as of this moment."

He pushed away from the desk and stood. "We hired you on Beth Maher's recommendation. You certainly won't get ours." He told Mallory, "Let me know when you're done," and left the room.

Claire sat in disbelief, her mind racing, trying to piece together the timeline from last fall. She'd processed so many documents, for different attorneys and cases. Late October would have been while she was going through chemo. She hardly drank during those months. But she remembered the brain fog and exhaustion. Could she have done something so stupid?

Mallory interrupted her thoughts by taking her laptop and giving her paperwork to sign, letting her know there would be no severance, since the termination was with cause. Then she offered to escort her out. It wasn't even nine o'clock. Claire got in her car and sat with the windows open, letting what happened sink in. Fired. And with cause. Aside from Sebastian's deception, it was the deepest humiliation of her life.

She drove around Hudson aimlessly, finally turning onto the street where Tamara lived. As she passed her building, she slowed down. It had been only a month since her reading. She'd left that building strangely buoyant, filled with acceptance and hope. It carried her for days. But now she remembered that, until Tamara ran energy on her, she felt defeated throughout most of the reading. And that the psychic warned her to emotionally prepare for what lay ahead. Was this one of the challenges she foresaw? Why didn't she warn her it would come so soon?

She should go home and call Unemployment, start that process. But facing it right now was unbearable. She circled back to the main strip, looking for any distraction. None of the shops along Warren were open yet, except for a few cafés. The yoga studio had a class at ten, but she didn't have her workout clothes. And she didn't feel like doing yoga anyway, even if it might be the best thing to calm her. What she really wanted was a drink. In a bar. With people.

When she pulled into the parking lot at Mackey's Grill, she could see it was open. She pictured herself walking up to the bar in her stupid professional suit.

It was laughable she thought it might preserve her dignity. In this context she would look only like a job-hunting loser with a drinking problem. She wondered if they were going to fire Richard, if there was any point in calling him to apologize.

Now that the initial shock was over, she thought about the ramifications of dismissing the case, beyond her own situation. The Eternals would be happy—of all ironies that she should be the one to help them. But for the Clays . . . and April. Now they would have to absorb this defeat, when they had already lost so much. The enormity of her mistake made her sick with shame. She was paralyzed with fear should it ever get out.

She remembered the last time she lost her job she ended up at Mackey's. Was that why she found herself there now? Fired or not, it was quite a different thing to go to a bar at night versus first thing in the morning. She'd never done that before and knew instinctively that once she did, she would have crossed a line that could be crossed again. Part of her wanted to debase herself, wallow in that subterranean world. Sit and drink with other strangers who were there to forget. But some reservoir of pride and propriety pulled her back.

"No," she said out loud, as she started the engine again. "I'm not that low yet."

Anna was putting dishes away in the café kitchen one afternoon when Zebiah told her to go up to the house and pick some vegetables from the garden. "We're running low, and we have to make the chowder for tomorrow. I'll need corn, cauliflower, and yellow squash—bring as much as you can. Parsley and basil too. Oh, and ask Esther for some bouillon."

Anna usually welcomed the chance to be outdoors, but the weather was unpleasantly humid, and it was difficult for her to bend down in the garden. She could manage to pick only one cauliflower and three squash before she felt her back spasm and had to stand, feeling light-headed. When she had gathered all she could, Esther gave her a small cart to load up the vegetables, and she made her way slowly back to the café, pushing the cart along the narrow, bumpy strip of sidewalk.

The sidewalk turned into stretches of long grass, which impeded the cart. She moved onto the highway, but after two cars passed by, she began to feel unnerved and decided the grass was safer. Up ahead, a large U-Haul van was parked in Duncan McAuley's driveway, with what looked like junk and lumber piled beside it. From what she knew, the house was set to be demolished soon. Everyone assumed Duncan had abandoned it and that there was nothing inside even worth stealing. Had someone come to clear out its contents?

She studied the exterior of his dilapidated house, intrigued despite her repulsion. There were several empty bottles of liquor on the porch. The windows were darkened and filmy with dust, and the roof was almost caved in. She heard he had no working plumbing and relieved himself behind a makeshift partition in his backyard. Since childhood, she'd associated filth with evil, and now she shuddered, imagining what might have happened behind those windows.

She pushed the cart faster, seeing a stretch of sidewalk past his driveway, farther up. Seconds later, the cart came to an abrupt stop. She pitched forward, crying out as her midsection bumped against the handle. Rubbing her belly fearfully, she leaned over as far as she could to inspect the cart. The front wheels were tangled tightly with strands of grass.

A voice said from behind her, "Looks like it's stuck."

She turned and saw Duncan a few feet away, carrying a large open cardboard box. She'd never seen him so close up, and now she took in his lanky frame, lean except for a small gut beneath his stained T-shirt; the stringy blond hair and gaunt face; and the hooded eyes and dry, thin lips. For a moment she was numb with terror. Her mouth opened, but no words came out.

He squinted in puzzlement. Then his expression settled into one of sullen injury. "You're one of *them*, aren't you? You think I'm gonna hurt you? Jesus." He set the box down and moved toward her.

"Get away!" she cried finally, nearly hysterical. She tried to force the cart forward, but it wouldn't budge.

"Lemme see that," Duncan said. Before she could stop him, he knelt down, pulling a pair of pliers from his pocket.

"Please go away," she pleaded, looking around for help. Deciding to just leave the cart, she started walking as fast as she could toward the café. She'd gone only a few feet when she heard him say, "Wait! Look, it's fixed."

Turning around, she saw he'd placed the cart back onto the highway. He gave it a push forward and it rolled toward her easily. "Just some grass got stuck, is all. Go on, take it. I won't come near you."

To prove his point, he stepped backward onto the grass. Still, beneath the guise of helpfulness, she sensed aggression. Slowly, she advanced toward the cart, looking at him warily. He didn't appear inebriated. Different circumstances would have required her to thank him—but of course that was out of the question.

"See?" he said, smiling. "I'm not a monster. I wouldn't hurt a soul."

The enormity of his lie made her go cold. "You hurt April's son," she said, her voice shaking.

His face darkened. "I didn't do nothing to that kid or anyone else, 'cept try to be friendly, is all. No matter what he or anyone says. You all want to turn me out, go ahead. I got nothing left here anyway. No home, no friends, nothing. You ever think how it feels, living like some kinda leper? Nah, I bet you don't."

His mouth shook and his face contorted; he almost looked like he was going to cry. It was such a naked, ugly sight, she had to turn away. Taking the cart, she steered it quickly onto the highway, heading to the café. When she turned to make sure he wasn't following, he glared back and spat in her direction. She walked faster, feeling a collision of emotions. There was pity, which shamed and confused her—for she well knew what it was to be an outcast. But above all, what she felt was revulsion, terror, and a conviction she'd just encountered something vile and grotesque, something she hadn't known since that long-ago day from her childhood, when she stood trapped in a foul embrace, hidden behind the sheets on a laundry line.

10
THE STORM

The screen on Claire's phone showed that Karl was calling. She was tempted to let it go to voicemail again, but if she did, he might get worried and come by the house. Then he would see her and really be worried. He and Evelyn had already left two messages. She picked up and willed her voice to sound upbeat. "Hi, Karl, how are you?"

"You're there! Honey, we've been trying to reach you for days. Where've you been?"

"Around . . . just really busy. I had to see a lot of clients in the city, and now, because of the storm, everyone's shutting down, so it's been insane." She was amazed at how smoothly she lied.

"That's why I wanted to check in. The governor's declared a state of emergency. They're saying it might get bad up here this weekend. You want to stay with us till it all blows over?"

"It'll be the same where you are as here," she said with a laugh.

"I know. But at least you won't be alone."

His words cut her, though she knew it wasn't his intention. She heard Evelyn in the background shouting, "Ask her if she has enough food and water! And candles, and a flashlight!"

"Tell her yes and yes. And a good book too."

"All right, we'll call you tomorrow."

"I'll be fine, don't worry. It'll be like a vacation."

Hanging up, she wondered how much longer she could keep the loss of her job a secret. She just got approved for unemployment benefits but would need to find another job soon, one with health insurance. The COBRA payments without income were unsustainable. On good days, she pursued job applications and picked up around the house. Other days, she did nothing but lie in bed, reading or staring listlessly at her laptop, scrolling through gossip about celebrity breakups. Every job lead turned out to be not quite as advertised. Dead ends everywhere. It was vicious, this business of living. Still, what choice did she have but to get on with it?

The first order of the day was to pick up some supplies: water, candles, non-perishable food. She'd also lied to Karl about being prepared. With everything else going on, she hadn't considered the impending storm except to dismiss it as the usual East Coast hype. People in the city, especially, overreacted, closing down schools and transportation for blizzards that produced a scant few inches of snow. As for hurricanes, she'd seen her share growing up in Tampa and Miami, and while people down there took them seriously, no one freaked out beforehand quite the way they did in New York. Though a state of emergency was something to consider.

Outside, it was overcast and warm, despite the breeze. She could smell the humidity and feel it like an extra layer on her skin. Looking up at the gathering clouds, she wondered if they'd actually get a real storm. By the time she got to the Hannaford in Greenville, it was close to noon and the huge lot was nearly full. Inside, it was mayhem. The supermarket was always crowded on Saturdays, but now there was a competitive urgency among the shoppers Claire had never seen before. She was dismayed the store was out of so many items. Several shelves were empty. In the crackers section, there were only a few packages of cheap saltines.

"Are you serious?" she cried to a stock boy passing by.

He shrugged. "It's been like this since yesterday."

"But—this is all there is? Nothing else in the back?"

"We've reordered, but nothing's getting here till next week."

Forgoing the crackers, she managed to grab some cans of tuna and white beans, a jar of almond butter, and three gallons of bottled water. She was searching for candles in the household aisle when she looked up and saw Jan Strauss heading toward her. Claire was glad she'd put on makeup before leaving the house. It had been several months since she last saw or spoke to Jan.

"I can't believe it," Jan said, leaning in to kiss her cheek. "Everyone's out shopping. I just saw April Ives in the other aisle—not that I said hello or anything. You know about her and the McAuleys, right? How that whole thing back-fired?"

"What do you mean, backfired?"

"You haven't heard?" Jan cried. "The McAuleys are thinking to sue her for slander—not for money, obviously, but to teach her a lesson."

"Oh," Claire said, startled by the news.

"Anyway, I'm off. I have to help Paul put the patio furniture into the shed. It's supposed to get really windy. We should have lunch or something soon."

"Sure," Claire said, though she knew neither of them meant it. They'd gravitated toward each other so easily when she first came to Caliban. She complained to Jan about April's hostility, rude manners, and dirty house, snickering while Jan, not to be outdone, dished about April's trashy reputation, her string of loser jobs and boyfriends. How strange that now, two years on, Claire felt more of an affinity with April.

As she continued to shop, scanning each crowded aisle, she realized she was looking for her. Once or twice in the last few weeks, Claire had felt the impulse to reach out and suggest going for a drink. But she usually had those impulses *while* she was drinking, and when sober, was grateful she refrained. After Frank Moder, the last thing she needed was another humiliating rejection.

And then she saw her. April stood in the cereal aisle hunched over her cart with her head cocked, completely focused on the depleted shelves. She wore a big yellow hoodie, cutoff shorts, and old sneakers. From afar she could have been a teenager, but as Claire pushed her cart forward, it was jarring to see up close how worn and aged she looked. "April. Hello."

April lifted her head with a dazed expression. When she saw Claire, her eyes widened. "Oh, hi. That's weird, I was just thinking about you."

"Were you?" Claire said, pleased and curious. "Why?"

"I don't know, just . . . something I remembered about the house." She shook her head. "Nothing important."

"Oh." Claire was disappointed. April wasn't unfriendly, exactly, but she seemed closed off and distracted. "How are you?"

She shrugged. "Been better. But hanging in."

"I'm sorry. I heard some things about you and the McAuleys, but I wasn't sure what was true."

April let out a brief, bitter laugh. "Yeah, I'll bet. Not worth your time trying to figure that out. Anyway, it's all old news."

Jan had implied otherwise, but Claire only nodded and said, "Well . . . I hope you can move forward." As soon as she said it, she realized how trite it sounded. "How's your daughter Maddy? Has she finished school and left the nest already?"

"She graduated in June. A-minus average." April allowed herself a proud, bemused smile. "Yeah, she'll be moving out soon—well, actually, all of us might."

"Really? Why?"

"My landlords are looking to sell their property and move back to Mississippi—that's where they're from. They came here to take care of the wife's mom, but she died a couple weeks ago, so . . . They feel bad, but I get it. Anyway, the new owners might still rent out, so we'll see."

"Oh. I'm so sorry. I really hope you don't have to move again." Claire wondered if this was what April meant when she said she was thinking about her and the house. The possibility made her feel chastened. For all the money and labor she'd put into the house, she had never been happy living there. Sometimes she'd even imagined the house rejected her, like a bad transplant. Whereas April clearly had a strong attachment.

"Yeah, we'll see. So, how 'bout you? Everything okay?"

"Yes, fine," Claire said quickly.

April gave her a sharp look. "You sure?"

Claire felt her throat constrict. "I'm fine."

April looked like she was about to say something. Then she pursed her lips and nodded. "All right, well . . . I better get out of this nuthouse. Good luck shopping and all. Stay dry."

"Yes, you too." Claire walked away, puzzled by April's abrupt parting. The sense of a missed opportunity nagged at her. She wished she'd been able to be more honest in her response. After all, besides Karl and Evelyn, April was the one other person she'd told about her cancer. Claire remembered being a little tipsy at the time. Still, why did she confide in April of all people? They were so different—yet that night, and in that moment, their differences didn't seem so vast. Even today, despite their awkward exchange, she still felt a strange bond. Was it because she herself had come down in the world? Or because she finally realized such things were no longer so important? But if her recognition of this was a sign of growth, why was there no joy in it, no satisfaction? There was only this dull feeling of arriving somewhere too late, where nobody cared or even noticed.

On the last Saturday in August, Anna woke up late, in a panic, upset with Luke for letting her sleep in. She would be the one to pay for his good intentions. By the time she went downstairs, it was past eight. To her surprise, the kitchen was empty. Everyone had already eaten. She remembered it was Shabbat. Normally it would be bustling at this hour, but during Shabbat, the Eternals retired to their rooms after breakfast to rest or read before the morning sermon.

The quiet made her feel strangely abandoned and unsettled. The week before, she'd told Luke about her encounter with Duncan, and how her whole body went cold with certainty he was dangerous. "There was something about him, Luke, that was so . . . *insistent.* But also pitiable. Like a feral stray that takes your scraps, then attacks you." Luke was profoundly disturbed and made her promise to avoid walking by Duncan's house again, especially alone. Her account cemented his own hunch about the connection between Patrick Clay and April's son, with the similarity of their injured arms.

He brought the matter to Hiram's attention, but the elder dismissed their concerns outright. "There's no proof, and I'm not going to the authorities with just conjecture, not when things in town are still so tense. We watch out for our own children but keep this to ourselves."

When Luke relayed their brief discussion, Anna sighed. "I know we have no proof. But if he had something to do with Patrick's drowning, how awful that he should get away with it."

Rummaging in the kitchen, she found some challah bread and a hardboiled egg and sat at the table, set in a nook with three large bay windows. She was cracking the egg against a bowl when a bird crashed into the middle window. The impact was deafening. She cried out, jerking back in her chair. There was a small star-shaped crack in the glass. She eased herself from the chair and made her way to the back door. Outside, it was warm and humid. She looked up at the sky and noticed gray clouds overhead. The air seemed to emit a subtle, electric vibration.

The dead bird lay a few inches away from the window. It was a brown wood thrush, remarkably intact. For a moment, she thought it might still be alive. She knelt down with effort, squatting on her knees and holding on to the wall to pick up the small creature. The body was warm, but its tiny black eyes didn't move, nor did its white dappled breast. "Oh," she said softly, "poor little thing." She was still cradling the bird in her palm when she saw Esther come out of the chicken coop.

"What are you doing?" Esther called out, crossing the lawn toward her. When she saw what Anna held, she grimaced. "That's the third one since yesterday. I think because of the storm that's coming."

"It flew into the window there, while I was eating." She pointed to the cracked pane.

Esther gave her a strange look and said, "It seems you attract them."

Anna winced but couldn't deny the truth of it. They only recently chased away the owl outside her window by cutting off all the sturdy branches of the hemlock tree. It found a new perch on the big elm facing the highway—still on the property, but at least no longer constantly in sight.

"Can we bury it?" she asked.

Esther looked aghast. "*Bury?* Today?"

"Oh, of course," Anna said, crestfallen. Plowing was forbidden during Shabbat, and while she didn't feel burying was quite the same thing, it wasn't worth debating. "What should I do?"

"Leave it as you found it. It's nature's way. God's way."

Anna placed the bird back on the ground. Death was death. She knew it would make no difference whether the bird was disposed of, buried in a garden, or left for the neighborhood cats to ravage. Still, the incident upset her. She'd heard that dead birds signified new beginnings, but it felt to her more an ominous sign than hopeful.

"I trust you're well rested?" said Esther.

Anna colored. "I'm sorry, Luke should have—"

"He spoke with Hiram and Zebiah this morning. Going forward, you are to be excused when you're tired. I hope you don't abuse their kindness."

"I won't," Anna said, startled by this concession. To appease the matron, she added, "Nor yours, I promise."

When the morning service was over, she helped prepare the noon feast. Then they all gathered at the dining table to recite the Kiddush. Shabbat was a time for thankfulness and celebration, and she wanted to enjoy the leisurely meal. But as soon as she sat down, she felt queasy and exhausted. She forced herself to take small bites from her plate.

"Are you feeling unwell?" Luke asked, noticing her poor appetite.

"I'm so tired today. I don't know why, I've had plenty of sleep." She thanked him for speaking on her behalf. Then she told him about the dead bird.

"Oh, I've seen that too. It's terrible, isn't it, holding those poor, broken creatures in your hand."

"But this one wasn't broken, Luke. That's what's so strange. It looked perfect, like it just fell out of the sky. Esther thinks it's because of the storm."

He nodded. "The elders are worried about that. We gathered all the candles we had this morning, in case there's an outage. And we'll check on the shutters later."

After the meal and cleanup, Esther allowed Anna to go upstairs and rest until it was time to prepare supper. She acquiesced gratefully. In their room, Luke helped her onto the bed, where she lay on her side so he could massage her lower back. Soon she fell into a heavy, dreamless sleep. Two hours later, the first cramp came on. She stirred, but it passed quickly, and she fell right back to sleep. The second cramp came twenty minutes later. This one was worse and made her sit up in the bed, fully awake.

Luke was gone, and the room had grown dim. She peered at the small clock on the nightstand: it was only a little past five, too early for it to be so dark. Using electricity was forbidden until Shabbat ended at sunset, so she lit a candle and got up to use the bathroom. Her body felt so heavy and awkward, it took her a long time to relieve herself. On the way back to the bed, another cramp seized her. This pain was acute and familiar, lasting for several minutes.

She bent over the bed clutching her abdomen, panting, thinking wildly, *It can't be.* Finally, the cramp passed. She checked the calendar tacked to the wall, where she'd marked past dates through with an X. She wasn't due for another month. Her first pregnancy went a few days past her due date. She never considered the possibility this one could come so early.

Outside, the wind made a steady, hissing sound. She straightened and walked over to the window facing the back lawn and creek beyond. She could see big ripples in the gray water and tree branches swaying back and forth. The sky was dark with heavy rolling clouds. A sudden gust of wind swung one of the shutters hard against the window, making her rear back. She opened the window and latched the shutters. The wind strengthened and continued to howl, even after she closed the window. A strong sense of déjà vu swept over her, and though it was still fairly warm, she shivered. She heard a low rumble of thunder in the distance. Shortly after, her water broke.

By late afternoon, Claire had organized as much as she could for the storm. She set out a hand-crank flashlight, candles, and matches; plugged in her phone and laptop to charge; and gathered all her nonperishable food onto the kitchen counter. Finally, she closed all her shutters. Afterward, feeling spent, she lay down on the living room sofa for a nap. Within minutes, her phone rang. It was still charging in the kitchen, so she had to walk across the room to answer.

She reached for the phone irritably, thinking it was Karl again, but when she saw the name on the screen, her heart skipped. It was Lars, Sebastian's brother. He'd never initiated a call before. "Lars?"

"Claire." He took a deep breath, and in that pause her mouth went dry. "I'm so sorry to have to tell you this. Sebastian took his own life yesterday. They think so anyway—"

"No!" She felt her legs give way and sank to the floor, clutching the counter for support. "Oh no, oh god—what happened?"

"Some hikers found him early this morning, somewhere in the Sandia Mountains. He was lying a bit away from his tent, and they could tell he wasn't . . . so they called the forest rangers. They found empty pill bottles all around his sleeping bag and his backpack inside the tent. His wallet and ID were in there, and two notes, dated yesterday. That's why they think . . . Anyway, the autopsy will confirm all that. One note had instructions to call me, so . . . I'm in Albuquerque now, at the morgue. I got here an hour ago."

The morgue. And Sebastian. She covered the phone and began to sob. When she was able to speak, she said, "You saw him, Lars? Was he . . . Could you tell it was him?"

"Yes." He cleared his throat. "Claire, the other note: it's for you. It wasn't sealed, just folded. I only saw enough to read your name, that's all. I'll express mail it today."

"Oh. But there's a storm coming, I might not even get it on Monday. And what if it gets lost? Can you read it to me now? Please, Lars, I don't mind." This wasn't entirely true; she was extremely private. But she had to know what Sebastian wrote to her now, not next week.

"I—to be honest, Claire, I don't feel like I should. What if I scan a copy to your email? I'll ask around here or find someplace. I'll do it within the hour, I promise. And I'll still mail it. Is that okay?"

"Yes, yes, thank you so much." She was deeply moved by his kindness and wondered, not for the first time, why Sebastian always kept him at such a distance. Lars had once offered to introduce him to collectors—Houston was full of them, and he had connections—but Sebastian curtly refused. "I'm sorry for your loss too. I know he was your only sibling."

"Yes. Well." The discomfort in his silence was obvious.

"Had you heard from him recently?"

"No. Not since he left here. To be honest, I was surprised he had them contact me. I suppose he didn't want to burden you. Anyway, as it turns out, I'm glad you were spared this."

She shut her mind against the gruesome image "this" suggested: Sebastian dead and decomposed, possibly mutilated by wildlife. She should also be glad she was spared, and part of her was. Yet it seemed one more nail striking home the fact that, even if the divorce hadn't gone through yet, she was no longer his next of kin.

"Okay," he said, "look out for that email soon. I'll let you know if I find out anything more."

She thanked him and hung up. For a long time, she sat on the floor, listening to the refrigerator humming. Her heart banged against her chest with loud, steady thumps. *Sebastian's dead.* She could feel the pain gathering and stood up abruptly. In the pantry, she found Karl's bottle of Macallan and poured herself a large neat shot. She rarely drank spirits, but she needed to feel numb, and quickly. In two gulps, she downed the drink, grimacing. Then she refilled her glass and walked to the living room, taking her laptop with her.

She pulled up her inbox and stared at the screen, waiting. Lars said he'd send the letter within the hour. How much time had elapsed since they spoke? Ten minutes, fifteen? There were several unopened emails; she looked at the column of subjects blankly as the letters blurred, became hieroglyphic. The scotch hit her suddenly, and hard. She lay back on the sofa and closed her eyes. Minutes passed as she drifted into senselessness.

The pinging of her inbox startled her and she jerked upright. The message was from Lars. There was no greeting, only an attachment. Opening it, she saw Sebastian's bold, precise handwriting:

Claire,

This will be short and, I'm afraid, painful. But I wanted to tell you goodbye. I'm sorry to put you through this, after everything else. I know you'll want more in the way of answers, but if I had any, I wouldn't be here, at this point. Which is to stop asking. Stop thinking. I'm very tired. Please don't worry about the paintings,

they don't matter. And there's nothing you could have done—so don't go there. If anything, you probably helped me hang on longer than I would have. I'm sorry I hurt you. You didn't deserve it, but I didn't know any other way. One of many things I wish I could change.
S.

She read it over three times before closing the laptop. Then she finished her drink and sat very still, her gaze unfocused, as sorrow and confusion turned to guilt. He said there was nothing she could have done. But she couldn't help wondering if her asking for a divorce had triggered this. It was only a month ago; the timing couldn't be a coincidence. Had he harbored some faraway hope for reconciliation? She found it unfathomable. There was remorse in his letter, but was there love? Sebastian was never verbal about such things. Still, for this to be his parting message. *You didn't deserve it, but I didn't know any other way.*

There was something poignant, even pitiable about his words. In that admission she could sense his self-loathing and despair. She tried to imagine his last days and what must have driven him to take his life. All those empty pill bottles. She remembered the antidepressants he was on, how they sometimes seemed to do more harm than good. Whenever she tried to talk to him about it, he got so irritable, making her feel like an overbearing nag. He so often made her feel that way.

But there were also times, especially early on, when he could defuse her anxiety with his dry humor, when he sought her advice and listened to it, when they were so aligned in their thinking they practically communicated in shorthand. Most precious to her were the moments when she made an observation about his work that resonated. Something behind his eyes would flicker as if to say, *You understand.* And then there was that terrible period after she had her ovaries removed, when she went through her own depression, and he was so stoic and strong. As his career stalled, things became more difficult, but they'd managed well enough, up until his accident. And then they moved up here. And then Anna . . .

It took her so long to get past her hatred and reach a point of acceptance. Now all she could feel was a clawing anguish for everything that was gone. The pain came rushing back, and this time, she surrendered to it. She wept with abandon, keening and howling, rocking her body from side to side. *I can't stand this. I can't bear any more.*

When she was finally spent, she lay back on the sofa and stared up at the ceiling fan spinning above her. The room had grown noticeably darker. She became aware of the windows faintly rattling. Slowly, she stood and walked over to open the French doors, stepping out onto the deck. The wind had picked up, and the sky looked menacing, dark and thick with clouds. She did a double take seeing the maple tree. Just the day before, it was full of yellowing foliage; now it was stripped bare, all its leaves strewn across the ground and onto the tarp covering the drained, unused pool. She'd had to install the tarp as extra precaution against liability, in case someone fell into the hole.

She remembered her first sight of the pool, how it seemed to her almost grand in its crumbling decrepitude. She looked upon it then as an arresting visual, like a photograph—not as an actual structure with a history and function. Now it was just an eyesore, an expensive one at that. The estimate to fill in the pool was almost as much as repairing it. *What an asshole I was,* she thought. *No wonder April hated me.* Only someone incredibly obtuse could find such neglect picturesque. Obtuse and privileged. That was her then. But no longer. Today, she had finally lost everything.

———————

Despite their long marriage, Claire had only a handful of photos with her and Sebastian together. He was averse to posing for pictures, and there were some years, especially when she was heavier, that she didn't care to either. She spread some of the older photos out on the floor of his studio: a grainy shot of them outside a flea market in Philly; a Polaroid of her heavily made up and him gesticulating, taken by a friend at somebody's art opening; a large glossy of them newly married, standing outside city hall in Lower Manhattan. How young she looked, and how handsome he was in his borrowed navy jacket, his arm draped loosely around her, squinting at the camera with a rare happy smile. Against the walls, she'd propped his paintings, as many as she could bring up from the basement. It took her multiple trips up and down the stairs, and now she was exhausted but too wired to rest.

She drank straight from a bottle of wine and stumbled around the room, surveying all his paintings. Their layered hues, seen in certain lights and distances, created an almost miasmic effect of movement. But his canvases were small—the largest was only twenty-four by thirty-six inches—and also invited intimate examination. Up close you could see he employed the repetition of natural, overlapping motifs—palm fronds, ferns, other leaves, and grass—rendered with hyperrealistic precision. Some critics pronounced his work revelatory; others found it gimmicky and claustrophobic, dismissing him as a mere colorist.

Sebastian was often jealous about others' successes. But Claire understood the source of his bitterness. He was a brilliant painter who, through the whims of fate and curators, got bypassed. Some of that was his fault. He could be urbane and charming one day, and cold and antagonistic on another. But she knew of artists who were far more unbearable, and their careers still flourished. What it came down to, she concluded, was a matter of luck. Some people had it, and others didn't. She suspected she didn't. Sebastian must have realized the same for himself.

In the end, the fact that he left all his work behind was more revealing than any suicide note. He simply walked away from everything he was. And she would never know what he experienced afterward. "Oh, Sebastian," she whispered, beginning to weep again. All this time she'd imagined him living a life of debauchery, freeloading off vulnerable young women—and maybe he had, but what did any of that matter now? He'd suffered greatly, just as she had. It cut her to the core, knowing they both felt unbearable misery these last few years and were unable to reach out to each other. *There's nothing you could have done— so don't go there.* "I can't help it," she sobbed, "you know I can't."

She began to shake so hard she lost her balance and fell hard on her knees. The bottle of wine clattered to the floor but was near empty and, remarkably, didn't break. She cried out with pain, hugging her knees to her chest. She was drunk, dangerously so. "I don't care," she moaned, "I want to die . . . just let me die."

In that moment, she pictured her mother glaring at her, affronted, tubes in her nose and mouth: *Oh really? You think it's so easy?* She flinched, recalling her torturous, horrific decline. It was what she most feared for herself. Sebastian's way was better. She stared at the floor, her mind churning, listening to the storm raging. Over the last few hours it had intensified, and now rain mingled with the fierce wind, rattling the shutters on their hinges.

She stood up again and, holding the walls for support, made her way to the front of the house and the bottom of the stairwell. Gripping the banister, she went slowly up the stairs. Finally, she made it to the bathroom. She stared at her reflection in the mirror with dull shock. She already looked like a corpse. In the medicine cabinet, she found her bottle of Zolpidem. She shook it all onto her palm and counted: eighteen pills, ten milligrams each. The prescribed dosage was one pill before bedtime, but she'd developed a tolerance and, on bad nights, took a half or even a whole extra. Would eighteen be enough? She didn't want to end up on life support. But her health directive prohibited that happening. Karl had a copy and would honor it.

Thinking of Karl, she faltered. Could she inflict on him the same pain she was going through? But it wasn't really the same. He would mourn her, but he had Evelyn. And while he would never say so, Claire knew she'd burdened him with her troubles since she moved to Caliban, with the scandal and her cancer. One day, the cancer would come back. Tamara had implied as much. This would be more merciful for everyone. Still, she owed him some kind of goodbye. Even Sebastian gave her that.

She filled her water glass and, clutching the pills, walked into her bedroom. Beneath the window was a cherrywood secretary she'd bought at an estate sale, back in the days when she did those things. She turned on the desk lamp, setting down the water and pills, and found a pen and paper. Then she hesitated—not for lack or resolve, but for words. If these were to be her last, what could she say? Besides Karl and Evelyn, who would care, now that Sebastian was dead? At least his paintings would live on; she'd make sure Karl contacted Lars. What would be her legacy? She sat for a long while, thinking on it. Then she picked up the pen.

She spent the next several minutes writing. As she composed the letter, she felt curiously detached, as if she were playacting. She worried Karl would find it cold but was grateful for this moment of calm. If she allowed herself to feel anything, she wasn't sure she could go through with it. And it was important for Karl to believe she wrote the note in a rational state. When she finished, she sealed it in an envelope, wrote his name on the front, and propped it against the lamp.

She took the water and pills and sat on the edge of the bed. Her heart beat erratically as she considered what she was about to do. She didn't want to live. But she was afraid to die. She wondered what pills Sebastian took. She hoped he simply slipped into a deep, endless sleep. It was what she longed for herself. "Come on, just get it over with."

Her hands shook as she put half the pills in her mouth and gulped down a large sip of water. She managed to swallow a few, then immediately began to gag and cough. Several pills spewed out of her mouth, rolling around the floor in all directions. "Oh, shit. God*damn it*!" She turned on her nightstand lamp and got down on all fours to search for the scattered pills. Just as she picked up the second one, the lights went out. She froze in disbelief. She waited several minutes for the power to come back on and for her eyes to adjust to the darkness, but neither happened. Carefully, she crawled in the direction of the window, found it, and stood up. She could feel how the window shook in its frame, could hear the rain pounding against the glass—but she couldn't see a thing. Never in her life had she experienced such complete darkness.

Finally, tiny haloes of light started to flicker across the road. With a groan, she realized her flashlight and all her candles were downstairs. She meant to bring some up before it grew dark, but after Lars called, everything was forgotten. Even her phone was downstairs. "Shit," she muttered again. Trying to navigate the stairs in the dark was out of the question. She wanted to die the way she chose—not by breaking her neck. As she stood debating what to do, a familiar, voluptuous numbness began to seep through her body: the pills were kicking in. A moment later, oblivion settled over her. Before she could even get to the bed, she felt herself sinking to the floor and gave in to it.

The pain was blinding, clawing its way through her and twisting her organs. Anna had feared but forgotten this agony, and now she lived inside it feverish, writhing, screaming. It was night. She saw the sky turn black just before they closed the curtains and asked Luke to wait outside. It seemed endless hours ago, but she couldn't say for sure how much time had actually passed. She was in the birthing and convalescence room downstairs. It was adjacent to the kitchen and laundry closet, making sterilization and changing linens easier. She had stayed in this room after she lost her first baby and was discharged from the hospital. Miriam and Rachel tended to her then as well.

Sometimes Anna got confused, seeing the midwives' faces looming over her, and thought she was back in that terrible time, that everything that happened since was only a dream. Sometimes she felt the room itself was a dream—a dream of hell, where she would be eternally mourning her dead child. Then a new contraction would jolt her back to the present, and she'd remember there was another baby, this one, still waiting to be born.

Her screams grew more strident. "Shh, Anna!" Miriam eyes were round with alarm. "Luke will hear, you'll worry him." She worked a knotted cloth into Anna's mouth. "Bite on this when the pain comes."

The storm was bearing down upon them. Rain pattered against the window as the wind shook the glass. Other women came in and out of the room: Zebiah, Esther, Tamar, and Shoshanna. Every light was lit, every wall festooned with sheets of parchment inscribed with holy texts. The Shir Hama'alos psalm hung directly above Anna's head. Whenever she cried out, the women chanted the verses in unison. They said it was to conjure protection, but hearing their low-pitched voices reminded her of the strange humming between Esther and Tamar that day she saw them in the kitchen. These words they chanted sounded more sinister than holy. Zebiah placed a silver amulet around her neck, and as she thrashed her head from side to side, its thin chain dug into her skin. She tried to pull it off, but the older woman pried her hands away, pressing them down against her sides. Her eyes gleamed with determination, and in that instant, Anna was convinced she was evil.

She screamed again, and Rachel pressed a cool cloth to her forehead. "Anna, hush, it's okay." She stroked her hand gently, and Anna ceased resisting. Rachel would make sure no harm came to her.

"Don't leave me," she pleaded.

"I won't . . . I'm here."

Outside, the rain continued to beat down while the wind hissed and howled. From a faraway distance, she heard Miriam ask, "Is the ambulance coming?"

"They can't get through," someone said, "the phone lines are down."

Anna tried to ask, *What's wrong?* but all that came out was a garbled moan.

"Shh," Rachel murmured gently, "everything will be fine."

At that moment, the lights went out. For a split second, no one moved or made a sound. Miriam said, "The flashlight, Rachel, there on the table—" A beam came on, matches were found, and soon the women were busily lighting every candle they could find.

There was a knock on the door, and Luke called out, "Is everything okay?"

Miriam opened the door a few inches. "The baby's coming. We'll do all we can. But her fever is spiking. If there are complications . . . is there any way to get help?"

"We asked some neighbors if their cell phones were working," Luke said. "Walter Edgar was able to call out, but the emergency dispatcher said the roads are bad. Trees and power lines are down. And it's pitch-black outside—there's no moon. It won't be light for a few more hours."

He peered into the room. It was unorthodox for men to witness childbirth, and even male doctors were exceptions only in cases of emergency. His eyes grew wide as Anna seized up with another contraction. She twisted her head, using her shoulder to dislodge the knotted cloth from her mouth. "Oh, oh! Oh God, please help me!"

Miriam pushed Luke firmly away from the door. "Let me tend to her. Find more candles if you can."

Anna cried, "Luke! Where's Luke?"

"He's just outside," Rachel said.

"Please, can he come in?"

"My God," Zebiah said, "the things she asks for, even now." Leaning close to Anna, she told her, "You must obey our ways, do you hear me? Do you want this child to be unholy?"

Anna turned away from her angry expression. On the wall opposite, the women's shadows converged and shifted in the flickering candlelight, forming terrifying shapes: a pulsing heart, then the outstretched wings of a large bird, and now the head of a horned goat.

No, no, no. Anna shut her eyes and clamped her lips tightly, gritting through the waves of pain as they came on stronger and faster, so fast she could hardly catch her breath. She gripped and pulled at the thick rag rope they'd fastened across the bed. Inside her womb a force was gathering . . . The baby began to crown between her widespread legs, stretching her pelvis so that she felt it might break. "Push, Anna, *push*," they were saying, an urgent chorus, and from the far reaches of her memory, Sebastian's voice echoed and joined them—"Come on, Anna, you can do it, just hold on"—as if he were there in the room again with her.

"Push, Anna, push!"

"No," she moaned, "go away . . ."

"Almost there now," Miriam said.

The pain crescendoed as the baby's head pushed through. She felt her flesh tearing and let out a high-pitched scream, a prolonged sound that seemed to come from somewhere outside her body. Then there were hands inside her, pulling, a gushing wetness. The metallic, unmistakable smell of blood. At last, a slippery release, and it was out of her—the baby was out. She sobbed with relief and fell back against the pillows, instantly losing consciousness.

When she came to moments later, Rachel was wiping her face with a cold towel. Anna said feebly, "Where's my baby?"

Miriam stood up from the foot of the bed, holding her newborn, a gray umbilical cord protruding from the stomach. "You have a boy," she said, bringing him closer to Anna. The sparse hairs on his head were dark, his eyes narrow and long like hers and tightly shut. Anna's heart leaped at first, then sank. He was so small, barely larger than the two hands cradling him. How could something so tiny have caused her so much suffering?

"Will he live?" she asked, adding fiercely, "Tell me the truth."

Miriam sighed and looked from the baby to the window, as if seeking the wind for a sign. Her profile was unreadable, obscured by long shadows. Finally, Anna heard her say, "If it be God's will."

A loud crash from outside shook the house and jolted Claire awake. For a moment, she had no idea where she was. She lay in a fetal position, her cheek pressed against the hard wooden floor. Weak sunlight filled the room. She could see several small white pills just a few feet away. The events of the night before came back to her, and then she remembered Sebastian. The reality of his death sliced through her with fresh agony. She squeezed her eyes shut, absorbing it. He was dead, and she was still here. She had failed—and she didn't think she would have the courage to try again.

She forced herself to stand up. Everything hurt: her joints, her stomach, her chest and head. The lamps were still unlit; the power hadn't come back on. She shuffled over to the window and opened it. It was noticeably cooler but still windy and raining. Leaning her head out, she gasped. Across the road two houses down, a huge pine tree had fallen onto the highway, blocking off most of it. She could see the roots sticking up on the other side of the road and shattered cracks along the asphalt. Several large branches had broken off and were strewn on the ground, along with pine needles, leaves, and bits of trash blowing around in the wind. A street sign lay in the middle of her yard, and just up the house to her right, a cable line hung loose from its post.

"Jesus Christ," she said. It was far more damage than she expected. And this was only on her street. She wondered what the rest of the town and surrounding areas looked like.

She closed the window, pulled on some sweats, and made her way downstairs. Her phone was in the kitchen; it was just past ten thirty. Neither Karl nor

Evelyn had called. She tried to call them and got a recording saying there was no service. When she opened her laptop, she had no internet.

She found her mackintosh and rain boots in the entry closet and went outside. The wind was strong and slanted the rain in her face as she struggled to keep her hood on. Her boots had poor traction, causing a near wipeout on a pile of wet leaves. Down the road, she could see some neighbors gathered around the fallen tree. Walt and Carol Edgar were there, standing next to Jerry Ingalls. As Claire got closer, she stopped dead in her tracks. At the very bottom of the highway, where it opened onto a wide intersection, a pool of brown water stretched as far as she could see, erasing the curbsides and traffic island that should have been there. "Oh my god."

Carol peered out from under her umbrella and called out, "Who is that? Oh, Claire!"

She walked up to them, picking her way carefully over the branches. She kept her hood low over her face, acutely aware of how awful she must look. "I heard the crash and—"

"Us too," said Walt. "Scared the dogs half to death. Looks like the roots of this thing just couldn't hold."

"That's crazy," said Claire. "Look at all that flooding down there."

Carol nodded. "The creek is rising too. I've never seen anything like it. I wonder what it's like everywhere else."

"That reminds me—do any of your phones work? I'd like to check on Karl and Evelyn."

Walt said, "Mine did last night, but now I've got no signal."

"That's 'cause the Eternals jinxed it," Jerry teased.

"What do you mean?"

Carol rolled her eyes. "Nothing. We were just telling him one of them knocked on our door last night, asking if he could use our phone. Someone was having a baby, so they were trying to get help. Walt got through to 911, but there was a backup and a lot of roads were closed. So, I don't know . . . Hopefully things over there are okay."

Claire listened in silence. A baby. It could only be Anna's. Her mind reeled with these strange, circular coincidences: yesterday, the news about Sebastian, and now this reminder of the girl who had ruined their marriage. Walt was saying something to her.

"I'm sorry, what?"

"Were you okay last night? You got enough supplies?"

"Oh. Yes, thanks, I'm fine."

"Because it doesn't look like we'll be going anywhere soon. We may not get power back for a while either."

"That sucks," Jerry said. "Well, I'm heading back."

"Let's go home too," said Carol. "I'm getting soaked."

Claire said, "I'm just going to walk around a bit."

"Be careful," said Walt. "Don't go stepping in that water down there—who knows what's floating around."

"I won't." Claire walked along the highway toward the intersection. Passing the Eternals' farmhouse, she looked across their wide front lawn and, as she had many times before, wondered at the life that went on inside. All the shutters were tightly closed. She could detect no movement or sounds from within. The house appeared as impenetrable as its inhabitants. She'd never been inside or attended one of their Shabbats. Sebastian admitted his indiscretion with Anna unfolded on the night he went but gave no description of the ceremony itself or what the house looked like inside: how many rooms there were, what the furnishings were like, how the Eternals *lived*. Ordinarily those were the questions she would have asked, but at the time she was too single-minded. She could only ask him again and again about the timeline and sequence of events that led Anna to leave her home and end up in theirs.

She looked away and continued down the highway. On either side were ruined gardens, fences missing their pickets, and, in one driveway, part of a chimney, smashed to pieces. Duncan McAuley's roof, from what she could see, had completely collapsed; his house looked like a box bashed in by a giant shoe. The parking lot of the Horizon Café was a wide, shallow puddle, the edge of it licking at the top step of the entrance. Approaching the flooded intersection, she saw water spread out for almost a block in every direction. To her left, looking north, cars parked in a row had water up to the tops of their tires, while to her right, along with other bits of flotsam, a lawn chair moved slowly with the lapping current.

The severity of the storm finally sunk in. *There must be over a foot of water,* she thought, *and this is only one road.* Walt was right; it would be impossible for the power companies to get to every area until the floods receded. But first it had to stop raining. She thought about Karl and Evelyn again. If only there was a way to get to them. They were six miles away, in Westerville. She wondered if she could drive there, imagining how surprised they would be to see her.

The truth was she didn't want to go back to her house and spend another night in the pitch-dark, left to brood on her own. *I'll go crazy again,* she thought, beginning to panic, remembering the hallucinations she had the previous winter. She hadn't had those same visions again, but she still awoke on occasion in the middle of the night to strange creaking sounds and saw ominous shapes in the shadows in her bedroom.

I'll get in the car and see how far I get, she decided. She turned around and began walking back up the road. As she neared the Eternals' farmhouse, she noticed that toward the rear of the house, one set of shutters on the lower floor was open. She hadn't seen it walking from the other direction, but now it caught her eye, partly because it was open and also because a large hydrangea bush grew beneath the window, with several white flowers somehow still intact. As she got closer, she saw flickering lights beyond the glass, dancing movements that seemed to beckon her. She crossed the lawn quickly and reached the side of the house. Keeping close to the wall, she inched toward the open window, pushing through trees and shrubs along the way. She pulled her hood down and crouched behind the hydrangea bush, peeping through the leaves at the room beyond.

On the other side of the windowsill, three tapered candles were spaced evenly apart, all burning at the same height. Anna lay on a bed in the middle of the room, facing the window, a faded quilt covering the pronounced swell of her belly. She was propped up by several pillows, her head turned sideways with her eyes closed. For a split second Claire felt light-headed, remembering the last time she saw Anna like this, and the shock of seeing Sebastian on his knees, pulling her dead baby out. This time, there was no blood or screaming or chaos. In fact, she was struck by the stillness of the scene before her.

By the side of the bed, a young woman with light brown hair sat in front of a lit fireplace with several blankets draped over her lap. Throughout the room, paper scrolls with elaborate cursive writing Claire couldn't decipher were tacked on to the walls. They suggested something strange and ritualistic, as did the three lit candles during daylight. She wondered if there had been—or would be—some kind of ceremony or sacrifice. If she were able to witness it, would she be enthralled or repelled? Were they the gentle, spiritual people of their pamphlets, or the perverse, secretive cult people cautioned against? They had ruined her life, and yet, in this moment, it was hard to imagine the latter. She tried to envision herself having the kind of faith that provided such peacefulness. But she didn't believe in a benevolent god, only a vindictive one.

A tall, fair-haired young man walked into the room—the husband. He carried some logs and set them down in the fireplace, then bent over the young woman and lifted something tiny and swaddled. As he straightened, Claire realized with a pang it was Anna's newborn baby. It looked impossibly small, barely human. The woman said something to him. He frowned and shook his head. After a moment, he placed the baby carefully back onto the woman's lap and went to sit at the edge of the bed. He rested a hand on Anna's forehead and smoothed back her hair. The tenderness in his face was almost unbearable.

Claire felt sick with jealousy. Whatever troubles Anna had gone or would go through, her husband loved her. He took her back. They had made a baby. While her own womb was scorched from disease, her husband gone forever. She realized how pathetic she was, chilled to the bone and hiding with the rain dripping down her neck, gaping upon an experience she would never have. Nor would this be the end of it. She would have to see them walking through town with their child, and perhaps more children in the future. And then she knew with sudden clarity: *I can't go on living here.*

Anna stirred awake. She lifted her head up to her husband. He brought a glass of water to her lips and she drank. She looked at the window, and her eyes met Claire's. Her face went still, then spasmed with alarm. She started to speak, but before she could, Claire bolted.

She saw a thicket of trees in the back of the property, about a hundred yards away, and ran as fast as her cumbersome boots would allow. When she reached the trees, she hid behind the largest one, her chest heaving, and peered back at the farmhouse to see if anyone was following.

Did Anna recognize her? It didn't seem possible. But it was uncanny how the girl's eyes found hers, as if by instinct. She could still feel the jolt of it. When she was sure no one was coming after her, she started moving farther back through the trees, toward the creek. She would walk west along its edge until it curved directly across the road from her house, then cut over.

Even before she came upon the creek, she heard the roar of rushing water. Her boots began to stick, and when she looked down, she was on a slushy trail of mud. Seconds later, she walked through a clearing in the trees and gasped. The creek had become a gushing river moving rapidly downstream, rising so high it spilled over the rocky bank and onto the backyards of her neighbors. Instead of neatly mowed lawns there was only a shallow, widening stretch of muddy water, making it impossible to gauge the perimeters of the original creek.

"Holy shit," she gasped. It was becoming difficult to walk through the muck and puddles, but she didn't want to go farther inland and be caught on private property. Since the Clay boy's drowning, almost every house along the creek had signs against trespassing. At least it stopped raining. She continued to make her way along the line of trees near the creek, trudging as fast as she could without losing her balance. After a few more yards, she felt dizzy and paused to rest. A large loose branch floating about three feet away caught her eye. She thought she could use it as a walking stick and waded toward it. As she bent to pick it up, her right boot slipped and she pitched forward, hands outstretched. She felt the shock of cold water and a sharp, cutting pain on her palms and knees. Somehow, she'd fallen into the rocky bank, now completely submerged by the flood. She spun around, disoriented, splashing farther into the water. Then the current took her.

Before she knew it, she was in the middle of the creek, her mackintosh tangling around her. She thrashed clumsily, swallowing water, trying not to panic as she felt herself pulled downstream. Her body scraped against more rocks and branches in the water. She strained to keep her head above the surface, the sky and trees rushing past in a dark blur. She was a good swimmer—her early life was spent in oceans and pools—but she'd never experienced a current like this. This water was alive, ferocious. She was as useless as a rag doll spinning in a wash cycle.

One of her boots slipped off and her mackintosh unsnapped. She reached out, both arms flailing, hoping to find anything that might stop this breakneck, turbulent ride. If she could only get to a part of the creek that was shallow and narrow. But the water appeared to be only widening around her. When she kicked, she couldn't feel the rocks under her feet. The other boot slid off. She bumped against something—a large, splintered tree log—and grabbed it. Slowly, she pulled herself along its length, inching closer toward the trees, until she finally felt mud under her feet again. When the water was only up to her knees she let go of the log, sloshing toward the nearest tree.

She'd taken three steps forward when something yanked at her right ankle, lifting her upside down in the air. As she fell backward, her head hit something. Then she was immersed in water up to her neck. It gushed into her nose and mouth. Grasping her leg for leverage, she raised herself up, coughing and spitting, her mackintosh trailing below her. Looking up, she saw that her leg was caught in a rope noose tied to a tree limb. The rest of her dangled uselessly in the air. She looked down at the pool of water less than two feet below. It was shallow and surprisingly placid, reflecting the gray clouds above. But it was deep enough to drown her, should she let go.

Her predicament was so bizarre, at first she couldn't think what to do. She jerked her caught leg wildly, hoping to dislodge or break the rope. All it did was make her spin around. Using all her strength, she hoisted herself higher, trying to reach the rope to loosen its grip on her bare ankle. The rope cut into her flesh and would not give. She couldn't even wedge in a finger.

In the distance, she saw the Eternals' farmhouse. The current had carried her back downstream. Now their proximity gave her hope. *"HELP!"* she screamed, again and again. *"Help me!"* No one answered. Blood trickled from her temple onto her chest. Only then did she register the throbbing pain in her head. *Think, Claire,* think*!* she commanded herself. But she was too frightened and cold and tired. Her arms trembled with the effort to hold on to her leg, which was beginning to go numb. Her abdominal muscles were cramping. She considered taking a deep breath to go back into the water in order to rest her arms. But she wasn't sure she'd have the strength to lift herself up again.

She glanced down. In the water's reflection, a piercing brightness tore through the veil of clouds. Sunlight flared and refracted, stunning her eyes. The beauty of it was surreal and terrifying. She had a sudden, profound intuition that whatever came next was contingent on her will—that if she fought hard for it, somehow she would survive. It was a staggering conviction, one she had never before experienced. *I can get through this,* she thought. *I can make it out of here.* Then another voice said, *But you don't have to.* She froze, unsure where the voice came from—if it was her own, her mother's, or Sebastian's. She listened for the voice again, hoping for an answer. None came. A strange calm suffused her, and she realized it didn't matter. What mattered were the words themselves—their simple, soothing revelation. She felt the truth of those words. She let that truth sink into her bones. And then she let go.

11
RECKONING

Dinner was eaten, the dishes were done, and the kids shooed into their rooms so April could finally have some quiet. She sat at the kitchen table with an old laptop a friend had given her and began to search for rentals. Earlier that day, Delia told her they'd found a buyer for their lot. He wanted to build something new and planned to start demolishing once the escrow closed in December. Delia felt awful about it, she could tell, but she and Ed really wanted to head back south.

"I get it, Dee," April said. "Don't worry about it." But in truth she was taken aback by the news. Their street hadn't flooded, but with the damage done to so many homes and roads around them, she figured no one would be rushing to buy anything soon. Now she had only two months to find something. She looked around the unit with its ugly plywood walls, brown carpeting, and linoleum flooring. It was never more than shelter, a roof over her head. But the thought of looking for a new place, the hassle of packing and moving, only to find something just as bad—she couldn't help feeling deflated.

She wondered if she should move away from the area too, find something closer to work in Cairo. The kids would have to switch schools midyear, but maybe that was better than staying and getting constantly hassled. Especially for Justin. Everyone in town knew about Eli and what happened with Duncan. It seemed every week she heard some new, bogus rumor about her and the McAuleys she would have to squelch or ignore. Though the latter was near impossible.

The McAuleys didn't sue her for libel, but they placed a full-page open letter in all the local papers:

> We'd like to express thanks to the friends and neighbors in our community who have supported us during these difficult months. Those who have loved ones dealing with addiction and other mental health issues know there are many challenges. These challenges require empathy and patience. Sadly, an individual of questionable reputation—the close associate of a convicted felon—chose instead to attack the most vulnerable member of our family with false accusations, exploiting his circumstances for her own gain. We are grateful that justice prevailed and these slanderous charges were swiftly dismissed. As we repair the harm done to our family and name, we caution others to beware of this opportunist who claims to be your neighbor. Please be alert and stay safe.
>
> With gratitude and concern,
>
> The McCauley Family

Her friend Polly was the one who told her first, asking her to swing by her house after work. As soon as April walked in, Polly handed her a copy of the *Catskill Daily*. After she read it, Polly added, "It's not just the *Daily* either, honey. Lisette said it's in the *Reporter*, the *Hudson Valley Mail*, the *Register* . . . It's really messed up. I just might lie low for a while."

"What exploitation?" April cried, flinging the paper across the room. "I never even asked for money! I just wanted that fucker locked up! Fuck!"

She was used to being the subject of gossip, but not of public condemnation, where people felt not only emboldened but justified in hurling insults at her and her children—at their schools, the grocery store and gas station, the flea market and post office.

She hadn't told the kids yet about moving because she wanted some options lined up first. But the options in her budget were as depressing as she feared.

Even if she could find a place nearby, would anyone rent to her? Forty minutes later, she had three possibilities tagged and closed the laptop. She'd call them in the morning and also put out feelers through friends and coworkers.

There were three beers left in the fridge. She popped one open, drank half of it standing, then grabbed another and slumped onto the couch. If only she could really get out and forget everything, instead of drinking on the cheap by herself at home. It was depressing and made her think of Claire.

The shocking news of her death the month before reverberated throughout Caliban and its surrounding communities. Two young men discovered her the day after the storm at the edge of the Eternals' property line, while they were taking videos of the rising creek. They were on the other side and looked across to see her hanging upside down, one leg caught in an animal trap, with her head submerged in the shallow bank. Some locals were at the scene when the police cut her down. Carol Edgar recognized her mackintosh.

Karl wasn't able to identify her until the Tuesday after the storm, because bad flooding had closed off roads between Westerville and Caliban. Later, when he went to Claire's house, he found the front door unlocked and, in her bedroom, a suicide note. That she drowned on the Eternals' property in such a horrific way reignited superstitious outrage against them. Then Karl declined to press charges, which incited the townspeople further, depriving them of any satisfaction. Even those who were supportive of the Eternals before now felt apprehensive. All these morbid events were too much, stretching their limits of tolerance. A lot of people felt they got off too easy when Brian and Jody's lawsuit fell through. They wanted accountability.

April kept her opinions to herself. She was sorry about Jody's lawsuit because, coming on the heels of her own tossed case, she knew her friend must be suffering. But hearing of Claire's death—and how she died—was a shock that rattled her badly. She looked unwell the last time April saw her, but she was friendly, even sympathetic. Still, their exchanges were always tinged with awkwardness.

In the beginning, that stemmed from hostility, but even after it abated, April felt no impulse to extend their acquaintance into friendship. The woman was so tightly wound and seemed to have such huge needs that April's visceral response was to keep away. She refused to take on any guilt about it now, but she was shaken and saddened by this proof that her instinct was correct. And despite her old grudge, she felt for Karl Udall, who had seen Claire's dead face and now would never be able to unsee it.

Over the last few weeks, more details about Claire's death emerged. Evelyn told close friends that Sebastian also committed suicide. They discovered through her email that she'd found out the day before she died. People connected their deaths to that of Anna's firstborn, saying the Pedersens brought bad luck to the house. But longtime locals remembered the terrible way April's father had died and the premature death of her mother, and decided the house itself was bad luck. It all circled back to gossip about April's latest troubles, adding fuel to the animosity of her enemies.

She thought back to the night Claire asked her point-blank why she stayed. At the time, she didn't bother to really examine the question. Now she thought hard on it. People came and went over the years, but there was always a core group of those who had a stake in the town, a history—and she was part of it. She was a Tremaine. Her family, all the way back to her great-grandparents, were buried on a prominent hill in the old cemetery. There wasn't much she could wield in the form of respect, but there was that. Now, even among her friends, she sensed mostly judgment. Though they believed what she said about Duncan and were appalled for Justin, they disapproved of her association with Eli, now that he was in jail. Several told her outright she was crazy, even negligent, to stay in contact with him.

Should she do as they advised and cut ties with him? She was supposed to take Justin to see him tomorrow. The thought of it filled her with dread. Among the least of her resentments toward Eli was that he added this extra weekly burden on to her already jammed schedule. Everything about the facility was unbearably depressing: the noise, the smell, the tangible shame. All the sad, fearful, angry faces. Moving to a new town wouldn't change that. And then, depending on Eli's sentence . . . She would have to see how much time he got. That this could be their lives for the indefinite future was unthinkable.

The temperature dropped suddenly, and on the third Sunday of October it was a chilly forty degrees. Anna had been awake since before the sun came up, stepping out of bed quietly so as not to wake Luke. She tiptoed in the dark to the baby's crib and leaned over, listening for his breathing. Oh, his powdery sweet smell! She could never get enough. It must be proof of their purity that babies alone smelled so heavenly. The fierce love she felt for him was unlike anything she'd ever experienced. It blindsided her and overwhelmed everything. And while it bound her closer to Luke, it amplified her suspicion and resentment toward the other Eternals, especially the matrons. Rachel was the only one she trusted. Luke could not understand her wariness.

"They delivered our baby, Anna, under the worst conditions. He's alive because of them."

"No," she said, "despite them. They did everything to make me sick and miserable while I was pregnant. He came a month early and almost died!"

One the one hand, she had never been so sleep-deprived, so somnolent. But another part of her brain was hypervigilant, fiercely attuned to her son's survival. When she heard his soft exhalation, she relaxed. Pulling his extra blanket around his neck, she sat in the rocking chair next to him, to keep watch. He was a quiet baby, unnervingly so. Sometimes she bolted awake in the middle of the night, convinced he was dead.

She remembered vividly her fear and exhaustion right after he was born: how weak he was, and how desperate they were to keep him warm. If the EMT hadn't arrived the day after the storm, he might not have survived. She developed a raging fever, and they kept her in the hospital for three days. But the baby weighed only four pounds and remained in an incubator for another week. Finally, they allowed him to sleep in a crib and, once he adjusted to that, let her nurse him. Two days later, she and Luke took him home. Now he was seven weeks old and weighed almost six pounds. Today they would finally have the bris and naming ceremony.

Her parents had come from Milton with Luke's family to attend. She hadn't seen them in almost two years, since she was first shunned by the Eternals. Their reunion was awkward, but they focused their attention on their grandchild, which helped to smooth tense feelings. They did not discuss the past, and while she was relieved, she was also unsure how to envision a future where she could feel at ease with them again.

The families insisted on coming to the bris, despite Hiram's warning of the volatile environment in the aftermath of Claire's terrible death. Nothing further had actually happened, but an eerie sense of watchfulness pervaded the town.

No one engaged with the Eternals. All their carpentry work was canceled or paid off mid-job. Local markets refused to stock their dairy and produce. The café had closed for two weeks because of flood damage and, once it reopened, only attracted out-of-town patrons on Fridays and Sundays. People treated them with fear and superstition, as if any contact with them might provoke another catastrophe. They braced themselves for violent retaliation, but even this quiet boycott, if prolonged, would be devastating. Hiram was reaching out to other Eternal communities for assistance with money and relocation. It was a sobering acknowledgment of their uncertain future in Caliban. The week before, he made the unthinkable announcement that anyone who wished to leave could do so. So far no one had. But in private rooms and hallways, some were considering it.

Anna didn't learn what happened to Claire until weeks after the fact. Her focus had been entirely on the baby's health. It was only when they brought him home from the hospital that Luke finally told her. She listened in disbelief. She remembered the terror of seeing Claire outside the window the morning after the storm. With her wet hair, sickly pallor, and piercing eyes, she seemed like malevolence incarnate. When Anna insisted someone was outside, they thought she was delirious. Later, she wondered if she'd imagined it. The incident amplified her fear of the woman. She'd wanted her gone—but not like this.

"Oh no," she whispered on hearing the news, "not again."

"Again?" Luke said, puzzled.

She shook her head, growing more agitated. What she feared about herself was too loathsome to voice. "It's such a hideous way to die, in that trap. And it's our fault!" As soon as she said it, she was sorry; she'd forgotten Luke was the one who set them. "I don't mean you. You only did what you were told. But it's so horrible."

"It was an accident," he said, his face ashen. "If the flood hadn't washed away the bank she wouldn't have drowned, even with the trap. And we had trespassing signs. Anyway, they think she meant to kill herself."

"Why do they think that?"

He hesitated. Then he took her hands in his and said gently, "Because, Anna, there was a note—and a reason. Sebastian also took his own life two days before."

Her mouth fell open, but she made no sound. She saw him search her face to gauge her reaction and said quickly, "I don't mourn him, Luke. I'm just . . . shocked. It's a terrible tragedy for them both." It was true; she had no feelings for Sebastian or Claire except shame, guilt, endless remorse. But she recognized her part in their macabre fate. And she feared what God might demand as retribution.

Not my son, she prayed silently now. *Please, I beg You.*

As the room grew lighter, she could see his face more clearly: his shuttered eyelids and small, open mouth. Everyone said he looked just like her, and indeed, there was very little of Luke in him so far, though Miriam told her that mixed babies sometimes looked less foreign as they grew up. Anna couldn't tell if she meant it as an assurance or insult. It felt like the latter. But there was no point in engaging with her provocations, so she said nothing.

She wondered whom he would resemble in temperament. She hoped he would be blessed with Luke's mild, forgiving nature and be spared her inconstancy and fears. For the first time in a long while, she wished she knew more about her birth parents, what traits of theirs her son inherited through her. She also wondered if her birth mother had felt the same intense attachment and, if so, what circumstances made her give up her own child. Seeing her adoptive parents again, she couldn't forget that, at least for the last two years, they had given her up too.

"I'll never do that to you," she said, leaning in to kiss her baby's forehead. "They would have to tear you away."

The night before, she hardly slept, worrying about what could go wrong during the ceremony, if the baby might be harmed during the circumcision, and if she would be able to comport herself with dignity. Luke tried to set her mind at ease. "It will all be fine. The doctor said he's healthy now. The worst is over."

"Don't say that. We must be careful never to say that."

When Luke woke up, she masked her nerves and tried to feel excitement. They dressed carefully in their finest white garments, and she swaddled the baby in a white towel. Then they descended the stairs to join all the other Eternals in the large front parlor. The candelabra had been lit with seven tapered candles, representing God's divine completion. Those who had a role in the ceremony gathered around an ornate chair designated for the spirit of Elijah. Luke's father stood next to Jonah on one side of the chair while Gabriel and Sarah stood on the other side.

Luke and Anna passed the baby to them, and Gabriel laid him gently on the chair of Elijah. At Jonah's nod, Luke lifted the baby and gave him to his father, who sat upon the chair. Then Luke picked up the surgical knife set on a nearby cushion and extended it to Jonah, saying, "I appoint you, Jonah, as my messenger to perform this circumcision." Jonah took the knife and held it aloft while he gave the circumcision recitation, the blade gleaming under the lit candles. Anna could not tear her eyes away from it. As Jonah lowered the knife over her son, she flinched. Then the flesh was cut—she heard his startled, bleating cries as Jonah wiped the blood from his blade on the towel. The baby continued to wail, and Anna bit her lip, willing herself to stay still. Everyone was watching. Steadying her voice, she recited with the others, "Just as he has entered into the Covenant, so may he enter into Torah, into marriage, and into good deeds."

Jonah turned to Luke. "What is the name you've chosen for your son?"

"Asher," Luke said in a clear, proud voice.

Jonah nodded. "That is a good name." He repeated it out loud so all could hear. A murmur of approval filled the room, and then everyone grew silent again as he continued to recite the blessing, dipping his finger into a goblet of wine and letting some drops fall into the baby's mouth. After a few moments, the crying ceased.

Jonah sterilized the wound and covered Asher with a soft white blanket. Then the baby was passed again in reverse order, until he was back in Anna's arms. Cradling him, she peered down at his face. To her surprise, his eyes were wide open, milky gray and staring straight up at her. She let out a short, delighted laugh.

Luke whispered into her ear, "You see, he's fine."

She nodded and kissed her son's forehead. "Asher," she murmured, inhaling again his sweet baby scent. It *was* a good name—simple and modest, yet hopeful. It meant "blessed."

Anna lifted her head and caught her mother's eyes, shining and proud, and saw her father beaming. Looking around the crowded parlor, she noticed the same joyful pride in everyone's faces: in Luke and his parents, Miriam and the midwives, all the elders, even Zebiah and Hiram. All their suspicion and judgment and withholding of the last year—gone. She had come back from disgrace and given her husband a son. They had all forgiven her.

―――――――――――――――

Three days after the bris, Luke's and Anna's parents prepared to return to Milton. Six other Eternals decided to leave with them, including Rachel, her husband, Samuel, and their two small children. Anna was despondent to see the young midwife go. Rachel had always been kind to her, even when others were not—especially in those dark days before her exile. And if she hadn't been present during this birth, Anna wasn't sure if she or the baby would have survived.

On the eve of their departure, Anna found Rachel alone in the room she shared with her family, busily packing.

"I wanted to give you something," Anna said, "in case I don't see you tomorrow." She presented two cotton handkerchiefs she had rolled and embroidered. "There wasn't enough time to make a proper gift, but hopefully these will be useful."

"Oh, they're lovely! I'll cherish them." Rachel tucked them into her pocket and embraced her.

"I'll miss you," Anna said, "but I hope you'll be happy in Milton."

"You and Luke should come too, with the baby. Why don't you, when it would make all your family so happy?"

"I know. They tried to convince us, and we'd like to, but . . . Luke feels we shouldn't abandon the community just yet. Not that you and Samuel are," she added quickly. "It's just—our situation is different. We have an obligation to the elders, Hiram especially, for absolving me. If not, I would never have been able to return to Luke and become a mother to Asher. So you see, for all these blessings, we're indebted to him."

Rachel's face quivered with a strange expression. "I'm glad for all that too," she said carefully, "but you're not indebted to Hiram. Not at all."

"Why do you say it like that?"

Rachel looked away for a long moment. When she turned to Anna again, her eyes were full of sorrow. "I have to tell you something," she said, her voice trembling but determined. "You're going to hate me, but I can't keep this inside anymore. I did something terrible. Your firstborn, Anna—he isn't buried in our plot. Hiram said he couldn't be, that he was stained by your sin and should be laid to rest where he died. The Pedersens were already gone the next day, so that night we buried him. I had no choice, Miriam said it was Hiram's instruction—"

"Miriam?" Anna whispered stupidly.

"Yes. She's the only other one who knows—and I suppose Zebiah. I've never even told Samuel. I was never going to tell you, but if you stay here for Hiram's sake—" She broke off and shook her head. "I had to tell you. God forgive me if I'm wrong for doing so."

Anna heard her own small, cold voice: "Where did you bury him?"

"In the backyard, behind a maple tree, just where the roots spread out. I washed him, Anna, and filled a pillowcase with lavender to keep it sweet. We made it into his shroud, and then we laid him to rest. I wanted to say a prayer, but Miriam said we mustn't, we had to hurry." She pressed Anna's hand urgently. "Forgive me. I had to obey Hiram. But all this time it's weighed on me."

Anna stared at her in stupefaction. She felt as if she'd passed through an invisible portal, where the world she knew fell away to reveal a different world, one that was monstrous, false, unbearable. Her mind refused to accept it. But in her blood and organs, she knew. For the first time in her life, she was the one who had truly been wronged, the one in the position to offer forgiveness—and found she could not do it. She took a step back, extricating her hand. "I have to go."

Rachel nodded miserably. "I'm so sorry. Please don't tell Hiram, I beg you—for my sake and Miriam's. I shouldn't have told you; he swore me to secrecy. I just wanted you to know you owe him nothing."

"No. Indeed I don't." Anna moved to the door and left without another word.

In the corridor she stood frozen, each dull beat of her heart pulsing in her ears. Hiram. Zebiah. Miriam. Rachel. She saw all their faces. Faces she had feared. Faces she had trusted. She saw Rachel and Miriam burying her dead baby in secrecy, in darkness. The image pierced her—for she understood that she too had hidden him away, in the furthest recess of her mind. Hiram told them he was buried as an Eternal, with a prayer of blessing for his everlasting soul. Instead, he lay alone, unblessed and forgotten, as one of the unjust. That the elder was capable of such treachery—it was unconscionable. She felt sickened, remembering how after the bris, she and Luke thanked him for his forgiveness and leniency. When she thought of Luke, her heart twisted. The truth about the burial would crush him.

She walked slowly to their room. Luke was in his nightshirt standing above the crib, holding Asher against his chest. "I got him to fall asleep," he whispered. "I was just about to set him down."

Watching them, she felt the rebuke of all her blessings. She had been absolved of her sin while her firstborn remained punished. Luke straightened up from the crib and asked, "Did you see Rachel?" Then he saw the look on her face. "What's wrong?"

The distance from April's mobile home to her old house in Caliban was just over a mile, an easy shot along the highway she could usually cover in two minutes. Today she drove slowly, dreading her appointment, but though she arrived at a little past noon, she didn't see Karl's car. She hesitated, then drove on, deciding to make a loop around some side streets to kill time. Waiting would only make her more tense, and she preferred he got there first. She passed a huge Victorian house festooned with orange-and-black papier-mâché and plastic skeletons, several elaborately carved-out pumpkins displayed on the porch. "Fucking A," she said. Her friends had mold in their basements, windows that needed replacing, roofs still leaking—and these assholes were decorating. She flipped the bird in her rearview mirror and accelerated.

She wasn't sure what Karl wanted but figured it had something to do with the house, since he suggested meeting there. "I'll explain once I see you," he said, and she was too perplexed to do anything but agree.

Before the phone call, the last time she spoke with Karl was back in late spring, at the annual firemen's pancake fundraiser. She went with Justin and Cara, and said a polite hello to him and Evelyn. He was polite in turn, asking about her brother and saying nice things about her kids. Then he said, "Claire told me how you dropped her credit card off a few weeks back, that you were good company. I want you to know I appreciate it." After a surprised lapse, she said, "Sure. It was nothing," and he nodded briefly before moving on.

Still, she didn't go to Claire's funeral. That morning, she was scheduled to work the flea market, and though she could have excused herself, she chose not to. She and Claire weren't close, and many people assumed they were still on bad terms. Claire herself was hardly popular, but April wagered the whole town showed up, if not to pay their respects to Karl, then out of morbid curiosity. She wanted no part of it—or them. Over the phone, Karl accepted her belated condolences and apology with a firm "Don't give it another thought."

Driving around, she couldn't help feeling anxious about what she would say to him. Given their strained history with the house, her old animosity toward Claire, and the horrific way she died, it was all awkward as hell. After a few more minutes, she headed back to the house. This time, Karl's silver SUV was in the driveway. She parked at the curbside and got out of her truck.

From what she could tell, aside from some missing shingles on the roof, a bent mailbox, and one tree with its trunk sheared off, the place hadn't suffered much damage from the storm. As she approached the steps, she took a deep breath. *Chill out. He probably wants to sell the house and needs some information.* She was about to knock, then remembered to ring the bell. Within seconds, Karl was at the door.

"April. Thanks for taking the time." He motioned for her to follow him inside. At first glance he looked the same, but the smile he gave her never reached his eyes, and his physical presence seemed diminished. She felt a surge of sympathy.

"Sure. Sorry I'm a little late."

He made a dismissive gesture. "Let's sit at that table over there," he said, leading the way toward the dining room with its formal mahogany table and six high-backed chairs. The inside of the house looked the same as the last time April was there. It was still spotless, sparse, possibly even more desolate, though that impression could have been due to the circumstances. He pulled out a chair for her and sat across the table behind a small stack of papers. She was about to ask how he was when he cleared his throat and said, "I guess I'll get right to the point. You're probably aware Claire meant to take her life."

After a startled pause, April said, "I heard something like that. So it's true?"

He nodded. "I think she planned to drown herself in the creek, and instead somehow . . . Anyway, she left a note for me. It didn't give much as far as answers. But then we learned about Sebastian, I'm sure you heard, and that she'd lost her job. I guess on top of the cancer last year—oh, wait. You didn't know about that."

She hesitated and then said, "Actually, I did. She told me back in the spring."

"She did?" he said, surprised. "She swore us to secrecy. Well, it's good she had someone else to confide in. We didn't know about the job. She kept that quiet too, even from us. Guess she was more depressed than I realized. Maybe the job alone wouldn't have been so bad, but all together, with Sebastian . . ." He sighed deeply and said, "Now this makes more sense. She mentioned you in her note."

April's eyes opened wide. "What did she say?"

He reached for a folded sheet of paper, opened it, and read: "If you are okay with it, I'd like April Ives to have the house back. Take whatever you want, but give her the house. I think that's the right thing to do." He set the note down and looked at her. "It took a while for me to contact you because, well, it was quite a process. First, the police kept the note as evidence, and then I had to review it with my lawyers. For the record, nothing in the letter is legally binding. But you should know she thought of you."

He waited for her to say something, but she was speechless. If it hadn't been Karl telling her, she would have thought the whole thing was a joke. After a moment, he went on: "I'd like to clear the air about something. I know you were upset with me about how I bought this house. You gave me a good deal because of your dad, and then I passed it on to Claire. I was trying to get her the best price, but . . . I should have been up front with you."

She nodded. It was more an explanation than apology, but she was hardly going to make an issue of it now, while he was grieving.

"Though if I'd known what it would all lead to . . ." he was saying. "I keep thinking if I never told her about this house, maybe none of this would've happened." For an instant, the muscles in his face trembled. Then he controlled himself. "This house is just hard memories for me—no offense. This town too. It's not just the Eternals. Believe me, I'm not advocating for them. But I don't see the point in making them the scapegoat. The whole town has turned in on itself, gotten mean. Claire felt it. I think you have too."

It was the first time he'd alluded to her troubles. Before she could respond, he continued: "Anyway, Evelyn and I talked about it, and we'd like to propose a compromise. I can't just *give* you the house. She and I are getting on, and we need to consider our retirement. But I can sell it back to you for what I paid. I hope you think that's fair."

Fair. She thought about the word and what it meant in this case. If he'd never mentioned Claire's note, she would have considered his offer to be generous—and on the surface, it was. But why did she feel that, in some way she couldn't define, she was being played again? He said he paid for the house—but hadn't Claire paid him back? And why tell her about Claire's wishes if he wasn't going to honor them? *Because he wants Claire to get credit for it. Just like he wants credit now for being "fair."* He knew she didn't have the money. It was all just for show, an empty gesture.

For a moment, she was tempted to call him out on it, grief be damned. *Don't be a moron, for once in your goddamn life.*

"Sure," she said. Why not call his bluff, let him dangle a little? And then she was struck with an idea. "Let me talk to Mark. He's doing better lately, and I know it would mean a lot to him, to both of us, having the house back in the family."

She had the satisfaction of seeing him look surprised.

"Well, okay," he said after a beat. "Talk to him. Let me know what you want to do."

<hr>

As soon as April got home, she called the Columbia County Jail to confirm Eli would be able to see her before visiting hours were over. After a moment's debate, she canceled the apartment viewing she'd scheduled for later that afternoon. Cara came home and she told her to stay put, then made sure Delia was around to keep an eye on her while she was out. Finally, she called her friend Suzie, who was watching Justin while he hung out with her son Ryan, to say she might be late picking him up.

Traffic on the way to the jail was slow, considering it was Sunday. Several of the smaller roads were still closed off and caused congestion on the main highway. "Move it!" she screamed, sighing with impatience each time she had to brake. In the car in front of her, everyone but the driver had their phones out the windows, snapping pictures of autumn leaves. They were from the city, no doubt, with their OCCUPY WALL STREET bumper stickers, and she felt a surge of resentment at their sightseeing in the midst of disaster.

It was close to three by the time she got to the jail. The contact visitors' area at the detention facility was a large, drab concrete room with six metal tables spaced apart and plastic chairs arranged around them. It was almost always crowded, though less so on weekday afternoons, which was when April usually went. She still disliked the pat-downs at the security checkpoint but was growing used to them, and she noticed a few of the guards were becoming friendlier.

The last time she saw Eli, a week ago, he told her he was taking the plea deal that the prosecutors offered. Jess, the girl who connected him to the traffickers, was going to talk, so he figured he might as well too. He said his jail time could be reduced to eighteen months. It was a sentence he could live with. She thought it was one she could live with too.

The security line for visitors was also long and slow. Once inside, she had to wait for half an hour before they finally called Eli. Usually, when she came with Justin, he was clean-shaven—as if grooming could distract from his orange-and-white-striped uniform, a ludicrous, clown-like outfit surely designed to be humiliating. This time, he was scruffy and unshaven; he wasn't expecting her.

"What's going on?" he said as soon as he saw her. "Everything okay?"

"Yeah, everything's fine," she said, feeling suddenly nervous. "Maybe even good."

They both sat. Frowning, he said, "Then why're you here? I mean, you never come on weekends. Where's Justin?"

"He's at Ryan's, he's fine. I'm here 'cause I have to talk to you." She looked around, leaned closer, and lowered her voice. "Remember what you said about that money in your safe deposit? That it was for me to keep for Justin?"

He blinked and took a moment to respond. "Yes . . . why?"

"Something crazy but kind of good happened today. I might be able to get my house back." She gave him a condensed account of Claire's suicide, her surprising note, and her meeting with Karl. She also told him about Dee's buyer, that she had to move and had been looking at other rentals for weeks now and how slim the pickings were.

He listened, rubbing his cheeks, and finally said, "So you want the money to buy the house. How does that help Justin?"

"I sold it to Karl for thirty grand, and he said that's all he wants back. The house for him is just guilt and bad memories. But for us, imagine . . . We can have a real house again, and it's all fixed up, she put a lot into renovating. I'm not being sentimental, Eli—it's a good investment, worth way more than he's asking. And down the road it'll be worth even more, I'm sure. If I ever need to sell it, that's money for Justin. College." She paused to take a breath. "And when you get out, if you want, you can live there too. Not like, you know, you and me as a couple. But as Justin's dad."

His eyes flickered with interest. "You mean that?"

"Yes." Though as soon as she said it, she wasn't so sure. "At least we could try it out."

He leaned back in his chair and looked up at the ceiling, thinking. Then he said, "Okay, I know you love that house, and it's a great deal. But are you sure you should stay in that town? I thought you said Justin wasn't happy there. You said you were starting to feel threatened. Maybe you should use the money to look for something else, and somewhere else, where you're not going to get harassed all the time."

"Where else am I going to find a house in good condition for thirty grand? I'm forty-four years old, Eli. I clean houses and work at CVS. I'm never going to get another chance to have a better life. Not just for me but the kids. Justin. And why should I let those assholes drive us out of town? And getting back my own goddamn house? This'll show 'em. Might even shut them up. People shit on us because we've got nothing. We can turn that around. And I think things will settle down. Plus, there's a lot Justin's still attached to there. He's got his friends, and now he could have them over and not be embarrassed."

"What if that creep Duncan comes back? He'll know where Justin lives."

She shook her head. "I don't think he'll come back. His house got totaled in the storm. And if he ever does, then I swear I'll sell the house and move. We'd make a profit. But we have to get the house first."

"And what if this guy Karl was just bullshitting? Or he changes his mind?"

"I won't give him the chance. When I give him this money, I will lay it on so thick about how tight I was with Claire and how much this house meant to my folks, how much my dad liked him. I will guilt him into an early grave if I have to. But that's why we have to move fast. I don't want to give him time to think on it."

"You're not giving me a lot of time either." He sighed heavily and was quiet for several seconds. Then he said, "Okay. I hear you. I get it."

She let out the breath she'd been holding. "Thank you. But, Eli, no one can know where the money's from. Ever. Once I put it into my account, that's it. I'm telling Karl it's a loan from Mark, and I'll make sure he backs me up. If Karl knew it was your money there's no way he'd sell me the house."

"He wouldn't want my dirty money, huh? But you're okay with it?"

She blushed but made herself look him in the eye. "I know there's no other way to get that house. So yeah, I'm okay with it. One other thing: once you give me that money, it's done, you understand? No future claims on the house or anything. This is an investment for Justin—for all of us. I just want us to be clear on that."

He thought about it for a long moment. Then he nodded. "I'm clear. I'm giving you my word. You're giving me yours." He held out his hand. They locked eyes as she shook it. "We're just going to have to trust each other."

After she left the jail, she headed to the storage unit in Ashland. The strip mall was nearly deserted, with only two cars parked in front of the nail salon. It was past five and getting dark. Her hands trembled as she unlocked the front door of the storage building, went down the long hallway, and opened Eli's unit. She lifted the lid of the metal box and stared at the stack of bills, the words *dirty money* flashing through her mind. She thought about the trafficked girl, barely older than Maddy. Somebody's daughter. "Fuck," she hissed, hitting her fist against the unit door. She couldn't push back the niggling thought that she was bartering her son for the sake of nostalgia and a bigger house. But wasn't having that house about her kids after all? Taking care of them, making a good investment, letting them grow up somewhere they didn't have to be ashamed?

The money was already here—and though it came from something bad, couldn't she use it for something good? Slamming the lid shut, she shoved the box into the large tote bag she brought and closed the unit. She cracked open the front door, her heart racing, and made sure no one was around. Then she walked as fast as she could back to her truck.

On their third sunset walk along the highway, Luke and Anna finally saw the opportunity they were waiting for. It was the time of day when their neighbors were usually inside having supper, but on previous evenings, they noticed a car parked in Claire's driveway and activity within the house. Tonight, the house was quiet and the highway completely deserted. "Now," Luke said, steering Asher's baby carriage quickly across the lawn toward the backyard. Anna glanced around once more before following them. When they were behind the maple tree, she was able to catch her breath; here they could not be seen from the highway.

She peeked into the carriage to check on Asher, who gazed up at her placidly. "Please, darling," she whispered, stroking his cheek, "be good and stay quiet." She reached under his blanket and pulled out her Bible, a small spade, and a cloth sachet. The sachet contained a lock of her hair and Luke's, Asher's tiny nail clippings, and sprigs of bay laurel and rosemary. It was a totem for the baby, so that the ground where he lay could absorb each of them too.

They found a small patch beyond the tree roots where the soil seemed more yielding. "This seems like a good spot," she said. They didn't know his exact resting place but hoped that anywhere near the tree was close enough. At Anna's nod, Luke knelt and began to dig a small deep hole. She stood watch, moving the carriage gently back and forth.

In the end, they chose not to confront Hiram. They discussed petitioning the elders for his removal but couldn't be certain they were truly uninvolved, as Rachel claimed. They also feared the elders might require the baby's exhumation as proof. Disturbing a soul's resting place was considered a desecration unless caused by an act of nature, war, or crime. If those causes could be proven, reparation blessings would be given at a new burial. If not, the soul would remain forever in unrest—a fate worse than returning to earth as an unjust.

"They must never find out that we know," Anna told Luke. "We must go to the grave and bless him, as his parents, and then leave this town as soon as possible." She had never spoken to him in that manner, commanding him to do something. But in that moment, she felt if he would not stand up for her and what had been done to their child, she would take Asher and leave. Something in her face must have made him understand what was at stake.

When Luke finished digging, she placed the totem in the ground, and they covered the hole with dirt, patting it down. The sun began to set, and the light was rapidly fading.

"Luke, let's pray together."

He knelt by her and lowered his head. She opened the Bible and began to read from Psalm 121, the first of three they selected. Her voice was barely audible at first, then gained strength as she went on. After a moment, he joined her. When the light grew too dim to read, they both recited from memory: "The Lord is your keeper; the Lord is your shade on your right hand. The sun shall not strike you by day, nor the moon by night. The Lord will keep you from all evil; He will keep your life. The Lord will keep your going out and your coming in from this time forth and forevermore."

By the time they finished the last psalm, the sky was pitch-dark. Anna placed the Bible open-faced on the ground, over the spot where they had buried the totem. They each leaned down to kiss the book. Then Luke closed it and said, "We should leave now. It's gotten dark and they'll wonder where we are."

She nodded but remained kneeling with her eyes closed. She said softly, "Forgive me, my son. Forgive us. We never meant to forsake you. Sleep in peace now, until we all reunite in God's eternity."

They walked back to the highway in silence. As they neared the farmhouse, Anna peered up at the large elm; the owl was gone. Had it been there earlier? She couldn't recall but felt palpable relief at its absence now. She asked Luke, "Do you think we amended what was done? Will our blessing him be enough?"

Luke took a moment to answer. "Yes. I believe God will sanction our blessing, humble as we are, for being sincere. He should certainly do so over the blessing of a false elder. In fact, I'm convinced it was by His design that we found out."

She said nothing for a while. Then she asked, "Why would He allow such treachery in the first place?"

He said carefully, "He allows us everything, Anna, including the choice to do harm or good. I don't know why Hiram chose as he did. I wonder if his corruption provoked all that's gone wrong for us in this town. Maybe that was part of God's judgment."

She was silent again, but it was too dark for him to see her expression. Finally, she said, "It seems to me if we can no longer trust our elders to guide us on His path, then they serve no purpose. Better for us to seek His guidance directly."

He stopped walking and took her arm. "Are you saying you no longer wish to be an Eternal?"

"No," she said. "I'll always be an Eternal. But I don't need an elder to show me how."

———

It was cold but sunny the morning April moved back into her old house. Delia and Ed were scheduled to leave the following week for Hattiesburg. They were packing too and gave April extra boxes and bubble wrap when she ran out. "I'll miss you," she said when she returned her set of keys. Dee hugged her and said, "Come down and visit any time." But they both knew she wouldn't and that what Dee meant was goodbye.

Ed helped April load up the U-Haul van she rented for her move, though he let Maddy's boyfriend, Eric, and his roommate, Tom, do the heavy lifting. Everything went in the van except for Maddy's belongings, which they piled into Eric's truck. She was moving in with the boys.

"You sure?" April asked again as they drove toward Caliban, following Ed in the U-Haul and the boys in Eric's truck. "Plenty of room in the new place."

"You mean the old place," Maddy said. "*No* thank you, been there done that. Movin' on!"

"Well, you don't have to act so happy," April said irritably. Maddy was hardly around anyway, and in truth, they got along better because of it. Still, it sucked to feel old and tossed aside. "Anyway, it doesn't look the same at all now."

When they walked inside the house, April was relieved that it no longer looked the way it did when Claire lived there either. Karl had removed all her possessions save for a few pieces of furniture he didn't need—a wicker lounge chair, two wooden bookshelves, a small bench for the entryway—which he told

April he'd leave if she wanted. They were flea market finds, he said, but useful, so she got over her pride and thanked him.

"Damn," Maddy said, looking around, "it's so *clean*."

"Yeah, you're welcome," April said dryly. She'd spent the day before dusting, scrubbing, and vacuuming the place. Claire had kept it pretty clean, so it wasn't hard work. But it was creepy to wipe down the bathtub and come across strands of her dark hair, to know that dust in the corners contained her dead sloughed skin. And in the downstairs bathroom, she noticed a strange rusty smell that hadn't been there before.

The minute they stepped inside, Cara and Justin ran upstairs to claim the rooms they finally agreed on. April let Cara have her old bedroom, the larger one closest to the stairs. She knew it had been Claire's bedroom too and, feeling strange about it, decided to take the back room downstairs, which the girls had shared before.

It took over three hours to unload everything. Throughout the day, neighbors drifted by, some to say hello, others to gawk. Those who were genuine in their welcome hugged her and left little gifts in the entryway. Suzie brought Ryan, and Polly and Lisette came together, bearing trays of food. Trudy Carson and Jerry Ingalls, who poked their heads in briefly, were downright nosy. They had heard but could not believe the story April's friends told them: that Karl had painful feelings about the house and sold it back to her and Mark for cheap.

Word had gotten around. The week before April moved back in, someone threw a rock at the living room window. She'd have to replace it eventually, but Ed had boarded it up for now and installed a security camera and Ring alarm.

At one point, a small group of men, led by Hank Winter and Harlan Shane, gathered across the street to watch silently with their arms crossed. It took everything in April not to go up and spit in their faces. She knew one of them had broken her window. But Ed told her to stay cool and de-escalate. Finally, it got too cold for the men to stay outside, and when Eric and Tom disarmed them by offering hot coffee, they grudgingly left.

As she walked out to the U-Haul for more boxes, Jerry followed her. "Mind if I ask what you paid for the house?" he said with a smile.

"I don't mind," said April, smiling back. "But I'm not gonna answer." *Fuck you,* she seethed inwardly, directing the thought not just at him but at everyone else in the town she knew talked trash about her. She didn't want an all-out war—he lived just across the street—but there was no need to be nicer than she had to. He was still yammering at her, aggressively cajoling, when she saw an Eternal couple far down the road, bundled up in dark clothing. The man was very tall and pushing a carriage in her direction. As they got closer, she realized it was Anna and her husband. "'Scuse me," she said to Jerry abruptly, and walked toward them.

Anna seemed astonished to see her. For a moment, April wondered if she was still supposed to act like they didn't know each other. Then Anna's face lit up. "April! What a nice surprise. This is my husband, Luke. Luke, this is April!"

"Hello." He nodded and smiled. "Anna has said such wonderful things about you."

"Oh, well . . ." April never knew what to say around earnest people. "It's nice to finally meet you."

"How are you?" Anna asked.

"I'm good, actually. I'm moving today—back into my old house. You didn't hear?"

"No," said Anna. She and Luke exchanged a quick, odd glance, and he touched her arm, as if in reassurance. "We haven't been talking much to people lately. Well, that's . . . I'm happy you'll be the one to live here." Then she asked her kindly, "How is your son?"

"He's doing better. Thank you. And I guess this is your little one." April bent to peer into the carriage. A tiny, pink-cheeked Asian baby stared up at her, frowning. "Boy or girl?"

"A boy," Luke said, smiling proudly. "Asher."

"Huh, that's different. But I like it." April straightened and said, "Justin's with his friend upstairs or I'd have him come out. But maybe we'll come by the café one day when you're there."

Anna said, "Oh . . . I won't be working there anymore. We're leaving Caliban."

"You are? When? To where?"

"Back to Milton, on Sunday. We're taking our last walk around these roads now, before it gets dark."

"Wow. You're leaving. And I'm just coming back." It occurred to April that the newcomers she'd grown to know—Claire, Delia and Ed, now Anna—would all be gone. "Are you going because of how people are after . . . you know, what happened?" For a brief, strained moment, Claire's death hovered between them.

Anna nodded. "It's partly that. And we miss our families."

"Should you be talking to us?" Luke asked, inclining his head toward Trudy and Jerry, who watched them from his lawn. "We don't want to cause trouble for you."

April looked over at them briefly, then shrugged. "Don't worry, I'm watching my back. Hopefully people here will settle down. Maybe things have to get really bad before they get better. Maybe this is the worst of it."

Anna gave April a wan smile. Then she looked back at the Eternals' farmhouse and shook her head. "I don't know if the worst has happened. But whatever the future holds, I pray that you and your family will be okay."

"Thank you," April said, staring at her, puzzled by her tone. This was not the painfully naive girl of two years ago. So, Anna had finally grown up. *Well*, she thought, *it's about time.*

Anna said shyly, "I hope you'll be happy, being in your house again."

"Thank you. I'm glad I ran into you. To wish you luck and say goodbye."

"Me as well," said Anna. They both knew not to embrace. Then Luke nodded, and they continued on their way. April watched as their dark, disparate figures progressed up the highway, crested over the hill, and disappeared from her line of sight. They were strange people she didn't really know. And yet she felt they were allies.

Maddy came up, interrupting her reverie, to say she and the boys were taking off.

"You sure? You don't want to eat something first?"

Maddy shook her head. "We'll eat after we drop all my stuff off."

"Okay, well . . . call me later." She grabbed her daughter in a tight hug, releasing her before she could complain. "It'll be weird, you not living with us anymore."

"C'mon, Mom, don't get sappy." In a nicer voice she said, "Look, we're just in Greenville. I'll still come over to watch Justin if you give me some notice."

She sprinted away with a wave. Soon after, Ed left to return the U-Haul, which seemed like the signal for everyone else to leave too.

Suddenly the house was quiet, interrupted only by the occasional sound of the kids' footsteps creaking above the kitchen, where April stood unpacking. As she stored her banged-up pots and pans in the empty cabinets and her perishables from a cooler into Claire's stainless-steel refrigerator, she couldn't help feeling like an imposter. All the appliances were so new and barely used, the renovated pantry immaculate. Would she be able to keep it so nice? Would she feel more comfortable if she didn't?

In her wildest imaginings, she never hoped to have the house again and was still incredulous Claire had left it to her. She couldn't fathom what compelled the woman—whether it was guilt, insanity, or some imagined sentiment of friendship. The impeccable condition of the house heightened her discomfort, as if to underscore how little she deserved it.

Christ, she thought, *get over it. It was your house to begin with.* Still, it was impossible to deny Claire's imprint. Twice she thought she smelled her woodsy scented candle, but when she inhaled more deeply, there was nothing. She pushed forward and continued to put things away, tackling the back room next. She worked quickly, methodically, barely registering the darkening sky, and looked up only when Justin startled her from the doorway, asking, "Mom, are we gonna eat?"

"We're starving!" Cara yelled behind him.

"Oh, shit," April muttered, hurrying past them into the kitchen. The microwave clock showed it was almost seven. "Sorry, shit, hold on." She quickly nuked the remains of Polly's mac and cheese, and they sat at the table wolfing it down, barely talking. When she was done, she got a beer from the refrigerator, popped it open, and clinked it against their water glasses. "Well, cheers. Here's to us being back."

Just at that moment, the light overhead flickered off. April said, "Oh, shit," and then an instant later, it came back on. She looked up at the ceiling and said, "That was weird. Guess I'll have to change the bulb. You guys all unpacked and got your rooms set up?"

Justin nodded. Cara, yawning, said, "Pretty much," which April knew meant the opposite. She looked at her daughter and sighed. More and more, she was just like Keith: artsy, pretty to look at, hopelessly disorganized.

"Okay, go finish and then brush your teeth, both of you. I'll come up in a bit when I'm done down here."

But more than an hour passed before she went upstairs, and when she did, it was completely silent. She poked her head in Cara's room first. The light was still on, and as expected, it was mayhem, the bed piled with heaps of clothes that the girl lay sprawled upon, sheets and blankets bunched around her. April flicked the light off and shut the door. Justin's room was dark, but from the hallway light she could see it was tidy, his boxes flattened and lined up in an orderly pile against one wall. He was in bed too, completely covered by his duvet. Obviously, he had no problem falling asleep in a new space, all alone.

She wasn't so sure she'd manage as well. She was exhausted, her body ached with fatigue, but her mind could not shut down. In the upstairs bathroom, she opened each cabinet and tested the faucets, turning the fancy spigots on and off. If she only had the energy, she'd keep on unpacking. Instead, she wandered quietly through the house, looking at each room from different angles, taking in the strange and familiar. All day long she'd had these jarring moments of trying to reconcile the two.

From the stairs, she could see the streetlight glowing through the naked windows into the living room. She put on her coat and sneakers, opened the front door, and stepped onto the porch. She thought about getting her cigarettes, then decided not to. Sometimes, when she was already wired, smoking made her more so. She'd have to quit again anyway, when all the disruption from the move died down.

She looked up at the sky with its indistinct stars, fewer than she was able to see from Delia's lot. High above her hung the moon, sliced perfectly in half but still bright enough to illuminate the houses nearby. She could see Jerry's TV glaring in his living room and the large cedar tree separating his property from the Tremmels'. Up the hill to her right were the Carsons' split-level, Lisette's quirky pink cottage, and the long slope of meadow leading to the cemetery. To her left were the Edgars, Duncan's demolished lot, Brian and Jody's emptied-out old bungalow. Across the road stood the imposing frame of the Eternals' farmhouse, candles flickering from random windows. She realized it was Shabbat.

She thought of Anna and Luke behind one of those windows, and then Maddy setting up in her new place. Delia and Ed on their air mattress; Karl lying next to Evelyn, grieving. Harlan out somewhere stirring trouble. Eli sleeping in his dank, cold cell. All the rest of the world and the unknown, yawning future.

She hugged herself, shivering, and went back inside, closing the door behind her. On the bench in the hallway were small piles of cards and housewarming gifts. She crouched down to examine them: dish towels from Suzie, jars of preserves from the Edgars, some foul-smelling potpourri from Trudy Carson. Two more cards and a box of little hand soaps. Tucked under the bench was a brown paper bag twisted at the top, suggesting the promise of alcohol. She pulled it out and her breath caught. It was a bottle of scotch—Macallan.

"What the hell?" She looked inside the bag and around the bench, but there was no card. Her heartbeat quickened. For a moment, she thought it might be poisoned. But checking the bottle, she could see it was brand new and sealed. She tried to think rationally. It had to be from Karl. He must have dropped it off or left it, which she somehow overlooked. But even as she reasoned this, she didn't believe it. And this scared her more than anything. Because she *knew*: it wasn't Karl's way. He had no reason to give her a gift—and if he did, he would have had it nicely wrapped. He would have left her a note.

She rose, gripping the bottle, and walked in a daze to the kitchen. She got a glass from the cabinet, cracked open the scotch, and poured herself a generous shot. "Fucking A, Claire," she said softly, bringing the glass to her lips.

ACKNOWLEDGMENTS

I'm indebted to my agent, Pamela Malpas, for believing in this book and advocating so tirelessly on my behalf. Thank you, Chris Heiser, for your vision, enthusiasm, and thoughtful edits; that you said yes to this debut fulfills a dream. All my appreciation to the fantastic team at Unnamed: Allison Miriam Smith, Penina Roth, Jaya Nicely, and Cassidy Kuhle.

My deepest gratitude to Nick and Mary Lou Nahas, and Chris Gordon: this novel would not exist without your generous hospitality over two eventful summers in the Catskills. The world you introduced me to turned darker in fiction—but the actuality was bliss.

Boundless love to Adam Klein for unfailing encouragement and commiseration, and for always being my first set of eyes and ears; every writer should be so lucky. Huge thanks as well to my other readers: Elizabeth Bull, Ryan D. Matthews, Kate Angus, Bella Pollen, Nicole Brodsky, and James Sidel.

I'm grateful to the following institutions for their support: Playa Artist Residency, Brush Creek Foundation for the Arts, Virginia Center for the Creative Arts, The Hambidge Center, and Poets & Writers, with special thanks to Get the Word Out program leaders Thierry Kehou and Lauren Cerand. Thank you to The New School and my instructors Helen Schulman, Dale Peck, Sigrid Nuncz, Shelley Jackson, Darcey Steinke, and Douglas A. Martin.

Thank you, Maggie Su and Gerald Maa. Thanks to Stephen Beachy for publishing an early version of "The Eternals" in *Your Impossible Voice*.

Thanks to Jena Smith, Jill Menard, and Scott Galante for indulging all my legal hypotheticals; and to Annick DeBellefeuille, for relaying hurricane anecdotes that served my plot.

For keeping me informed, amused, and otherwise sane, thank you to Kelley Yasbek, Katie Madarasz, Michelle Chavez, Daina Zivarts, Eva Wreigard, Diane Scharff, Jon Murata, Peter Kuang, Joanne Walsh, Richard Hand, Stéphanie Stindel, Meg Garvey, Darcy McKinnon, Tara Cox, Isa Murdock-Hinrichs, Sarah Holt, Mary Groebner, Megan Culhane Galbraith, Laurie Stone, LJ Sysko, Julie Bloemeke, and Dustin Brookshire.

Most of all to my family, given and chosen: your love and support carry me. It's everything.